THE
LOST
MIGRATION

ANDREW S. VADAS

THE
LOST
MIGRATION

THANKS

When I started this book I was naive and hopeful. Without my beautiful wife, Eleanor Cleverly, I would have never adopted the standards it takes to hone and finish a project of this nature. She pushed me to be better in my writing, my editing and most importantly, my life. Thank you for your support, I love you.

To my Uncle Arthur who read my manuscript with patience and care. The feedback you provided influenced this final draft in many ways.

I also want to thank Paul Katz, Brian Coe, and Stacy Emmons. You all took the time to read a manuscript full of flaws and helped me turn it into what it is today. Without your volunteer hours, I would have been lost.

Yasmin Gruss, you spent many hours editing this book and without you it would be barely legible. I took this work as far as I could and you took it over the finish line. Thank you for your keen eye and enduring focus.

Elijah Toten, you took a photo and my vague descriptions and turned them into the exact design that I wanted for the cover of the book. Thanks for your help!

ONE

My mother, Sarah Mae Billings, told me to take the trash out to the burn pit. As I carried the bin to the far corner of the acreage, I wondered if it would be the last time I set fire to my family's refuse. Holidays would bring me back, and of course, I would do chores just like before, but would this be the end of carrying trash out to the burn pit as a part of my routine?

I opened the ammo can next to the fire ring and took out the box of wooden matches. The crumpled paper at the bottom of the pit lit up like rabbitbrush. The smoke that came off the trash had that sweet chemical smell. As the center burned out, I folded the unburned paper from the edges into the middle of the pit until everything was ash.

In the August sun and the heat of the fire, I was dripping sweat. I took my shirt off and slung it over my shoulder for the walk back to my house. Fence posts and water troughs rolled around in my vision like the ticking hands of a clock. Stacks of hay sat in the hay barn; how long before their division and distribution?

Back at the house, my mother was waiting for me on the porch.

"Your father's ready for you," she said.

"Yes, ma'am. I'm going to get washed, and then I'll head over there."

My father, Wesley Billings, didn't like to cut dirty hair. As per tradition, I shampooed and ran a comb through my locks before I dressed and walked over to the barn. When Dad cut my hair for the first time, I was blonde. In the mirror, as I combed my hair, it was as if my head was a sand dune and all of the golden sand had blown away, revealing the wet brown below. My facial features were not quite feminine, but they were not nearly as masculine as I would have liked. Growing up, people had always told me I looked just like my mother, and when I looked at myself in the mirror, it was hard to argue. I had her light brown eyes, her sharp nose, and both of our foreheads were a little too small for our faces. My thin-lipped mouth came from my father's side.

After my shower, I tucked my snap-button shirt into my wranglers and pulled my calfskin cowboy boots over my feet. I preferred a pointed toe, even though square-toed was the fashion at the time. With my western shirt and my jeans, my cowboy boots, save for the toe, I blended in well when I went into town. Kermit, Texas, was the closest town to the ranch, but it was more of a collection of houses propped up next to the gas wells than it was a real town.

My father was standing next to the stool he used for cutting hair. He was brushing off his clippers when I entered the barn. Like someone was carrying me, my body set itself down on the stool.

"How you doing, son? Have a seat," he said, even though I had already landed on the stool.

"I'll have the usual," I told him. In every step, I followed the unwritten script of our ritual. "What's new with you?"

"Oh, you know me. Ain't been up to much. Workin' like always."

"Football's about to start back up."

"That's right. Same with school, as you well know. We're leaving early tomorrow. You going to be ready and rarin' to go?"

"Yes, sir, I'll be ready."

"You going to be ready, ready?" my father asked.

"Hard to be ready for something I don't really understand all the way."

"What don't you understand?"

"Nothing. Just that if you told me to get ready to go fishing, I'd know what I needed to do."

"You seem to know."

"Why'd you say that?" I asked him as he let out a faint chortle.

"Cause you're you. You got your stuff together before your mother had to ask. You never need any pushing to study or do your chores. Just the way you are, I got faith in you."

My father's hands moved fast as he worked the sides of my head with the clippers. Then he took his time touching up the top with scissors. Even with his care, the job didn't take more than fifteen minutes. When he finished, he dusted off my shoulders and pulled the canvas sheet off with a big whoosh. The sheet cracked like a wet towel; my little hairs sparkled in the air as they fell to the ground. Outside, the sky had darkened and the wind picked up.

"Looks like a storm's coming," I said as we stood looking out from the barn.

"It'll threaten, maybe even piss a bit, but I don't think any real rain's going to come. Lord knows we need some, but that don't mean we'll get it."

Outside of the barn, the storm had dulled all the color out of the sky, like a black and white photo come to life. Off in the distance, thunder cracked. Standing side by side, we watched the wind blow through the grass, kicking up sand and dust. "Whelp, I'm going to double-check I got everything, I don't want to hold us up tomorrow. Thanks for the cut."

"You're welcome." My father thought for a second and said, "Hey, you know I'm the only one that's ever cut that hair?"

I nodded yes.

"I suppose that'll be changing. I don't know how they do things up there in New Mexico, so just be careful. I don't trust half the barbers we got here in West Texas—who knows what they got up there in that territory."

"I'll be careful."

Walking back to the house, one of the mesquite trees that sat along the drive caught my eye. It stood in full bloom, covered in tiny yellow flowers, a strange sight for late August. Looking back around the ranch, porch lights were starting to turn on even though the sun hadn't set yet. The many families of the ranch flipped on their lights in preparation for the darkness that would greet them when they left the mess hall after dinner. I must have known that the families all did this, but on that day, it seemed important to me.

My mother, again, was waiting on the front porch for me; maybe she had never left.

"Your hair looks nice," she said. I had a seat on the bench next to where my mother stood. "Your uncle wants to have a word with you before we sit down to dinner."

"Yes, ma'am. I'll go see him right now."

"It's weird, isn't it?"

"Yes, ma'am. It does feel strange."

"Well, it ought to," my mother said as she looked out over the porch railing and onto the land around us. "You're a part of this place. And when this place changes, people take notice."

"They sure do."

"It's like you're getting married or something."

"Or dying," I said before I could stop myself.

"Don't say things like that. You may be joking, but I don't find that funny."

"It feels like people are preparing for my funeral. Weddings are supposed to be joyous, and this doesn't feel joyous. Everyone's somber, like they know something bad is about to happen to me."

"It's hard for folks to imagine a life that exists beyond this ranch. Even for me, you know I barely ever leave this place, let alone the state." My mother didn't break her stare from the land. "Go ahead and see your uncle now," she said. She turned to the house without facing me and went inside. I sat for a minute and looked out at the same land my mother's eyes had been locked on. There was so much there, but for me, it wasn't enough.

My uncle's office was the original homesteader's cabin, built by the squatters that claimed the land in the late 1800s. The pine siding on the building had all the blonde pulled out of it, leaving it the color of weak coffee. Every time I climbed the small set of stairs to the front door, I wondered if it would be the day that the porch peeled off from the front of the cabin. I stepped on the wood planks of the porch with great reverence. In my mind, this little building was a part of Uncle Grant's body. Like always, I knocked before I entered.

"Come on in," Uncle Grant said through the door as if he knew it was me. I walked into his office and had a seat in the leather chair that sat in front of his desk. A matted, gummed-up cigar was wedged into his clamped-down molars. Without saying anything, he let me know he'd be with me in a minute. He continued flipping through a packet of papers, scanning each page, signing at the bottom. All the while, my eyes wandered around the cabin, examining the dust that had settled into the worn-in crevices of my uncle's office. On his spotless ranch, it occurred to me that this cabin might be the only place that was out of sorts in any way.

Out of the corner of my eye, I saw that Uncle Grant had made it to the end of the packet of papers. He looked so much like my father, only less handsome and less muscular. He slipped the pages into a manila folder and tucked it away into a drawer. He looked up at me and settled back into his chair, signaling that he was ready to talk.

"Thanks for coming to see me. I wanted to sit down with you for a minute before you take off," Uncle Grant said.

"What did you want to talk about?"

"I want to know what it is you think you're going to get out of college."

I thought for a second and said, "I think education is important. I'm pretty good at school…" I was sputtering in the absence of a fully formed thought when Grant cut me off.

"That's not it," Grant said. "What're you trying to get from college?"

I composed myself until I felt that I had a better answer. "I want to learn a profession, I guess. Figure out what I want to do with my life."

"They aren't going to teach you to do that." Grant spun his cigar in his mouth and chomped back down on the soggy tarred stick.

"Are you saying I shouldn't go?"

"No, no. Of course not. I'm real proud of you, Otis. You know I never went to college, right?" I nodded my head. "I never went, but I know a little bit about it. I know that you don't go to college to learn a trade."

"No?"

"Well, you may *go* to learn a trade, but you won't come out the other side with one."

"Why do you go then?" I asked.

"You go to prove that you're worth a shit," he said with a little chuckle. "I've been having you help me with the books, and I've seen you doing chores your whole life. Since you were a little boy. I know what you can do. If you flunk out of college, you'll always have a home on this ranch."

"Thank you, sir," I said.

"Here's the thing though, just cause I know what you can do, doesn't mean nary a soul in this world knows what I know. College is a chance to show that you can work for four years and accomplish something. The rest of the world can see that degree, and it shows 'em you can finish something. See what I'm getting at?"

"I think so."

"Do you? I can tell by looking at you that you're not understanding to the fullest," he said, so sure of his assessment. "Let me put it another way. If college doesn't work out, we'll be excited to have you back here, but there won't be anybody else that is. You got that?"

"Yes, sir. That makes sense."

"That's what I think you'll get out of college. Now tell me what you think *you'll* get out of college?"

I resettled into my seat while I thought about Grant's question. "I want to be great." I felt right away that I had, again, said too much. Uncle Grant breathed in my proclamation. He watched me like I was an animal that had just walked into a carefully placed snare, one that he had set.

"Is that right? You want to be great, do you?" he asked the walls of his office. "The way you say that tells me you don't think you can be great unless you leave here. Is that right?"

"Hadn't thought about it that way, but I guess I believe that."

"You got a right to believe it. Shit, I left home when I was your age and I built this place, didn't I? If I didn't think I was greater than what my folks could provide for me, then we wouldn't be sitting on this property, would we?"

"It's not like that. I love the life you provided for me."

"I know you love it here, I'd be able to tell if you didn't. But you want to be greater than a farm boy, don't you?"

"Yes, sir. I believe so."

Uncle Grant smiled and pulled the cigar from his mouth. He laughed and sat back in his chair. "We'll be here when you're done with college."

"What if I don't come home after college?"

"We'll be here when you're done with that, too," he said. Together we marinated in silence. A nice long snap of quiet usually meant the conversation was over, but I could see that Grant was laboring over something. He looked vulnerable, like a wild boar out in the open. After a while, he sat forward and said, "Alright, Otis, I got some work to do before dinner."

Waiting for me outside the cabin door was the high desert heat. I knew Uncle Grant meant well, but the sound of doubt in his voice had me a little pissed off. In my routine, I felt that I could find refuge from my thoughts. I raced up the stairs of my house and into the bathroom to wash up before dinner. Water on the face calmed me down a bit, and my mind shifted to the hunger in my belly.

Just about every dinner I had ever eaten was eaten in the mess hall. The meals of my youth ran on a continuous loop, shifting and morphing seasonally, but more or less, we ate a rotation of the same twenty meals, over and over again. A never-ending cycle of meat, usually pork or lamb, buttered vegetables, beans, and some kind of potatoes or rice. Amid all of life's uncertainties, heading into the mess hall for dinner wasn't one of them.

As I walked in, food was coming out of the kitchen on great serving dishes, but nobody noticed. I took my seat next to my mother and father. We were sitting next to the Sandoval family, their kids all washed up and sitting in place. The gears of my mind were grinding and gnashing, but I did my best to keep my body still. I noticed Mr. Sandoval's hands as he took hold of his fork and knife. The muscles stretched and swelled as he manipulated the utensil, and when I looked down at my hands, I wondered why mine didn't look like his.

My mother asked me if I was hungry, and I told her I was. She smiled and looked pleased. She was always most comfortable at the dinner table. My father ate with his normal eagerness. The Sandoval kids watched me as they scooped rice into their mouths. I realized I wasn't eating—I was watching everyone else to see if they were watching me. Other than the two Sandoval boys, nobody was.

We ate quietly, without ceremony. When the meal was coming to an end, I excused myself and slipped out into the night. I hopped the pasture fence and walked towards the congregation of sheep as fast as I could without breaking into a run.

The washed-out lights of the property barely showed on the sheep as they grazed the barren pasture. With their heads down and their breath dusty, they never gave up the hope of finding something green.

TWO

The morning of my departure to New Mexico, I wasn't able to sleep through the sunrise. Up out of bed, I stepped softly through the house, letting memory, not light, lead my way down the steps and out through the front door. I watched the sun come up, painting the eastern horizon. Working hands streamed out across the property to start the day, and I took the cue to go back inside and finish packing.

On our front porch, I stacked my belongings, everything that I owned. When I was finished, my mother called me to breakfast. Waiting at the table was a plate piled up with bacon, eggs, and toast. My mother, with a delicate smile on her face, watched me eat.

"You showered and ready?" my father asked.

"Yes, sir, just about. Still need to go through my room and make sure I didn't miss anything."

"Good. We're going to take off right after breakfast."

"You don't need to be off with him so quick," my mom said.

"Got a long drive ahead of us."

"Albuquerque can wait, I promise."

I didn't rush through my meal, and I could tell my mother appreciated my casual dining. My father finished his coffee and went upstairs to clean up and change his clothes before the trip. While I finished my breakfast, my mother watched. Normally, this would have bothered me, but that morning, it wasn't intrusive or annoying.

My mother had all the trouble in the world when she had me, and she took every chance she got to remind me of the difficulties of her pregnancy and labor. Every time I rode my bike or swung an ax, she promised that I'd be the one to put her in her grave one way or another. Such a busy woman, her superpower was working so hard while always having one eye on me, her only child.

"I wish I knew why you were heading off. It's my fault, isn't it? Education is so important. Guess I should have figured it would take you away from me." From the way she was talking, I could tell she wasn't looking for a response.

I offered one anyway. "You did too good of a job raising me. You always told me to stay out of trouble, study hard, and I did. If you would've let me run wild, skip school and all that, there'd be no way for me to go off to college."

My mother laughed, unable to help herself from being charmed. "You don't need to go so far. They've got a college in El Paso, you know. And that school in Las Cruces gave you plenty of money."

"Not as much as the Albuquerque State gave me."

"Your uncle would have let you go anywhere you wanted."

"You know I wanted to do it all on my own."

"I'm sure your uncle appreciates it, but I don't." She smiled and her cheeks pushed up on her eyes until they were just slits. "You'll be fine, you'll be back before I know it."

"Thanksgiving isn't far off at all."

My father returned to the kitchen; it was time to load up the truck. My mother followed as my father and I carried my bags outside. We walked down the front steps of our porch and right into a surprise party. At least half the ranch was gathered outside, mulling around, waiting for me to come out. I lugged my bags out towards my father's truck while my audience looked on.

Uncle Grant stepped through the crowd and cut me off from the truck. "Where you going?" he asked, a big smile hung upon his face.

"About to pack up the car, we're fixing to leave soon."

"You ain't taking your dad's truck," he said with a dramatic pause at the end, mustering up as much theatrics as he could manage.

"What do you mean? We got to."

"I mean you aren't taking your dad's truck."

"How are we going to get there then?" I asked, bracing myself as if a big right hook was about to come for my cheek.

"You're takin' your truck." His smile grew wider.

"I don't have a truck. We gotta take Dad's," I told Grant, wishing he would get to the point. My father was now standing behind me, smiling just like his brother. I knew what was coming, but I didn't want to let myself believe it.

"Follow me. Need to show you something," Grant said, walking towards the barn. All the folks there to see me off followed without invitation. I stood still at first, trying to process the events that had unfolded over the last thirty seconds. My mother, following Uncle Grant, looked back and waved me on.

After my initial hesitation, I gave chase, and just as I caught up with the building rabble, we all entered the big airy barn. Sitting inside was an old two-tone blue and white Ford F-150. Grant walked up to the truck and set his hand down on the hood like he was petting a horse.

"A man needs a truck," he said to me, smiling bigger than I had ever seen him smile before. Uncle Grant handed me a large key; on one end there was a black rubber square with the word Ford etched into it.

"This is for me?"

"You like it?" Grant asked. Rather than answer, I hugged him. With tears stipping down my face, I didn't want to leave my uncle's arms. The tears were coming from a place that I didn't understand, and I wasn't sure what I'd have to do to make them stop. As ashamed as I was to be crying in front of all those people, it felt good to let those tears run.

My new truck wasn't new at all. It sat on rusty leaf springs, and the bed had more than a few scrapes and dents. Some good old boy had ridden it hard before it got to me, but I couldn't take my eyes off of it. Owning a truck had been a wild fantasy of mine since I was a little boy, and now it was a reality. It felt like I had hit the lottery.

My uncle released me and laughed. "Shit, boy, it ain't that nice. Didn't cost much at all."

My father entered the barn with my bags and tossed them into the back of the truck. "Start her up, son," my dad said. Everybody was looking at me as I got into the truck and turned the engine over. It came to life, I put it into first and eased out of the barn until I was clear of the doors. My first ride in the old Ford was all of one hundred feet. I turned the truck off and hopped out to a parade of friends and family trailing behind me. The crowd mobbed me with hugs and handshakes, farewells, and good lucks. I hugged my mother and kissed her on her cheek. I hugged Uncle Grant and thanked him again.

We drove off the property on an incredible high, fueled by love and excitement. By the time we made it through Kermit, my high wore off and I was left raw. My father sitting in the passenger seat of the truck looked like he was superimposed. My mind couldn't accept the positions we were sitting in. A sensation came on to me, dissociation from the self I had always known. I didn't see it coming, and I wasn't sure where it came from, but I knew the end result. At that moment, the ranch ceased to be my home.

THREE

Most of the driving I had done up to that point in my life was on dusty gravel roads or going back and forth between the ranch and my high school in Kermit. The interstate was a place I had been before as a passenger, but as a driver, it was alien.

My father thought it would be good for me to drive the entire way to Albuquerque. I accepted the challenge, eager to show that I had dominion over my new truck. We hummed past phone poles, billboards, tumbleweeds, roadkill, cellular towers, oil wells, towering overhead power lines, sprawling cattle ranches, and dried-up mountain ranges without stopping. I had the urge to pull the car over and examine each hillside and every billboard, wanting to linger on the side of the highway and take my time. Instead, I drove on with a sense of duty—a mission that needed completing.

In the weeks before my father and I drove to Albuquerque, I spent plenty of time contemplating this looming six-hour drive. Six hours seemed like far too long to sit still. As the day wore on, I got more confident behind the wheel and less cautious. My knuckles blushed back into pink, and my arms loosened up and bent with comfort. The vibrations from the tires rotating on the road made me forget why I was driving to New Mexico in the first place.

"Whatcha think the kids'll be like?" I asked my father, breaking a long stretch of silence.

"Not sure. Just like you, I guess."

"How do you mean?"

"I don't know," my father said, looking out the window.

"I'm thinking there'll be all kinds of different kids. From all over, don't you think?"

"Maybe. Just the same, I'd assume it'll be kids from ranches, small towns, and the like."

"A bunch of kids from Albuquerque, too. The lady I talked to, the one at admissions, said lots come from Albuquerque."

"Well, there you go. Seems like you already know then." My father rested his chin in his hand but didn't take his eyes off the window.

As we neared Albuquerque, we exited the highway to stop for lunch. Driving down the main drag of the nondescript town, surveying the buildings on the side of the road for something good to eat.

"I saw a sign for Russell's when we pulled off the highway. Should be up here somewhere," my father said. Russell's Chicken and Biscuits was his top choice when it came to dining out.

As we drove, I saw a sign unlike any I had ever seen before. The billboard advertised a business called *TJ's Showroom* and featured a generously bosomed woman wearing nothing but what appeared to be a fifteen-foot long belt that was wrapped around her body four times. The belt strap barely covered her nipples and ran straight down between her legs, covering up the space between her thighs. She was laid out in an uncomfortable position, with one of her legs pointed straight up into the air.

As I pored over my new favorite billboard, my father spotted Russell's Chicken and Biscuits. "Here we go. You see it up here on the right?" he asked, trying to make sure I didn't miss it. I nodded my head, but my attention had been kidnapped by the beautiful sign.

As I turned the old Ford into Russell's parking lot, I sneaked another peek at Ms. Belt Straps. The placement of the sign gave off the effect of her lording over Russell's lot. As the truck pulled its long body into the lot, the sign reached out and grabbed me. Not the sign with Ms. Belt Straps, but the sign that said, "Welcome to Russell's." It reached out and grabbed the old Ford on the passenger-side door and ripped my mirror clean off.

I've never killed a man, but the shock that went through my body once I realized what I had just done must have been the same as watching a man fall dead after you shoot him. Fear, adrenaline, and regret blew through my veins as I parked the truck.

"Damn, Otis! You ain't even had the truck for twenty-four hours before you take the doors off it!" my father said as he looked out the window at the damage.

"Shit. I can't believe I just did that," is what came out of my mouth, but what I meant was, 'Did you see that fucking sign?' He had seen the sign, and he knew that I had seen the sign.

After we ate, my father asked the kid at the register to speak to the manager. Asking for the manager at fast-food restaurants was something he enjoyed doing. If he had a question, regardless of context, he felt like he should ask the person with the most authority.

When my father asked the manager if there was a junkyard nearby, the manager let out a laugh. Little did we know that New Mexico was littered with junkyards. Just about every person in the state has one out in front of their house. The manager gave us the number to his cousin's junkyard two towns away in the direction we were going. We called up, and just like my father predicted, they had an old Ford truck with both the mirrors still on it. We stopped at the junkyard, my father swapped out the busted mirror for the newish one, and we were back on the road like nothing had happened.

"Fifty bucks is a cheap price to pay for a lesson on keeping your dern eyes on the road," my father said, smirking.

"Yessir. Took my eye off the road."

"Didn't have anything to do with that billboard, did it?" my father asked, his smirk doubled in size.

"What billboard?"

"The one with the tits."

"Oh. That one," I said, blushing.

And then we were there, in Albuquerque. My father took the wheel as soon as we entered the city, and I helped him navigate his way to the college. Once we arrived, we carried my belongings to the dormitory, my new home.

The dorm I was assigned to was a massive adobe building, artfully crafted but with a tinge of sterility. Walking through the halls of the building felt like being in a hotel you knew you were going to be stuck in. I couldn't wrap my mind around the idea that a utilitarian complex of rooms could be somebody's home.

FOUR

My father watched as I loaded my dresser up with my clothes. As I finished, he looked into my empty duffel bag and then at the open drawers of the dresser.

"Where're your knickers?" he asked.

"I don't have any."

"How come?"

"Cause I don't wear any," I said.

"Damn, Otis, you don't wear no chonies? Your mother knows this?"

"No, sir. I don't think so. But I haven't worn them for some time, so she might."

He shook his head, his face a mixture of disgust and disappointment. I laughed as I folded the empty duffel bag up and tucked it into my closet.

After settling in, my father took me out to eat. The restaurant was full of other kids eating their last familial meal with their parents. My father and I ate quickly and quietly. He had booked a one-way flight to Odessa that was set to take off that night, so he had me drive him out to the airport straight from dinner. He was three hours early for his flight but didn't seem to mind.

As I drove away from the airport, I was bombarded by sadness. Overlooked emotions un-numbed themselves and began to terrorize me, affecting my ability to control my body. My eyes got all wet and hard to see through, my breath became heavy. In the chaos, I gasped for air, then let out a deep snort. The snorting and the crying built up a massive tickle inside my head— tickle that could only be alleviated by an unavoidable, impending sneeze. The sneeze came without my consent and blew through the cab of my truck like a chinook wind. Paralyzed momentarily, when I regained movement, I found that a shot glass worth of liquid shit had painted the inside of my jeans. I marveled at the fact that a sneeze could be so powerful that it caused me to lose the ability to pucker my asshole. It had never occurred to me that such a sneeze was possible. I remembered something just then that I had forgotten since the last time I had eaten Russell's Chicken and Biscuits, which was that Russell always left me with diarrhea.

I got back to the dorm and duck-walked my way up the three flights of stairs to my room to grab some new pants and my toiletry kit. Walking through the hallway of my dorm, I tried as hard as I could to make myself invisible. Finally, I made it safely to my room only to be greeted by a smiling, happy Mexican family.

A mother and a father, a daughter, and two sons stood in front of me, all eager to meet their son's new bedfellow. One of the sons was sitting on my bed, and the other son was laying sheets out on the bed that I had already decided I didn't want. Frozen in front of that nice family, words were hard to find.

"Hi, I'm Ruiz," the guy making the bed said. He extended his hand and I shook it. Ruiz's hand was skinny and full of bones, as was the rest of him. His thick black hair stuck straight up out of his head, framing his sunken face. He was a little shorter than me and looked like he was half my weight. Later on, I'd learn that he had been brought up in Albuquerque and knew the place well. He worked throughout his entire childhood, sweeping job sites after school and roofing in the summer so that he could save enough money to live in the dorms. Albuquerque State was a commuter school, having no more than 2,000 kids that lived on campus. The rest of the massive student body lived at home with their folks, and Ruiz wasn't interested in being one of them.

"Otis Billings. Nice to meet you," I said politely to my new roommate.

"This is my dad and my mom," he said, looking over to the two older people in the room. "My sister Maria and my brother Juanito." As he introduced them, I shook each of their hands, my butt cheeks clenched as tight as possible. "Ruiz is my last name, but that's what everybody calls me." Ruiz had a confidence in him that told me he knew something I didn't and was deciding whether or not to fill me in.

"Yeah, I figured that. Never met anyone with the first name Ruiz," I said, intending to be playful but landed flat. We sat in silence as his parents looked me up and down. Ruiz's sister didn't pay much attention to me, and despite the secret in my pants, I wished she would have.

"OK, let's go," Ruiz said to his family. "We're going to eat. See you when I get back." I said goodbye, casually leaning against a wall as I watched them walk on through the room and out the door. As soon as the door closed, I scrambled to grab new clothes and my toiletries, then headed to the showers to wash my accident away.

The communal bathroom was empty and still clean; the onslaught of kids had not yet set upon the tile-floored temple of hygiene. Lingering in the steamy grotto of the locker room style shower stall, I reflected on an eventful day. I moved from Texas to New Mexico, acquired a truck, wrecked a truck, got a roommate, and shit my pants all between a single sunrise and sunset. The day ended in a hot, stale-aired room with a stranger. Ruiz snored delicately as I lay in my new bed, staring at the ceiling. Having never been to summer camp, I couldn't be sure, but I imagined that going to college must be similar. Away from my family for the first time, meeting new people, eating in a cafeteria, and bunking up with strange kids from places I knew nothing about. That first night while I stared at the ceiling, I had no idea what was in store, but it didn't stop me from guessing.

FIVE

Just like at home, meals were taken in a communal fashion at the university. A half dozen Mexican women stood in front of giant trays of food, waiting for students to request a scoop. When called upon, the women artfully slopped generous portions down on the waiting plates. When we were all lined up, ready to receive our meals, the people around me looked just like large children dressed up for a special occasion—all with their own style and haircuts and shoes. I don't know why I was surprised to find that the other kids didn't look like me, but I was.

I took my tray full of fried bits and cheesy noodles to a long table and sat down on a plastic chair that, upon seeing it, seemed too small, but when I sat down, it fit just right. As the cafeteria filled up, people moved closer and closer to me until they were sitting with me. My table filled up with men, and the table next to us with women. The tables went like that throughout the cafeteria; I guess the natural order was to segregate ourselves by gender.

Eating our food in silence, everybody looked so vulnerable. We were all new, we didn't know anybody, and we had no status—a collection of lone wolves eating off the same carcass. I liked looking around at all the wide eyes.

"Have you guys found weed yet?" one guy asked the table. "I'm in the market if so."

I said no, and so did a few other people, but the rest seemed to not hear him. He spoke up again, "Anyone have a fake ID?"

The question was answered with sheepish denials and head shakes, then one guy spoke up, "I have one, it's not that great but it works."

The eyes of the table shifted to the diminutive guy who had just spoken. He had slicked-back black hair and a seasonally inappropriate leather jacket on. The guy barely passed for an eighteen-year-old college student, let alone a twenty-one year-old man, but that didn't deter anyone from putting their faith, and money, in him. In the time it took me to finish my meal, he arranged to buy beer for a few of the guys at the table. I went back to the dorm with a belly full of casserole.

When I returned to my room, Ruiz was sitting on his bed, messing with the stereo on his dresser. I lay down on my bed and thought about the guys in the cafeteria.

Ruiz seemed to be indifferent to me. He was friendly enough, but we hadn't had a real deep conversation yet or even much of a shallow one. I hesitated to engage him, but my curiosity got the better of me.

"Hey, Ruiz."

"Yeah?" he asked, turning to face me. "What's up?"

"You a big drinker?"

"Fuck yeah," he said, nodding his head.

"Cool." I went back to staring at the ceiling.

"Why do you ask?" Ruiz turned back to his stereo.

"No reason. Some guy in the cafeteria was talking about fake IDs."

"Those are pretty cool, I guess. My cousin will buy us booze, though. Don't worry about fake IDs and all that shit. I got you covered." Ruiz had a certain pride in his voice as he spoke. His confidence on the subject put a spotlight on my insecurity.

"I never really drank before," I said, knowing it would come out sooner or later.

"What do you mean?"

"I've never been drunk before, never even tried a beer."

"Never tried beer? How is that possible?"

When I was fifteen, I went for a ride with my Uncle Grant in his truck. We drove around the ranch looking at all the sheep and talking about what needed to get done in the following weeks. From under his seat, Uncle Grant pulled out a bag of Levi Garret chewing tobacco and balled up a pinch of brown sticky leaves in his palm while he drove with his knee. He opened his lips and tucked the wad back into the side of his mouth next to his bottom molars. He grabbed the wheel with one hand, and with the other, he picked up the pouch of tobacco out of his lap and offered it up to me. I looked at the pouch and then up to my uncle, and he made a "Go ahead" gesture. I took a pinch of the brown moist leaves and plopped it into my hand, balling it up just as I had seen him do. The little brown marble of chaw fit perfectly in between my cheek and molars. I looked back at Uncle Grant and he smiled, then turned his head and spat a giant goop of molasses-colored liquid out the window. Mirroring his movements with less grace but the same result, my spittle hit the dusty road below.

And that's it, that's all I had done. Chewing tobacco with my uncle was as close to doing drugs as I had ever been. Uncle Grant's unwritten rules for the ranch included no drinking and no smoking; therefore, booze was never around. The kids I went to high school with stole their dad's beer and went to great lengths to get whiskey and cigarettes, but I never felt like going through all the trouble just to try something I didn't know if I liked.

Ruiz, however, was ready to share his stories of a different high school experience. His cousins got him drunk and high at a young age, and he spent his high school days partying. His parents were strict, but they both worked and weren't around enough to keep him away from substances. After a few conversations, it was apparent that getting fucked up was Ruiz's favorite hobby. He loved telling me about all the different types of weed he had smoked and all the alcohol he had brought to various parties. He was quite the storyteller.

"We'll start you off on the light stuff," he told me, excitement on his face. "Liquor will fuck you up too bad. Do you like cigarettes?"

"Never tired one."

Ruiz taught me how to inhale smoke into my lungs and exhale it out of my nose. The hot smoke hurt like hell, and I coughed so hard I was sure the lining of my lungs was coming apart. As bad as the cigarettes burned and as bad as the beer tasted, I loved it all. When I was a kid, I idolized cowboys, and smoking cigarettes and drinking beer made me feel like Gus and Woodrow. After a little while, the beers started to taste alright and the cigarettes didn't burn my lungs so bad anymore.

School wasn't nearly as rigorous as I had anticipated. Go to class for a few hours each day, do some homework, and I still had a whole lot of day left to do as I pleased. With all the free time, Ruiz was able to get me up to speed on partying, which, according to him, was the entire reason for college. The dorms at Albuquerque State were small, but there were still plenty of guys around who were interested in getting fucked up. I started smoking pot every day after class, and at night, Ruiz and I would walk around looking for action. The action we typically found was a group of guys sipping beers in a dorm room.

Ruiz knew I had no experience with drugs and alcohol because I told him so. What I didn't tell him, however, was that I was also a virgin. Most nights, I lay in my bed and thought about not only my virginity but the concept as a whole. I wondered why female virginity was so sacred while male virginity was so shameful. If only the roles could have been reversed. When the guys in my dorm talked about sex, I would nod my head and say things like, "Yeah" and "Cool," hoping they wouldn't turn to me for any type of input.

Ruiz, of course, was well versed in the ways of women. He liked to tell tales of his sexual conquests almost as much as he liked telling stories about getting high and drunk.

"I met this girl at a party up on the Northside, the rich part of town," he had said. "We were hooking up when the cops showed up and broke up the party." When he told these stories, it was almost like he was back there, reliving his missed opportunity.

After hearing a few dozen of Ruiz's salacious tales, I started to notice a pattern. The story would start out promising: "We were about to fuck," he would say, then lament, "but then these dudes got in a fight." Or, "Her parents came home just as I was about to put on the condom."

I waited in the shadows, deciding to ambush him the next time he spoke of a failed sexual encounter. He gave in to my trap. "We were about to fuck and then her nose started to bleed. It was crazy! I guess she gets them all the time, but it totally killed the mood," he said.

"You tell a lot of these stories, and they all end the same," I said. "Do you have any stories where you actually get lucky?"

"Well, I don't like to kiss and tell," he said.

"Bullshit. You tell at least two stories a day that involves you kissing some girl. I noticed you never get laid in any of them, though." I handed him a beer to help ease the blow of my confrontation. I opened one myself and laid down on the bed. "Look, it's not a big deal. You never hear me tell stories about chicks."

"True, you don't. Why is that?"

"Because I don't have any." It was only right to admit my secret if I expected him to admit his.

"I don't have any either... successful ones, that is," he said just a little louder than a whisper.

"Really? I thought you were so experienced."

"Nope, not really. I've hooked up before but never got it in," he said, looking over his shoulder as if other people were in the room and he didn't want them to hear.

"We're in college, right? From what I hear, it's supposed to be some kind of big pussy party," I said.

"So they say. In movies, they make college look like a four-year orgy. Seems like that might not be the case," Ruiz said.

"Who would have thought movies lie?" I asked, and we both laughed.

This conversation got my wheels turning. Without the stress of keeping my secret, I spent time pondering the reasons as to why we might not be having any success. The first thing that seemed off was that we weren't often in contact with women. Our nights typically involved listening to music, drinking beer, smoking cigarettes, and playing ping pong. All of these activities were done in the company of men. But outside of our limited exposure to women, other issues needed to be addressed. After all, we weren't completely isolated from the opposite sex. On the off chance that we did hang out with the ladies in our dorm, we had no idea how to behave. We drank until we puked, or we smoked weed until we couldn't talk. In my limited experience, I had found that women liked talking, and they didn't like barf. My deep contemplation on the subject led to some sort of epiphany, quite possibly the first epiphany I had ever had. My breakthrough was this: If there was some way to restrain myself, if I could only have a few beers or only smoke a little bit of weed, I may have more success with the ladies.

Going forward, instead of drinking six or seven beers, I paced myself with four. Instead of ripping bongs, I took a few puffs on a joint. Right away, I could tell that I was maintaining my composure better, and I was enjoying myself a lot more. Even with the newfound restraint, progress on the female front was slow. Cutting back on drink and drugs was a start, but I knew I needed to do something other than hanging out in my friend's dorm room if I wanted to get laid.

SIX

Going into college, I didn't know what I wanted to study. Trying to pick a career when I was eighteen seemed as reasonable as picking one meal to eat for the rest of my life. As a scholarship student, I needed to declare a major in my first semester, and the school mandated that I visit a student counselor in order to do so. The counselor was supposed to help me with my decision, and I assume it was also their job to make sure I made one.

"What are you good at?" she asked me straight away.

"I don't know. I'm good at all sorts of stuff."

"What was your best subject in high school?"

"Hard to say. My school wasn't too challenging. I got good grades in every subject. That's why y'all are letting me come here for free."

"You're not giving me too much to go on here," she said and laughed, although she didn't seem to be joking around. "What was your *favorite* subject in school?"

"Probably English. Read a book, write a paper, easy enough. No studying, no tests."

"Good. You should join the English Department. You can take a few classes and then decide whether you want to study Literature or Creative Writing."

"That's it? Am I declared now?"

"That's it. That's all you gotta do. When you decide which track you want to go down, let me know, and we can chat again." The counselor was ready to wipe her hands clean of me, but I didn't budge.

"One more question, if you don't mind?" She smiled and nodded her head yes. "What job will I do when I get a degree?"

"Whatever job you want, I suppose."

"I mean, what job can an English degree get me?"

"An English degree is a very broad and flexible degree. It will open a lot of doors. Of course, if you study creative writing, if you go down that track, then you'll want to be a writer. If you study literature, you could go into editing or publishing. But it doesn't have to be so specific, our English grads go on to do all kinds of work."

"A writer?"

"A most competitive field. Not a lot of folks hiring writers, but there will be some jobs out there. Do you like to write?"

"I like to write papers for class."

"Good. Keep writing, maybe someday you'll be famous." She smiled again, seeming to be pleased with herself.

I walked out of that office with a head of steam. For me, having grown up on a ranch in West Texas, greatness was measured in acres and by heads of cattle, the size of a man's truck, the X's on the band of his hat, and the quality of his boots. Greatness was well defined, and everyone on the ranch had the same idea of what it looked like. It looked like Uncle Grant. He had all the money, all the smarts, all the power. I never wanted to be Uncle Grant, but I was thirsty for his greatness. This counselor lady reminded me that fame and greatness came in more than one flavor. From that day forward, there was a chemical change in my body. All the atoms that made me up changed over and morphed into some new phase. I was reborn. Writing would take me where I wanted to go. I was a writer.

My first semester at school was loaded up with the beginner-level English classes that I was required to take, and they proved to be well-stocked with women—a pleasant surprise. My nights with the boys did not include much exposure to females, but my days were shrouded in feminine energy.

The first few weeks in class, I spent my time scanning the room, ogling all of these new women. I had a favorite in every class. There was Jenny in my writing and rhetoric class; plain looking but quick-witted and smart as a whip. Sarah was in my Western Lit class; she was a stunner, almost too beautiful. Annabelle was in my Modern Contemporary Lit class; she was personable and not the least bit shy, and her confidence was alluring.

Late at night, once Ruiz was asleep, I fantasized about having sex with my classmates, not just the crushes. Every woman in my classes, even the female teachers, played a part in my masturbation rituals. My fantasies typically included an educational theme. I would imagine undressing my teacher in the middle of class, or make up an elaborate scenario where I ran into a classmate on the quad and seduced her in the library stacks. I was much better at creating fictitious sex than I was at creating fictitious stories for my writing classes. 'Maybe I'll write romance novels,' I thought, half-serious.

Growing up on a ranch, nestled up next to a small town, I knew everybody around me, and they knew me. At school, I was an unknown, and it took some getting used to. After a while, I settled into a life of anonymity. One day after class, I was walking home when someone tapped me on the shoulder. I thought I must have dropped something, but when I turned around, one of my favorites was standing there. Annabelle's big chestnut eyes were looking up at me. She was a small person but she had a big presence.

"You're in my dorm, aren't you?" she asked.

"Uh, which one are you in?" I asked, pretending not to know.

"Coronado. Same as you. I've seen you in the cafeteria."

"Oh, yeah. Now that you mention it, I think I've seen you around," I said, squinting my eyes like she was at first blurry but now coming into focus. "How's it going? I'm Otis." Approaching someone I didn't know and telling them that I recognized them seemed like something that could get you thrown in prison. The courage of this brown-banged woman baffled me.

"Annabelle," she said as she reached out a hand to shake. I shook it, and she said, "What do you think of Modern Lit? I noticed you're in my class."

"You notice a lot, huh?"

"I do. Sorry if I'm being nosey."

"No, not at all, I'm impressed."

"I was hoping Modern Lit would be a great class; the jury's still out, I guess."

"It seems ok so far. I liked *A Brave New World,* but I guess we'll see how the other books go," I said.

"The rest of the readings look pretty good. Still getting a hold of this whole college thing, ya know?"

"I do," I said, shaking my head in agreement.

"I think maybe I've been partying too much. I mean, I'm having a blast, but it's a lot."

"I can relate," I said.

"Yeah?"

"The first few weeks in the dorms were a little out of control. I wasn't a big drinker or anything in high school, and now I'm drinking all the time." Annabelle nodded and I said, "Actually, I worked out a little system."

"What's that?"

"If I stick to just three or four beers and go easy on the pot, then I'm ok. No puking, no paranoia, no spins."

She laughed a delicate, irresistible little laugh. "You're pretty funny. I thought you were some kind of tough guy from the way you look. But you're harmless," she said.

"Thanks."

"I meant that in a good way." I took her word for it. We made it to the dorm, and instead of saying bye, she asked, "Why don't you show me this system you've got? What are you doing Friday? If you want to hang out and party a little, I'll be around."

"Sure. Sounds good," I said, trying my absolute hardest to play it cool. "What room are you in?"

"1550. See ya Friday?" I nodded my head, and she hopped on the elevator. I took the stairs.

Before I had ever been on an actual date, the idea of dating conjured a very formal experience in my mind. You are supposed to ask a woman out, and if she accepts, you pick her up, open the car door for her, buy her a milkshake, and win her a few carnival prizes, then you take her home, and maybe you get a kiss. Then, Annabelle asked me to hang out. Upon careful review of my interaction with her, I realized I had no idea what had just been agreed to. The invitation was vague; maybe she just wanted to be friends, or maybe 'partying' was a euphemism she used for wild sex. Racked with a mix of anxiety and excitement, Friday couldn't come soon enough. One positive to come out of all this was that jerking off had never been easier or more vivid than the days leading up to the planned "hang out" with Annabelle.

After class on Friday, I took a shower and dressed in my cleanest clothes. I fussed with my hair, shaved my face, and put on an extra dab of aftershave. Annabelle didn't give me a specific time to come over—a form of torture for a prompt person like myself. I fought off my eagerness and waited until nine o'clock before heading up the elevator. When I showed up to her dorm room, I was disappointed and, in a way, relieved to find that there were ten other people jammed into her tiny room.

Annabelle let me in the door, hugging me as I entered. Inside, pop music echoed off the walls, the room bustling with people drinking light beer. The kids in the room looked as if they had been cast for a made-for-TV movie about the dangers of teenage drinking. Annabelle introduced me, "Y'all this is Otis. He's in my English class."

"Howdy, partner!" said a guy who was abundantly stronger and more handsome than me. The other kids in the room let out a collective laugh. The handsome, strong man who had greeted me belched out in victory, which elicited another round of laughter. In a dorm with plenty of ranch kids and small-town nobodies, I had been identified as both, which happened to be the lowest caste.

"Don't be a dick, Josh," Annabelle said to my saluter as she sat down terribly close to him.

"I'm only kidding, buddy. How bout' a beer?" Before I could answer, Josh hurled a cold can of light beer right at me. Miraculously, I caught it and popped it open, spray and foam splashing all over my arm and hand. All was forgotten, as even the biggest assholes on the planet were tolerable when they were willing to share their beer.

Sipping beer, making small talk with strangers, all the while, I had a tough time finding a comfortable place to sit. Focusing on the fascinating conversations that were happening around me was difficult. My mind was on Josh, who was right at home amongst his peers. He had the confidence of a man who was getting laid regularly. His chest was rigid and showed through his tight-fitting t-shirt. His baseball hat sat perfectly on top of his coiffed hair. Guys like Josh didn't have to do anything special to attract women, but they did it anyway. His outfit was neat and clean, and his clothes fit him well. It felt like every person in the room was sitting next to him, waiting for him to speak.

The way Josh sat next to Annabelle, I feared that maybe they were an item. And those fears were confirmed, over and over, as Josh cuddled, flirted, and kissed Annabelle throughout the night. My disappointment was seeping from my pores, but I tried my best to not let my emotions show. I drank beer and shot the shit with everybody in the room *but* Annabelle and Josh. Biding my time, I waited for an opportunity to excuse myself.

When I finished my beer, I stood up and said, "Annabelle, I'm going to take off. I'll see you in class on Monday." Then, I addressed the room, "It was nice meeting y'all."

"Aww, Otis. Thanks for coming." Annabelle got up from her bed and walked me the short distance to the door.

I thanked her for having me, and she looked over her shoulder then back to me and whispered, "Come back in an hour, ok?" and shut the door before I could say yes.

I returned to my room, trying to wrap my head around what had happened and what would potentially happen if I returned to her room in an hour. Ruiz was playing video games when I got back. He was slouched over, sitting Indian-style on his bed, oblivious to the outside world. His eyes were set back into his skull; he looked stoned and sad. I lit a cigarette and laid down on my bed.

"How'd it go?" Ruiz asked without taking his eyes from the television screen.

"Hard to say."

"What does that mean?"

"I showed up, and there were a bunch of people in her room, including some asshole that sure seemed to be her boyfriend."

"Damn, she has a boyfriend?" Ruiz asked, pausing the game and looking over to me.

"I guess so. He's an asshole."

"Well, you win some, you lose some, I guess," Ruiz said.

"When I left, she told me to come back in an hour. Pretty confusing."

Ruiz's eyes glowed like a jack-o-lantern. "She said that? Like, in front of everybody?"

"No. She showed me to the door and whispered it to me. Nobody else could hear."

"Jumping Jesus! She's gonna suck your dick, dude. You mother fucker." Ruiz unpaused his game and began clicking buttons on the controller in his hand. "Now that I think about it, you should probably just send me. I'm ready to go. I can tell you're scared." Ruiz spoke fast when he was excited.

"I'm trying to stay calm. Your crazy ass howling at the moon isn't going to help," I told him.

"Can I have one of those?" he asked, looking at the lit cigarette in my hand. I handed him one. He paused his game again and lit the cigarette. He took a long, deep drag. As he exhaled the smoke, he shook his head from side to side. "You lucky bastard," he said while his internal gears turned, jealousy coming off of him like steam.

"Will you take a picture?" he asked after thinking for a minute.

"Of Annabelle? No. Are you insane?"

"Why not?"

"You *are* insane. If I get lucky enough to get her naked, I'm not going to fuck it up by asking her if I can take a picture. What kind of psycho would do that?"

"Come on, man."

"Get the fuck out of here. You can jerk off while I'm gone."

"Fuck, I need to. My schedule's been all fucked up since I started living here."

"I believe it. It's pretty weird that they make two grown people live together like this."

"Every time I try to yank it, I look over and you're sleeping there. It kills the mood. I have to go to my closet or I can't jerk off at all."

"The closet? Well, that's ok, I guess."

"It's my only option."

Ruiz's honesty cut through our excitement and we descended into silence. He unpaused his game.

I went to the bathroom and brushed my teeth for the fourth time that day, a new record. In the mirror, I looked alright, but I shuffled my hair around a little anyway.

Sixty-two minutes after Annabelle whispered me out the door, I headed back to the scene of my earlier frustration, hoping for redemption. I knocked softly on her door, and after a few long seconds, she answered. She was wearing an oversized t-shirt and no pants, and my jeans almost combusted. Calmly, as smooth as possible, I followed her into her now empty room and sat down on her bed. She grabbed two beers out of her university-issued miniature refrigerator and handed me one. We made idle chit-chat and sipped our beers. I pretended to adjust myself while inching closer to her.

The moments before kissing a woman for the first time can be smooth and organic, or it can be a tense situation full of doubt and hesitancy. In this case, we piled onto each other in a wave of lips and tongues. Our teeth clinked and our noses mashed, but we didn't give up.

Persevering through the rough start, we settled into a rhythm. My nerves calmed and my horniness spiked. What was playing out in real life felt like a fantasy. The chill music that Annabelle had put on was interrupted by a loud knock on the door. I froze, and Annabelle jumped up. She quietly sprung to the door and peeked through the peephole. She turned back to me, frantically waving her arms in a pattern that I instinctively knew meant to get under the fucking bed. I obliged just in time for her to open the door.

"Hey, babe." It was Josh at the door. "Pretty sure I left my phone in here. Can I look around?" Josh asked as he let himself in. It was as if I was watching a scene from a movie play out, and the acting was done solely by foot.

"Are you sure you left it? I didn't see it anywhere," Annabelle said as Josh's feet shuffled around the room.

"Why are you being so weird tonight?"

"I just have a headache. I'm trying to sleep." She sat down on the bed; Josh was still standing. "Your phone's not here, is it?"

"I wanted to talk to you."

"I told you I wanted to be alone. I don't feel well," Annabelle lied.

"Alright. Sorry to bother you," Josh said, defeated. "Sorry for trying to spend time with you."

"You know it's not like that. Don't be a drama queen." The tough guy from before was getting pushed around by a tiny little bully, and I loved it.

"Then what is it?"

"I told you, I'm tired and I want to sleep without anyone bothering me." Without anymore talking, I saw Josh's feet walk toward the door and let himself out. After a moment, I grabbed Annabelle's dangling foot, startling her.

"Jesus Christ. I almost forgot you were under there." I rolled out from under the bed and hopped up next to her. We kissed through our adrenaline rush. She pulled her giant t-shirt shirt up over her head, revealing a tiny pair of cotton panties and bare breasts the size and shape of Bartlett pears. My shirt came off, but I left my pants on out of fear of getting naked too quickly. Our skin-to-skin embrace shot a bolt of electricity through my body. With her warmth against my chest and her legs wrapped around me, I fell into a pleasant fever.

While we kissed, I debated my next move. Should I go for more? Should I be happy with what was going on and not ruin the moment? The ambitious side of the debate won out, and I eased my hand down into her panties. I didn't make it far before she stopped my fumbling hand and removed it from her underwear.

We made out for a little while longer, and then we transitioned back to drinking our beers. We smoked a joint while we lay next to each other on the bed and talked about school. I told her I wanted to be a writer, and she told me she wanted to work for a publishing company. Her dream was to live in New York but would probably have to settle for LA, a nice consolation prize, as far as I could tell. Stoned and a little drunk, we cuddled our way into sleep while Cat Stevens played in the ether.

In the middle of the night, I awoke in a state of confusion, unsure of my whereabouts. Annabelle's room was pitch black and I couldn't see anything. As my eyes adjusted to the dark, I realized that Annabelle had woken me up—she was sitting on my pelvis. I was foggy and still a little drunk, and it took me a second to realize my cock was inside her. Completely naked with an arched back, she rode back and forth gently, making soft, concentrated hums. She went up and down a dozen times, and then everything came into focus. As I came to, I realized an imminent explosion was building up deep inside my loins. A naked, rather attractive woman was on top of me, I had no condom on, and I was about to come. Half gently, half hurriedly, I pulled her off of me just in time to evacuate on my stomach. I didn't know what to say, so I said, "Hold on!" For what? To this day I have no idea what I expected her to hold on for.

Never have I been so conflicted about an orgasm. Shame, pleasure, fear, confusion, embarrassment, and ecstasy all at once. Annabelle let out a shallow sigh and laid back down on the bed. We both sat in the dark, not speaking, not moving. I waited until her heartbeat was the consistency of a sleeping puppy, and then I carefully got out of bed and dressed. As

I snuck out of her room, I felt like at any moment, a great big prison spotlight would shine on me and I would have to explain why I came so fast.

Back in my room, I smoked cigarettes in my underwear and looked out the tiny open window—the only window we had in our dorm room. Next to me as I smoked, Ruiz was sleeping a deep, virginal slumber. He was free of the embarrassment and unexpected vulnerability of being a person who has had sex. I tried to reconcile the shame of my premature ejaculation and did so by remembering that I was no longer a virgin, my life's biggest achievement up to that point. Sex with an attractive woman was a feat, and if I squinted and focused only on this objective truth, I felt good. But relief was fleeting, as the circumstances of the night before were too hard to forget, and I couldn't help but fear the uncomfortable days ahead. 'Why do people have sex with people they know?' I asked myself. 'There should be a service that allows people to have sex with strangers so they don't have to relive their shame when they see each other in Modern Contemporary Lit on Monday.'

I didn't ever want to see Annabelle again, but I also desperately wanted to see her again. Wanting to hold her and find out about all the things she loves and all the things she hates and see if they match the things I love and the things that I hate. There was also the fact that I needed practice having sex—would she be willing to give me another shot? There was no way of telling, but it was killing me not to know. The only thing I could do, in the meantime, was smoke cigarettes and worry.

The next morning, I had no choice but to tell Ruiz what had happened. I explained the scene, Josh's intrusion, me waking up in the middle of the night, and my premature ejaculation.

"It's not that bad," he said, to my surprise.

"Really? I don't know if I told the story right."

"What's the big deal? You busted too quick. Pretty sure chicks expect that. See, I knew you should have sent me, I knew you weren't ready."

"You think she expected it? I don't know, she seemed pretty disappointed."

"I'm sure she was. But I bet she gets it. Sounds like it wasn't her first ride."

"Seemed to know what she was doing."

"Of course she did. You just woke up and she was on top of you? That's so awesome. Straight out of a movie," Ruiz said, and he seemed to be imagining the scenario in his mind. I left the room to take a shower. Ruiz didn't notice; he just sat on his bed, looking out the window just like I had the night before.

SEVEN

My first day of being a non-virgin was suspiciously uneventful. Before I had ever had sex, I spent a lot of time thinking about my first time; however, I hadn't thought much about what would happen afterward. There were no universal truths uncovered, I wasn't cooler or more interesting in any way. As far as I could tell, I wasn't any more of a man than I was the day before. I didn't get stronger or smarter or any more mature. Women weren't drawn to me like a fish to a lure. Not knowing what I should expect, I hadn't expected any of these things to happen, but it was a bit disappointing to find out that nothing would change. Losing my virginity was so important to me, and then once it happened, it felt so unimportant. An anticlimax on top of an anticlimax.

With nothing better to do, Ruiz and I got drunk. We drifted from room to room looking for something to happen. The dorm was abnormally sedate for a Saturday night. We smoked cigarettes out in front of the building, trying to keep the night alive. After a while, Ruiz rubbed his eyes and said he was too tired to stay out. He went to bed and I stayed outside, convinced that sipping my whiskey flask under the moonlight was romantic.

The next morning, when I woke up, the first thing I saw was that my notebook was open on my desk. On the open page was my handwriting. It read:

In the waning hours of my childhood, I don't feel like a man. Am I supposed to? I have been asking the age-old question, when does a man become a man? And society's answer seems to be a shrug of the shoulders and a best guess. I've done the things I thought I was supposed to do, checking as many boxes as I can find. And still, I repeat, I don't feel like a man. I am a long child that smokes cigarettes and uses adult language. Nothing more, and certainly plenty less. I came here to New Mexico to find out who I will become, but I am no closer to that answer. In all measurable ways, I am further away. I am restless. When does life become fun? When will I have dominion over it? It's apparent that these questions need answering, but who will answer them?

The handwriting was bad, but the content was interesting to me only because there was something there on the page. Written words that conveyed my feelings, which was something I had never done before, regardless of medium. My memory of the night before didn't extend past drinking outside by myself. When questioned, Ruiz told me that he had woken up in the middle of the night to find me sitting at my desk, writing.

Back then, in my youth, my hangovers were very manageable. I didn't get sick or throw up or anything like that. The main side effect of hangovers for me was the slowing of my brain. Typically, I felt dumber than normal, but that morning, I possessed the clarity necessary to have a full-blown revelation. The revelation that I was a drunken writer. Like Bukowski, Kerouac, Hemingway, and countless others before me, my writing came out whilst drunk. This was an exciting discovery because I wanted to be a writer, but I hadn't found myself writing very often. I felt as though I had finally unlocked my potential.

The other exciting angle was that the writing worked. Not in the way of it being good writing, but it worked on me. In just one night, my mind went from anxiety over Annabelle to romanticized fantasies of being a famous author, which, as far as mental states are concerned, was a vast improvement. Fantasies were a most pleasurable distraction from the shame I had accrued the night before.

The idea that I may be a prolific drunk was especially exciting to me. In my high school and college years, I focused my reading curriculum on the bums, the rakes, the drunken assholes, the scumbags, the recluses, the hobos, the train hoppers, the drifters, the one night stands, divorced absent dads, the borrowers, the broke, and the down and out lonely members of our society that wrote a perspective nobody asked for and nobody could get enough of. Like many aspiring writers, I wanted to be one of these fringe members of society who were able to provide a glimpse into the other side. The magic of reading, to me, was the idea that you could be safe at home, and at the same time, through books, be in the middle of some dangerous world. And the idea that I could be the one creating and living in that world was all too intoxicating.

The easy part of all this was that I enjoyed getting drunk and doing drugs; however, as I set out for a life of debauchery, there was one area where I drew the line. I was a scholarship student, and the life I was living was completely enabled by Albuquerque State University. I got drunk at night and high all day, but I read the books I was supposed to read, I wrote the papers I was supposed to write, and I maintained the grades I needed to maintain. I had to—I had no other choice. I loved my new life too much to go back to the ranch a failure. I was just as focused on my intoxicated experiences as I was on getting my degree, and I walked the line well. My grades were not only good, they were very good.

I didn't view intoxication as a hobby; even though it was a great source of recreation for me, it was more like field research. My literary heroes had lived a certain type of life, and if I wanted to write like them, I needed to do the same. Believing this made it easy to justify my poor writing. Of course, I wasn't any good; I hadn't done anything worth writing about. Whether it was worth admiration or whether it was worth jail time, the point was, I hadn't done anything, good or bad. I told myself that I just needed to keep my head down and my nose to the beer-soaked grindstone. Day by day, I would amass a collection of sordid tales like the ones my literary champions told, and voila, I would have interesting material to write about.

After all the worrying and contemplation, Annabelle and I remained acquaintances, never advancing to a friendship or a romantic relationship. It was disappointing, but with drugs, alcohol, and literature moving to the forefront of my interests, women and sex took somewhat of a back seat. Sex became less important to me, but it wasn't completely absent from my life. Desperation wears heavy on a man's breath, and women seemed to appreciate the fact that my focused mind wasn't focused purely on sex. I wasn't all that handsome. Not quite six feet and no big broad shoulders or hard muscles. I am now, and was then, an average man. Despite all my averageness, I did ok with women in college.

Even without dating anybody seriously at school, I honed my sexual skills into a respectable shape through one-night-stands and short-lived affairs. I enjoyed the company of women, and not just for sexual reasons. They were avid readers compared to my male counterparts and made much better conversationalists. The women in my English class respected my ambition to be a writer, and I quickly learned that proclaiming this ambition was a powerful tool. As a self-proclaimed average Joe, anything that can differentiate you from the mediocre masses should be considered a valuable resource.

Dropping a line about my writing in casual conversation affected women, and in turn, it had an effect on how they viewed me. I became a multi-dimensional human in their eyes, a man with crevices, nooks, and cavities full of anecdotes, quirks, and curiosities. Without doing anything other than announcing that I would become a writer after college, I had become an interesting person.

EIGHT

The snow began outside of Roswell and fell diagonally over the highway all the way to Loving. There wasn't any real accumulation on the roads, but the white crystals hitting my windshield drove home the fact that it was Christmas time. Spending holidays in Albuquerque, void of family and tradition, had made it hard for me to get in the holiday mood. Heading south on U.S. Route 285, the snow flurries and the open high desert all signaled a proper holiday, one spent in Texas.

Crossing the border of New Mexico into Texas meant the end of the trip was near, the ranch only another fifteen miles south. Bundled up in their coats and hats, the people of my childhood greeted my arrival with hugs and holiday tidings. My mother and father were there to greet me, but my uncle wasn't.

Out in the cold gray air, I could see the desk lamp twinkling through the window of the old cabin office. After settling in, I crossed the frozen sand plain that lies between my folk's house and Uncle Grant's office.

A fire was going in the ancient cast iron stove, and when I walked through the door, Grant was down on his knees, loading wood into the maw of the sinister-looking thing. He stoked up the fire and then got to his feet. He plopped down in his chair, looking a little disoriented and dizzy.

"Welcome home, college boy," he said, smiling.

"Thank you, sir. It's good to be home."

"If it's so good then where the hell you been? We missed you this summer. Your mother came in here wanting me to call and order you to come visit. She thinks I got some type of pull over you or something."

"She misses me, I guess."

"She sure does. You're her baby, always will be."

"I suppose so."

"Glad you could make it down for the holidays. How's life up North?"

"It's good. Getting close to finishing school. Graduating in the spring, ya know?"

"I suspected it was about that time. Been four years already?"

"Yes, sir."

"Well, that's good. What'll you do with yourself?"

"Not sure yet. I haven't put too much thought into it, I guess."

"You gonna move back here?" he asked me.

"I don't know. I'm leaning towards staying up North."

"So you *have* been thinking about it. That's fine, take your time. We don't want you back here unless you're ready. It won't work well if you ain't ready."

That night, I didn't sleep much. The wind blew up against the house, growling and creaking through to the morning. I got out of bed and went down the stairs before the sun or my parents had come up. Drinking coffee and smoking cigarettes on the front porch was a fine way to watch the chili pepper sun rise up over the land.

That morning, my mom served me a breakfast of biscuits and gravy with two eggs on top. She watched me while I ate, and as soon as I finished, she said, "Now, Otis, we need to talk about the future. You're finishing school soon."

"Yes, ma'am."

"When you graduate, you'll have a decision to make," she said. My father watched me as my mother spoke.

"Yes, I have to make a decision. If you're asking me what that decision is, then you'll have to wait a little longer. I haven't quite made up my mind."

"Be real careful with that tone," my father said.

"Yes, sir. I'm sorry. Didn't mean to take a tone. Seems like everyone wants to know what I'm going to do, but I just don't have an answer, is all."

"Sure it feels like a lot of pressure, but it's just the first of about a million decisions you're gonna need to make as an adult," my mother said.

"We got faith you'll make the right decision, but your mother and I wouldn't be doing our part if we didn't have this talk with you."

"Alright then, go ahead," I said, not sure if they intended to say more.

"I'm sure you're getting a pretty good taste of what's out there. Hell, I'm sure it's tempting, being out on your own and all. But you got a responsibility to this family," my father said, at war with his words.

"Yes, sir," I said. "Just so we're clear, what is that responsibility?"

My mother looked at my father, and he looked at me. My father's teeth were clenched tight—his mouth looked like it belonged to a wounded animal.

"I never told you this, but I think you already knew it. I was hoping you could take over for me. Take my job when it's time."

"When your uncle retires, your father will need your help," my mother said.

"We'll see what happens. Nothing's for sure other than we just want you back here when you graduate. Your Uncle Grant does, too."

I loved my independence and I loved my family. I feared being trapped by life on the ranch, but I feared the insecurity of having to support myself. Surely the easiest thing would be to do what everybody wanted me to do, but that doesn't mean my decision was easy. I had thought long and hard about what I was going to do, and I was no closer to a decision than the day I left home. There was no doubt in me of what I wanted, but I had lots of doubts as to whether I was going to be brave enough to go for it.

The day after Christmas, I packed up my stuff, getting ready to hit the road. My parents were up and ready to see me off, but Uncle Grant wasn't there. I said my goodbyes, gave out hugs, and thanked everyone for their gifts. After I loaded up the truck, I stopped off at the office to say goodbye to my uncle.

When I sat down in front of his desk to say my goodbye, Grant looked strange to me. He was dressed the same as normal, his hair was combed, his face shaved clean and all that, but for reasons unknown to me, at that moment, he looked different somehow.

Grant wished me well, but before I got up to go, he stopped me. "Don't go just yet. There's this other thing I got to talk to you about. Been thinking about it for such a long time that thinking about it is almost a part of me. Everybody on the ranch thinks you'll be coming back here soon, but I don't think that's the case, so I figured I got to tell you now before you leave." Grant looked up from his desk. "There isn't any natural way to say this, so excuse me stuttering over my words. Wesley, he ain't your real dad. Not biologically, anyway."

Instead of sinking somewhere dark, I felt light, like I was floating. Like I was watching my body sit still in my chair while the rest of me floated away. My uncle came into focus, and I saw that he was waiting for me to speak.

"If he isn't, then who is?" I asked.

"Me," Uncle Grant said with an unfamiliar softness to his voice.

With the utterance of one word, my childhood fractured into a pile of sharp little pieces. My uncle continued to speak, but I couldn't hear anything he said. When he stopped talking, I rose out of my chair and left the cabin.

In the old Ford, tumbling down the gravel drive that led to the main paved road, the property got smaller and smaller in the rearview mirror until the horizon swallowed it up. My decision was made. There would be no return to the ranch, not to live and not to visit.

NINE

Through the drinking and the drugs, the late-night writing sessions that produced nothing of worth, the classes, the cigarettes in my dorm room, and surface-level male bonding, I made my way through college and achieved a degree. A degree in English with a focus on Literature. Declaring as an English major, I had every intention of learning how to be a writer, but that didn't work out quite as I had planned. In my sophomore year, I applied to the school of creative writing and was rejected. The skill and discipline necessary to be a good writer were qualities I knew I didn't have, and the shittiest thing was that you didn't necessarily need to be good to get into the writing school. To get accepted to the school of creative writing, you just needed to be average, and I couldn't even muster that. Disappointed but not entirely shattered, I stayed on the literature track and did well. I enjoyed the books I had to read, and I liked writing the papers I had to write. I was always so convinced that I needed to be a fiction writer, though it was pretty obvious, even back then, that I was much better at writing facts.

In anything I did, I always wanted to be a natural. Wanting to be a writer, it would have been convenient for me to have been born a good one. Finding out that I wasn't natural, good, or naturally good was disheartening and uninspiring. Writing was something I was going to have to work on, and I couldn't bring myself to do so.

I didn't tell anyone that I had been denied entry to the creative writing track. Whenever the topic of my major came up, I would dole out some bullshit excuse as to why I wasn't in the writing program, something like, "In order to be a great writer, I feel that you must first become a great reader," or I would say, "I wanted to focus on reading literature before I felt that I could write literature." Excuses were probably the best lines that I wrote in college. Hard to say whether or not people bought my bullshit, but I just couldn't come clean with my friends—shit, I couldn't come clean with myself. I had worked hard on the short story I submitted to the writing school, and when I submitted it, I knew it wasn't any good.

Aside from my inability to get accepted to the creative writing school, there was one other secret that I held, one that was much more challenging to explain. The secret was that other than my short story submission, I wasn't doing any real writing at all. At night, while drunk, every once in a while, I wrote about my day or about the people that I thought were terrible, sometimes it was the places I wanted to see or the food that I missed in Texas. This glorified journal keeping, however, was infrequent. I was writing on average two pages a month, maybe. Even though I was rarely ever writing, I couldn't shut up about how I was a writer. I was addicted to it. Telling people that I wrote and explaining the intricacies of being a writer was much easier for me to do than sitting by myself and actually writing. Fraud was the word that filled my head as I regaled people, mostly women, with tales of my authorship. Even though I knew I was an imposter, I didn't govern myself. Realizing that my true creativity came in the form of conversation, not prose, I couldn't stop myself from indulging in my lies.

The night I met Beatrice Sibson, I was busy telling a group of people that I was a writer, crafting a self-narrative of an introverted extrovert who spends as much time at my desk as I do at social gatherings discussing literature. In between conversations, I laughed to myself as I realized I didn't even own a desk. Standing at the keg, I was pouring myself a beer when I noticed a smiling blonde-haired woman making eyes at me. Her french bob haircut framed her cheekbones and the black horn-rimmed glasses that sat on top of them. She refused to break eye contact with me, but I was shy and didn't approach her.

After an hour or two and a few more beers, Beatrice sat down next to me on the sofa. I was sitting by myself, looking around at nothing in particular.

"You look bored," she said.

At first, I wasn't sure if she was talking to me. I looked over to her, and she was staring right at me. "Oh, I'm fine. Just one of those party lulls."

"Party lulls?"

"You know what it is. When you aren't in a conversation with anybody, and everyone else at the party is engaged, and you don't want to interrupt them, so you just fall into a lull."

"I know exactly what you're talking about."

"It's weird, right? I assume everybody experiences party lulls, yet we don't ever talk about it."

"Until now," she said, smiling a nice smile.

"I try not to let the lulls overwhelm me. I try to enjoy them and just relax. It's only normal to fall into a lull from time to time."

"I didn't realize I was sitting down next to a philosopher. From the looks of you, I would have figured you were a rancher's kid."

"That's right, sweetheart, I'm a real deal cowboy. Born and bred."

"Sweetheart, huh? I bet you think I'm a city girl, don't you?"

"Well, yes. I do believe you are," I said, feeling comfortable.

"You're wrong. I was born on a farm. Full of cows."

"If you were raising cattle, wouldn't you have done it on a ranch? A farm's where you grow vegetables and what have you," I said, getting lost in the playfulness of the atmosphere we had started in.

"We raise cows for their milk. On a farm. A dairy farm is what they call it, Mr. Smart Ass." She smiled a delicate, victorious smile.

Beatrice and I didn't go on a date after that; in fact, we didn't follow any of the traditional courtship rituals. We found ourselves around each other more and more until we were inseparable. A month after our first kiss, we fell into a rhythm of seeing each other every day.

Beatrice defied my expectations of what a woman was supposed to be. She was from Northern New Mexico and came from a long line of blonde-headed dairy farmers. The Sibson family wasn't religious, but they were as close to perfect Christians as people can be. The family was built on the belief that you respect your elders and you take care of those who can't take care of themselves. They believed in honesty and integrity, education and wisdom. It was these values that defined Beatrice and peppered her every action, thought, and word. When I looked at Beatrice, I saw a direct path to her upbringing. When I looked at my upbringing, I couldn't find a straight line anywhere in the mix.

Children and animals made Beatrice happiest. She could listen to me talk all night about the ins and outs of raising sheep in West Texas. She was almost a hippy, maybe about eighty percent, but at her core, she was much too practical. She was pretty, but her beauty was subtle—it grew in my presence. She had soft features and a generous build. She kept her large breasts a secret under sweaters and loose t-shirts. She didn't dress fancy, but she loved to shop, perusing the second-hand stores on the outskirts of town. A flannel shirt and well-worn jeans were her signature look, but she had no problem filling out a dress.

When I met Beatrice, she had half a semester left before she would graduate. She was to be a middle school teacher and already had a student teaching gig lined up at a public school in Albuquerque. Responsible and mature, she had direction. Why she chose to date me, I had no idea.

TEN

After leaving the ranch, I was sure I wasn't going back to Texas, and once I met Beatrice, my future in Albuquerque was cemented. School ended and I moved into a small studio apartment that my uncle paid the first month's rent on. It was a surprise when he offered, and I accepted because I had no other choice. He made sure to make me promise not to tell my parents that he had done it.

The next month's rent was up to me, so I applied for jobs around town. A small publishing company in the city was hiring, so I filled out an application. Never heard back from them. I applied to a local newspaper, and they immediately emailed me with a generic rejection message. A free magazine detailing the numerous tourist attractions in Northern New Mexico had an opening for a Junior Editor. I had a phone interview that went ok, but when I sent in a sample of my writing, that prompted them to never call me or respond to my voicemail messages again.

I applied to every entry-level writing job in Albuquerque—there were only a few more than a handful. After a few weeks and a lot of silence on the other line, I began applying to jobs outside of the writing industry, eventually landing at a small insurance company doing what most would describe as bitch work. My boss was this green turd named Mr. Taylor. Taylor had me doing odd jobs like building cheap furniture, filling out paperwork that I didn't understand, filing paperwork, finding things that went missing in the office, cleaning windows, and answering the door when clients came by, as well as many other mundane tasks that aren't worth noting. I made $12.50 an hour, which was enough to pay my rent, my car insurance, get drunk on the weekends, and get high any time I wasn't at work. I hated the job, but it felt good to be making money and supporting myself for the first time in my life.

While wrapping up my first few months at the new job, Beatrice graduated. She was hired by the school where she did her teacher training program, just as she had planned. She was a sixth grade English and Writing teacher. She loved her kids, and by my standards, she made good money. One of her coworkers at the school lined up a job in the summer for her, working at a day camp in the Sandia Mountains outside of town. She was happy with her life.

In the time it took Beatrice to graduate and settle into her life as a teacher, I had become miserable at the insurance company. I felt hopeless when I got home, and I took it out on Beatrice. Part of me was jealous and part of me was angry with how my life was shaping out. She was so considerate and empathetic, but my attitude took a toll on her. One day, I went to her house after work in a particularly foul mood.

"You're not happy, are you?" she asked.

"What do you mean?"

"You're hard to be around. I'm just going to be honest with you, I haven't been excited to see you in a while."

"What are you talking about?"

"You've been an asshole lately. I know you aren't good at understanding your feelings, but surely you can see that this job is making you miserable? And you're doing your best at making me miserable," she said, and then we fell quiet.

I hadn't realized how much work was affecting me until Beatrice confronted me. I owned up to it, at least the part about hating my job and being unhappy, in part because I didn't want to talk about it anymore. Admitting I was an asshole was easy for me, but fixing it seemed insurmountable. I thanked her for being honest and told her I would look for other work. This fight would take place over and over again during the course of our relationship, manifesting in different ways, but at the core, it was the same issue.

Agreeing to look for a different job was different than actually looking for a job, and on that front, I was slow to act. I didn't start looking for a new job until I had to. Mr. Taylor came in late to work one day pissed off, looking hungover and acting like he was still drunk. He staggered into his office and sat down at his desk. Through his open door, Mr. Taylor yelled out for the administrative assistant, Nancy—a short, round lady in her mid-forties. Nancy was scared shitless of Taylor, and he seemed to prefer it that way.

Nancy cowered into his office where he reamed her a good one. She came out in silent tears and sat back down at her desk. This wasn't the type of thing that happened every day, but it wasn't the first time, and once was more than enough. Normally I didn't say anything when he verbally abused my coworkers; I kept to myself, tried to fly low. On this particular day, I was just as hungover as Mr. Taylor, and all the unhappiness I had been ignoring flooded my brain. I walked into his office like a bull rider about to hop on a bad old rodeo bull.

"Mr. Taylor, Nancy just came out here in tears. I think you ought to go apologize to her," I said, masking my fear.

Taylor looked up from his computer and set his bloodshot green eyes on me. "What the fuck did you just say?" he asked me.

"You oughta say you're sorry for yelling at Nancy like you did."

"Well, howdy-do. John Denver's got some shit to say today." He let out a nice belly laugh. "I'll be damned. Your country ass hasn't said a meaningful word since you started working here. And this is the morning you choose to stand up and start talking out your ass, huh?" Taylor delivered his words in a calm manner, but I could see there was an evil, rage-filled undercurrent inside of him. I hated when he called me John Denver, and I was just as full of anger as he was.

"Yessir. Today is that day."

"Go wash my car, kid," Taylor said with all of his ego.

"Yessir. I'll get to washing your car right after you go apologize to Nancy." Taylor let out a little chuckle, almost like a cough. "I mean it," I said to him.

"Listen to me, boy. When you tell your boss you aren't going to do something, you might as well just save your voice and walk on out the door."

"I ain't quitting."

"You don't need to. Your ass is fired. Go on and get your shit, and get your stupid country ass out of my face." Taylor leaned back in his chair and put his feet up on his desk. "Go on," he said again.

I walked out of his office and back to my desk. "Nancy, Mr. Taylor said he's sorry for yelling at you." Nancy had heard the entire exchange between Taylor and me.

"No, I didn't!" Taylor yelled from his office, feet still up on the desk. I resisted the urge to run into his office and punch him in his face, mostly because he was bigger than me and seemed like the type of guy who had been in a few fights. I grabbed the only thing I owned at that office, my coffee mug, and left without saying anything else.

ELEVEN

When I left the office, I called Beatrice to tell her what had happened, but she never picked up her phone during the workday. Ruiz was a teller at a bank, and he had random days off in the middle of the week, so he agreed to come to meet me for a drink at the Tin Star. I got there before he did and had a seat at the sheet metal-topped bar. The bartender brought me a beer and a basket of peanuts. Those all-you-can-eat-free peanuts were a Tin Star specialty that had been my dinner on more than one occasion.

While I waited for Ruiz, I drank like a nervous animal. The bartender, watching me, asked, "You alright, pal?"

"Yeah, I'm fine."

"Not working today?"

"Got in a fight with my boss. He canned my ass," I said.

"Figured. You'd be surprised at how many people come directly to see me after they lose their job."

"Makes sense. Gettin' drunk was the first thing that came to mind when I walked out of my office today."

"At least you got fired, it'd be a lot worse if you'd quit."

"Yeah? Why's that?" I asked.

"Cause you don't get unemployment when you quit."

"I get unemployment for getting fired?"

"Sure you do. That's what it's for."

Ruiz walked into the bar, plopped down next to me, and waved over the bartender. "Beer me. And a shot of tequila for my friend."

"Sure thing," the bartender cracked open a beer and poured a shot. He put the beer in front of Ruiz and the shot in front of me. I took the tequila without blinking.

One of the reasons I loved the Tin Star was their staff's indifference to smoking weed in the alley behind the bar. Besides Ruiz and me, the barkeep didn't have any other customers to tend to, so he joined us on this specific occasion.

"Did you know you can get unemployment if you get fired?" I asked Ruiz.

"Yeah, that's the only way to get it, as far as I know." Ruiz hit the joint and then looked at it with his head tilted. "Did you get fired today?"

"I did."

"That's why you wanted to hang out?"

"That's not *why* I wanted to, it's why I'm *able* to."

"What happened?" he asked as he passed the joint to the bartender.

"My boss and I got in a bit of a disagreement, and he told me to get my shit and get out."

"Damn, man. Sounds like an asshole," the bartender said.

"You hated it there, didn't you?" Ruiz asked.

"I was going to start looking for other jobs anyway. Guess I have to now."

"You'll be fine. I'll ask the bank if we're hiring," Ruiz said.

"Thanks, man, I'm not too worried. Can't get worse than working for Taylor."

"You told B yet?" Ruiz asked.

"I called her, but she doesn't answer during the day. We're supposed to hang out tonight, though."

We finished the joint, went inside, and had a couple more beers. Ruiz had to go home early, so I made my way back to my apartment. As I walked through the parking lot of my building, Beatrice pulled up on her bike.

"Hey, Otis. Did you call me earlier?"

"I did. Had kind of a rough day."

"Work stuff? Or something else?"

"I got fired."

Beatrice set her bike down and hugged me. She kissed me on the cheek, and while she did, she sniffed me. Something caught her attention, so she sniffed me again.

"Are you drunk?" she asked.

"I think so."

She was disappointed and spent the rest of the night telling me so. Getting fired, disobeying my boss, and getting fucked up with Ruiz were things she would never do. She didn't need to tell me that, but she did. I told her I would get unemployment and get a new job and cut back on drinking. It felt like I was pleading with my mother, and I bet she felt something similar.

I filed for unemployment and was surprised to find a rejection letter from the state. Mr. Taylor lied to the unemployment office and told them I had quit. I appealed the decision and got lucky when Nancy stepped up and vouched that she had witnessed my termination. The decision was overturned,and the state sent me $325 a week in unemployment assistance. I wasn't about to complain about free money, but I could barely live off the amount the state was giving me. With the stress of being poor and the strain that being unemployed put on Beatrice and my relationship, I was motivated to find a new job.

I applied to a bookkeeping consultancy firm, and to my surprise, they hired me. The company was called Ledger Partners, and they specialized in bookkeeping for small businesses that didn't want to do it themselves. It was the education Uncle Grant gave me, not my degree, that got me the job.

They paid me $45,000 a year on salary. In the grand scheme of things, they were probably underpaying me, but I thought they made a clerical error when the offer was sent out to me. I calculated what my monthly salary would be and it was $3750 a month, which to me meant I was rich. Every day I could smoke ten joints and drink a twelve pack of beer and still have money left over.

Beatrice was real pleased when I got the job. I bought her dinner and we had a nice little celebration. She built me up and made me feel like I was worth more than what they were paying me. She told me I was handsome and said she was lucky to have me. I have always been susceptible to flattery.

"Why do you love me?" I asked her. "You're so much better than me. It doesn't make much sense, really."

"I just do. You're intelligent, funny, and most of the time, you're kind. I'm no better than you, just different."

"You got me beat by a mile in smarts and humor and by ten miles in kindness."

"I may, but I'm not keeping score."

"What happens if you ever do?"

"Well, I don't know, but I'm not sure why you bring this up now? I think about this stuff, but I never thought you did."

"I'm just happy with you, and I love you."

"I love you too."

I realized then that I was scared to lose Beatrice. I shook off my fear and held her close to me. We had sex and then talked for a while longer. While telling her my thoughts and my feelings, I kept an eye on the door—it felt like someone would break it down any minute. For Beatrice, this outburst of intimacy seemed to keep her optimism from running dry.

The next morning, Beatrice slept in. I woke up early and slid out of bed on my tiptoes. The sun was coming up, and I opened the window to my studio as far as it would go.

Leaning out the window with my hip bones resting on the sill, I smoked a cigarette. The orange and red New Mexican sun rose over the Sandia mountains to the east. I breathed that cigarette smoke in deep and let it out like a popped bike tire, hard at first then petering out to barely a breeze. I loved smoking, I loved tobacco, I loved the way smoke went in and peace came out. My mind didn't race when I smoked; I could just focus on the moment. I had a real problem with scanning the past and jumping to the future, analyzing, projecting, assuming what could have been or what might be on the horizon. When I smoked, I could enjoy the sunrise and the slow progression of shadows crawling down the mountains until they were completely illuminated in the bright light of the day.

When Beatrice woke, she made skillet potatoes and eggs. What a cook she was—her potatoes were better than the ones I was raised on. We sipped coffee in our underwear and enjoyed the quiet, cool morning air. We finished breakfast with a joint and she went to the couch to read her book. Beatrice and I could relax for hours, not say anything, and still be on the same page. We cooked together, we drank wine while we watched movies, and went for bike rides when the weather wasn't too hot. We hiked, swam, and hung hammocks up in the mountains. She helped me ease out my potential, and I gave her a partner with which she could do the things that she enjoyed. I had nothing to compare our relationship to, but it was the best I'd ever had regardless of the fact that it was the first.

TWELVE

Ledger Partners was a fine company. I settled into the job, made some good money, even saved a bit. More than that, my boss respected me and treated me well. The office was nice, the free coffee was good, and my commute was short. Some of the clients were assholes, some were tolerable, and a few were very nice people. Working at Ledger Partners was as good of a job as I thought was possible.

My life became easier, more comfortable, but my dream of being a writer was slipping away, and it pulled at me. Settling into an average life felt like I was accepting that I wasn't special. The idealism of my youth was gasping for breath, but it hadn't been fully killed off by kids and marriage and a mortgage. Every day, I sat in my office and felt the pain of my dreams evaporating.

This isn't to say that I was doing much writing—I wasn't. It's not like I was spending my nights and weekends working on a novel. An actual enjoyment of writing wasn't the thing that fueled my longing for a different life. In college, it was apparent that I needed more seasoning, more character, and more experience. I hadn't done enough in life, and without an interesting perspective to draw from, what could I possibly offer the reader? Even though I was aware of my lack of tools, I had trouble waiting for them to grow. I didn't want to wait to get experience to be able to write well. I was restless in college, and that restlessness just grew inside me as a young adult—it permeated my entire life. I wanted to be a writer, not a bookkeeper. The urgency of my youth seems trivial to me now, but then, it was suffocating.

All of the things that were conjured in the minds of college girls when I told them I was a writer, that's what I wanted to be. The drinking, the lifestyle, the revelry and acclaim, and of course, the fame. I spent many days in my cubicle thinking about the notoriety I would one day have. This future vision of myself would walk around parties with a beer in hand, a joint hanging from my lip, all the buttons of my shirt unbuttoned, my hair messy, oversized sunglasses hanging off my face. During the day, I would drink coffee and smoke cigarettes at quaint coffee shops, striking up meaningful conversations with strangers who knew who I was but had the integrity not to say anything. At night, I would engage in good old-fashioned bacchanalia, then return home to jot down something beautiful and timeless and transcendent. Life would flow like a dream; spontaneous, creative, whimsical, and vague.

When I told people I was a bookkeeper, the little pilot light in their eyes flickered then went out. As a person who cared what people thought about me, I hated being boring. I was supposed to be special, but I didn't feel special. At the time, asking myself why I was so entitled was out of the question, but reflecting on it now, maybe it was the fact that I was an only child, or that I was the only one to carry on the Billings name. It could have been Uncle Grant's fault; he always told me how smart I was. He would say, "You're the smartest kid on the ranch, shit, you're smarter than some of the adults."

My mediocrity was painful, and even though things were going well, I sagged back into unhappiness. Malcontent created tension between Beatrice and me. She loved me for who I was, and I longed to be something I wasn't.

One day, while I was at work, supposed to be looking over a marketing company's P & L, I slipped into fantasy and decided, at that moment, with a head full of conviction, that I wasn't going to give up on my dream of being a writer. The problem with my dream was that it felt far-fetched. I figured the only way I could achieve greatness would be to take a practical approach. Leaps of faith were too scary, but I was saving money from every paycheck, and I knew that if I tightened up my lifestyle a bit, I could save even more. The plan that I devised was simple: If I had $25,000 saved up, then I could quit my job and start writing full time. $25,000 was enough money to sustain me while I completed a novel. I hadn't even completed a short story worth a shit, but I decided I was going to be a novelist. The grand gesture of writing a novel excited me, and the idea that I would no longer have to keep books anymore aroused me beyond imagination.

I had $1,900 in my savings account already, and with my cheap rent and inexpensive lifestyle, I was on target to save $800 a month. At that rate, it would take just a little over two years to save the $25,000.

Like a shot of morphine, my plan to become a writer alleviated the pain of my day-to-day life. Working a job that I hated was much more tolerable with an end in sight, even if that end was far off. The lack of immediacy was also a perk. Quitting my job scared me, but I didn't have to deal with that fear since I was so far away from my end date. I was less grumpy at home, and things with Beatrice smoothed out. She told me that she respected my decision and was proud of me for chasing my dream. Beatrice especially liked that part of my savings plan involved cutting back on boozing. I rationed my weed, and I stayed away from the Tin Star. I didn't hang out with Ruiz as much and opted for staying home more often than not. Everything in my plan was a win for Beatrice except one thing—I was a writer again, or at least, I was telling people I was.

At cocktail parties, work functions, around Beatrice's friends, basically any chance that I could get, I was telling tales of my writer's passion and my new goal to realize this passion. Not a passion I possessed, but a passion that I would pursue once I saved up enough money to do so. I could see her mood change when I went into my spiel. After a while, I noticed that when I went into my pontifications, Beatrice would walk away from the conversation.

One night after a dinner party, Beatrice was quiet in the car. We were about a mile from home when she spoke. "I love that you're saving your money, and I like your plan. I don't necessarily agree with it, but I think it's inspiring."

"I'm glad you said that. When I first thought this up, I was nervous to tell you about it. Your approval means a lot to me."

"You need to understand something, though. I won't be a part of this lie."

"Lie?"

"You aren't a writer, Otis. We've been together for a few years now. How many pages have you written?"

"Well, I know I haven't written a lot..."

"How many?"

"I don't know. Not a lot."

"Not a lot. That's right. Not a lot." I had never seen her incensed like that. She was normally a calm, methodical person, but at this moment, she had lost the carefulness that she was so well equipped with. "I don't want to hear it anymore. I don't want to hear about your writing, not until you start doing some."

"That's fine. You won't have to. I'll shut up and I'll start writing. I'm going to be great, Beatrice. I'm not going back to the ranch."

"You don't have to be great. Greatness isn't going to keep you away from the ranch. And why are you so scared of the ranch? It sounds like a wonderful place."

My first instinct was to get defensive, but I breathed through it and settled on silence. To me, that car ride was like being wrapped in a piece of tissue paper—any movement, and the thing would be ripped wide open. Beatrice seldom got mad, and I had never seen her so blunt. Her telling me that my bullshitting bothered her meant that it bothered her, and in that silence, I knew she wanted me to talk it out with her, but I wouldn't. We didn't say a word to each other until the next day. In the end, I didn't stop lying about being a writer, I just avoided doing so in front of her.

In my defense, my lie wasn't whole and complete. When I was just the right mix of stoned and drunk, I would get out the silver pen my mother gave me when I graduated college and I would write a page, sometimes more. My writing was an island, small sandy snippets surrounded by vast stretches of nothing. If I would have put the pages together, none of it would have fit or made any sense. The greatest deterrent for me was that my writing wasn't good, I could see that. I never found any momentum. I had serious doubts about how I was going to write an entire novel, but I ignored my sensibilities, smothering my second thoughts in cigarette smoke and the promise that I wouldn't have to do any more bookkeeping.

One of the unexpected consequences of my plan was that my performance at work improved. I got a raise, which allowed me to save an extra $200 a month. The end of my bookkeeping career and the beginning of my writing career were fast approaching, and I tensed up. As the months got shorter, I stopped telling anybody who would listen that I was a writer. I got quiet. In order to become a writer, changes were going to have to come, but I wasn't sure I had it in me to do so.

THIRTEEN

Beatrice made exceptional dinners during the fall. The farmer's markets were full of hot green chiles, sweet corn, and fresh fruit from the orchards down south of Albuquerque. On one of the cooler nights, we ate in the little shared courtyard of her apartment building. To Beatrice, this was just a normal meal, but I was so nervous I had to force myself to eat. We finished off our meal and lingered for a while as I smoked my after-dinner cigarette. A full belly and a cigarette calmed me enough to find my composure. Without grace at my disposal, I blurted out what was on my mind. "I want to move in together," I said, breaking our silence.

She looked at me with a conflicted face and asked, "You think that's a good idea?"

I had expected a yes or possibly a no, but I hadn't expected a question for an answer. "I do. I love you, and we've been together a pretty long while."

"Yes, we have. I would love to move in together." She paused and urged herself on. "But I want to make sure you're ready.."

"It'll be great," I said, thinking I knew what she meant. We both got out of our chairs and hugged each other. I kissed her on the cheek and then on the lips and we hugged tightly.

With the clarity that comes from time, I can see my motivation for wanting to move in with Beatrice was centered around wanting to save money, but at the time,

I had myself fooled. Knowing that money wasn't reason enough to share my life with her, I told myself that I loved her, and that became reason enough.

When Ruiz found out that Beatrice and I were moving in together, he articulated exactly what I had been ignoring.

"You gonna marry her?" he asked.

"Not thinking about that yet."

"You better start." Ruiz took a sip of his beer and set it back down on the bar top. "I don't know shit about women, but even I know that when you move in with a woman, you better be ready to marry her."

"Yeah?"

"You may not be thinking marriage, but she is. Guarantee it."

We drank our beers and then went out to the front of the bar to have a cigarette. I had forgotten to bring a coat, and the chilly air moved through my shirt with ease. "What do I do?" I asked Ruiz.

"What do you mean?"

"What do I do? About all this. Moving in with B and all that."

"You sleep in that bed you made. What do you think? You're moving in together, and now you got two options, stay together or break up. You can't un-ask to move in with her."

"That's what it was before we decided to move in together."

"But if you break up now, it's going to be messy as hell." Ruiz bowed his head as he sucked the last bit of smoke out of his cigarette. He dropped the butt under his foot and stepped on it. He picked his head back up, and we both looked out into the street. It was empty, nothing moved. The cold air was blowing down from the Sandia mountains, and we both shivered at the thought of winter coming on.

"I'm too young to get married," I said.

"Agreed," Ruiz said. I finished my cigarette and we walked back into the bar.

After discussing the situation with Ruiz, I thought it best to avoid any kind of relationship conversation with Beatrice. Considering we were set to move in together, I couldn't dodge her all together. At the bare minimum, we would need to discuss logistics, so whenever I saw my soon-to-be live-in girlfriend, I made sure to keep our conversations tactical in nature.

Beatrice didn't want to move into my place. It was too small, not very nice, and it wasn't hers. The lease on my apartment had gone month to month by then, so it was easy to terminate. After careful consideration, Beatrice decided that it made sense for me to move in with her.

The move went smoothly; I was able to get all my stuff put up in a day. And just like that, our lives were completely entangled. Well into my twenties, and somehow, I didn't own hardly anything. The things that I did own weren't worth moving. Beatrice made subtle suggestions to abandon my third-hand furniture and all of my nonsensical decorations. I conceded and dumped my belongings off at the Goodwill near her place. Beatrice's apartment was already well-appointed, so we didn't need my stuff anyway. I appreciated the effort and touches she put into our newly shared apartment. In contrast to my old studio, the new place was a world of comfort and functional luxuries. When the moving was over, we had built a place together that we were both proud of, even if it was mostly Beatrice's building.

FOURTEEN

After making big decisions in my life, I looked for little affirmations that made me feel as though I had made the right choice. There were plenty of signs when I moved in with Beatrice, but none of them were affirming. We argued about the usual things—toilet seat placement, dirty dishes, utilities, lights left on. Aside from the regular squabbles, I felt like Beatrice's attitude towards me shifted and got away from a healthy place. Our relationship turned into a tug of war. She lost her tenderness, and I became distant. It felt like she resented me for moving in with her, and even though I lived there, it stayed "her place." I was a guest in my own home.

The fragility of my new living arrangement didn't derail my plan to quit my job in pursuit of greatness. When I put my two weeks in at Ledger Partners, my relationship with Beatrice dropped deeper into turmoil. I was on the brink of not having a paying job, and I had no idea how to become a working author. While taking a leap of faith, there is certainly a moment when you leave the ground, and while suspended in the air, you have no idea where you are going to land.

"Been doing any writing lately?" Beatrice asked me out of the blue. Her hands were busy in the sink washing dishes. Her tone was inquisitive; however, my internal defense systems triggered.

"Some." Her eyes hardened and focused. I forced myself to speak. "I've been doing a lot of mental writing."

"Mental writing?"

"I think a lot of writing is done in the mind before the pen hits the paper. It's like typing on the computer—that's not writing. Writing is a process that takes place before you actually sit down and put the words together."

"Interesting," she said. "There's so much time in the day. Maybe you could do your mental writing and some actual writing. Before you leave your job, don't you want to have something to show people?"

"I think that would be nice, but it's hard to just pump out a novel for the sake of showing people."

"A short story, a few essays, some poems or something. You're quitting your job to become a writer, and it doesn't seem like you have any idea what a writer does."

If I would have had the courage to ask her what she was thinking, what her concerns were, her fears, it would have helped our relationship. She wanted me to stand in there and dance through the conflict. Instead of working through our issues, I doubled down on my bullshit, moved further towards the bottle, and, most of all, I avoided conversations with her.

When I first conceived of my plan to quit my job and become a writer, I cut way back on drinking and smoking so that I could save extra money. Somewhere during the two years that it took me to save the 25k, I had worked my way back to where I had started, and by the time I quit my job, I was beyond that. I shot pool with Ruiz every Saturday night, and I ran up tabs at the Tin Star at least one day a week. Each morning before I went into the office and every day at my lunch break, I got stoned in my truck.

Quitting my job to become a writer was supposed to be a re-awakening, a shot of adrenaline to the heart. Instead, I disassociated from myself and those around me. Beatrice felt the effects the hardest; as I pushed on into my stubborn dreams, she was pushed to her end. I had hoped that this new change would cause a ripple of happiness to wash over our lives, but it was having the opposite effect. Often, at home or in my cubicle, I fantasized about my life as a writer, and I noticed that those fantasies rarely included Beatrice.

On the week of my resignation, my boss came to my workspace. He leaned his butt cheek up on my desk, looking down at me. "You're stoned aren't you?"

"I don't know why you would say that."

"Because you smell like pot. And you look stoned."

"I'm just tired."

"Sure. Look, you used to be one of my best workers, but you've been dragging ass for a while now. I know you're done at the end of the week, but I figured I'd offer you an out anyway."

"An out from what?"

"An out from all of this bullshit. Quit smoking weed at lunch. No more coming in late and leaving early. Go back to the worker you were, and I'll forget you ever said anything about this writing nonsense."

I thought about it for a second. I was so close to freedom, there was no way I was going to cave the first time someone gave me a chance to scrap my plan. "I can't do that," I said.

"Fine. You've made up your mind, I can see that. Shit, I actually think you're pretty brave. Figured I'd be doing you a disservice if I didn't tell you that when you walk out of here on Friday, there's no coming back. Don't come back here in a month or a year or a decade and ask for your job back. Ok?"

"Yessir."

"Good luck, you crazy bastard." My boss laughed a little and looked out the window next to my desk. "Shit, I'd come with you if I wasn't sure my wife would hunt me down and put a bullet in my ass." We both laughed, my boss much harder than me. He patted me on the back, stepped his butt cheek off my desk, and went back to his office.

I left Ledger Partners at the end of the week and fell into an incredible amount of free time. The first few days, I sat around and got high, smoked cigarettes at Beatrice's desk, and tried to write. Nothing came out of me, nothing productive. The only thing that came to my mind was the fact that in the last year, I had stopped hiking, and I wasn't reading much anymore. I had stopped doing the things that made me the person Beatrice fell in love with. Signs were everywhere around me, and they all pointed to me making the wrong decision. Luckily, I didn't believe in signs—I believed in leaps of faith.

Before I moved in with Beatrice, we had plenty of disagreements. They were carefully worded and resolved without the deep wounds that claw a relationship apart. When I moved in with her, our small squabbles seemed to spill into each other like a bunch of little creeks finding the main channel of a river. Nothing was resolved, just pushed to another day, another conversation, a different topic. After a few months of living together, she came to me with something on her mind.

"Otis, I have to tell you something."

I froze, and she waited for me to speak. "Ok," I said after some hesitation.

"My life just isn't where I want it to be." She was already crying, and she looked like she would unravel at any second, but she kept talking, "I need you to move out," she said without making eye contact. I waited for a long speech, but it didn't come.

"Are you sure?" I asked, hoping to hear her explain her decision. I wanted to find a hole in her story, poke through it, break her of her seemingly feeble conviction.

She shook her head and said, "I am."

"But we're in love with each other. I love you too much to let this happen. You love me, don't you?" I asked, pleading to her emotions.

"I was in love with you, but you wore me down, you gave me nothing to love. I mean, come on. What's left of the relationship we started?"

I started to cry. She had never seen me cry, but she didn't want my tears, she wanted an answer to her question. I stuttered and stumbled like an old truck trying to get started. She gave up on me saying anything of worth and started to sob.

"I wish we could go back. I thought if I could become a writer, it would make me happy, and that would make us happy."

"I don't want to go back."

"I know we can't. But what if I changed? What if I quit drinking and getting stoned all the time? What then?"

"You can do all those things. It'd be great if you did all those things. You're just going to have to do them alone though."

The only time I remembered crying before this moment was when I was a kid. The feeling of crying everything out was a sensation that I had forgotten. That calm, pleasant feeling that comes after releasing all of the shit you've been holding onto. Beatrice kicking me out of the apartment was devastating, but at the same time, it felt good. Our relationship was either going to flourish or go up in flames, and since we had moved in together, I could feel the impending heat. And now it was all over, and I felt nice.

After the crying and all that tension, we held onto each other. We didn't hate one another, and even though Beatrice's decision was final, we still loved each other enough to want to provide comfort to the other.

Beatrice and I agreed that two weeks was enough time to make plans to live somewhere else. My mind swiveled back and forth between obsessing over the breakup and obsessing over my next move and what it would be. When thinking about what someone would do when faced with a decision like the one I was faced with, I figured a normal person would probably get themselves a job, rent a room with some roommates. A normal person would try to get their life back to normal. Well, I wasn't a normal person. I was a writer now, and writers don't do what normal people do.

When I went to the bar with Ruiz to shoot pool, I operated under a freedom I hadn't felt before. I didn't have to govern how many beers I had, I didn't have to watch the clock. I could let go, and, in my mind, letting go was exactly what I needed to jump-start my writing. A couple more disasters, and I would have a hell of a story to tell.

FIFTEEN

With no place to live, I began my home search. There were no restrictions on the type of housing I could occupy. My search was a raw canvas spread before me, limited only by my creativity or lack thereof. My mind painted ideas and I let them flow, no matter how far-fetched. In the end, I came up with an old and simple idea, getting inspiration from my childhood. Extra workers were needed on the ranch, depending on the season. These seasonal workers stayed on our property, working long hours during a short window of time. We didn't have beds for every man, woman, and child that came during those busy days, so many of them stayed in campers or RVs. Buying an RV seemed like a great way to get out of paying rent every month, so I started looking around.

Straight away, I learned that RVs were very expensive, and I readjusted my search to a camper shell that I could set into the bed of my truck. Albuquerque was chock full of campers, so finding one for a good price was pretty manageable. The internet connected me to a retired plumber who had a camper for sale. The shell was old but in good shape and fit perfectly into the bed of my truck. After I told the old man my story, he knocked the price down from $800 to $500, and I gladly handed over the cash. Pity was an effective bargaining method.

The camper was simple, little more than the exterior shell. A small stove that ran on propane and a dry sink made up the kitchen area. There was a bunk for sleep and a bench with a small table that folded down from the wall. The floor was made out of some sort of fake laminated wood. The shell was made of fiberglass and aluminum. There wasn't a bathroom or a shower, and there wasn't space for much, which didn't bother me because I came out of living with Beatrice owning almost nothing. It was easy to install, and Ruiz helped me set it into place and fasten it down.

I was so excited about my new home that I moved out of Beatrice's apartment before the two weeks were up. Anyway, it's hard to drink away your heartbreak when the person who broke your heart is standing over you. I wanted her to take me back, but I wasn't ready to make the changes she wanted. Getting a job and canceling my quest to be a great writer was out of the question, and because of this, I knew that Beatrice and I were through.

When I fired up the old Ford, I couldn't think of any place to go but Ruiz's house. He lived with four other guys in a big rundown house in an overlooked neighborhood of Albuquerque. Ruiz and his roommates lived as if they had never left college. They had a giant stereo in their living room that blasted music eighteen hours a day. Their refrigerator had nothing but beer and leftovers in it. Someone was always visiting them, crashing on the couch or there just to party. I parked my truck out front of their house and didn't move it for the next few weeks. Ruiz let me use his shower and toilet whenever I needed to. He was always up for getting high and drunk, so me staying there worked out famously.

Ruiz and all of his roommates were Mexican guys. Some of them already knew me, but they were curious as to why Ruiz let some white Texas hick park his camper in front of their house. I bought a bunch of beer to share with the house, and after a few days, they warmed up to me. We drank every night for two weeks straight. I lived on burritos and smoked a pack of cigarettes a day. Ruiz took me out to the bars in his neighborhood to help me get over Beatrice.

Ruiz seemed to know everyone at these bars, so it was easy to piggyback off of him, which was nice because my confidence wasn't in great shape. I didn't have a job, I lived in a camper, and I was fresh off a breakup. When Beatrice and I were together and I had that relationship ego going, I thought that every woman who looked at me was interested. Now, when I looked around at all the ladies in the bar or out on the street, I was convinced they wanted nothing to do with me. Ruiz seemed to intuit all of this and made sure to go out of his way to introduce me to people and include me in conversations.

Ruiz partied hard, but he had his life together during the daytime. He liked his job at the bank and they liked him. He'd been promoted, made good money, and had some respect. When it came to boozing and partying, I knew so few people who could walk the tightrope and keep their balance. Ruiz was one of them. He ran the house that he lived in like some kind of den father. He made sure all the bills got paid and kept the peace when things got heated. He did all of this on the sly, never letting anyone know that he had an eye on things. That's just how he was. When Ruiz walked into a room, he surveyed for trouble, looking to see what he could get out in front of. We all felt safe around him.

One night, Ruiz and I went to a karaoke bar by his house to meet some of his friends. Drunk assholes were singing Guns & Roses songs, and a round-faced girl sang a song in Spanish with the gusto of someone trying to get discovered by a talent agent. The group of friends that we were there to meet was about twenty people strong. Ruiz's friends had overtaken a section of booths that lined two of the restaurant's walls. We weaseled our way into sitting with two girls, and one of them tangentially knew Ruiz.

After introductions and a brief conversation, Ruiz took the woman he barely knew up on stage to sing a duet, and I was left isolated with a dark-eyed young woman named Marisol. She was much smaller than me and very beautiful. I tried not to stare at her but failed.

"So, how do you two guys know each other?" she asked.

"We were roommates in college," I said. "We went to school here in Albuquerque."

"Really? You went to State?" she asked, her excitement confused me.

"Yep."

"That's where I go now. I'm a sophomore." She was younger than I thought. "Are you guys still roommates?"

"No. Well, kind of." My throat tightened and dried.

"What does that mean?" she asked. She was so pretty, and I wanted to impress her, but I figured I would be found out if I lied.

"Uh. I live in an RV. A camper, really. Thinking about doing some traveling."Technically, I had thought about traveling before, so I wasn't lying.

"Cool," she said, catching me off guard. Her lips were painted with mauve lipstick and I couldn't help but stare at them. "I've heard about that. You like, don't pay rent and just travel around and stuff?"

"I don't pay any rent. I paid for the camper in cash."

"I wish I could do something like that. I live at home with my parents. When I graduate, I want to do some traveling."

"It's great. So freeing." She looked so pleasant while I spoke, listening to my words, making eye contact. "Where do you want to travel to when you graduate?"

"I don't know. Europe, I guess. Maybe Australia—I love animals. Oh, and Mexico. I have family there, it would be fun to see them."

"I would love to go to Mexico, never been before."

"Really? We're so close to the border, you should go down there."

"Yeah, it's crazy, right? I grew up in West Texas, not far from the border at all. I'm going to go get a beer, want one?"

Marisol came with me to the bar and I bought her a beer. She put her hands up on the bar and pressed her rib cage into the counter. We talked about her classes, her major. College kids have a built-in template of things to talk about, so the conversation went easy. Marisol smiled in between sips of beer and she laughed at my jokes, reaching out to touch my arm as she laughed. It didn't take an expert in body language to realize she was showing signs of interest, but it didn't feel like it was possible that someone so beautiful could be interested in me. If I could have watched myself talking to Marisol from afar, I would have guessed that her boyfriend was about to walk in and whip my ass.

We met back up with Ruiz at the table; he was alone.

"Linda's going to the bathroom. We were talking about going to the Corner Store for a nightcap, you guys in?"

The Corner Store was a dance club, and dance clubs worried me. Marisol's slender body and fluid hips left me with no doubt that she was a fantastic dancer. Dancing was not in my body, I didn't mind doing it, but my skills were subpar at best. Thankfully, I was in that perfect zone of being drunk enough to put my shortcomings in the back of my mind.

We made our way over to the Corner Store and I bought a round of beers. We stood on the outskirts of the dance floor, sipping our beers and watching the herd of people sway and bob. Marisol grabbed my hand without saying anything and led me out onto the dance floor. I was clumsy but willing, and she didn't seem to care. She smiled and brushed her hair out of her face. I drank and jolted my angular body around to the pumping music.

The DJ announced the last call for alcohol and informed the drunken, sweaty dance floor that the last song of the night was coming up. Marisol and I went in search of Ruiz and Linda. They wanted to finish out the last song, so Marisol leaned her body back into me and I rubbed my body on her to the beat of the music. We were laughing, and I spun her around and brought her in, and we kissed. We danced on and kissed intermittently when our dancing proximity allowed for it. After the music stopped, the ladies decided to come back to Ruiz's casa with us.

Back at Ruiz's, we listened to music and lingered in the living room, smoking cigarettes and weed, trying to make the night last longer. Eventually, Ruiz and Linda left the room. Marisol and I were alone together.

"Is your camper here?" she asked, breaking the silence.

"Yeah, it's out front."

"Really? Can I see it?" Marisol made things easy. She was organic, nothing forced, a real gem. We left the house and went out front to tour my new home. I was so excited to be walking through the front yard with Marisol that I almost broke into a promenade. The official camper tour lasted twenty-five seconds before we transitioned to making out.

Her shirt came off, and then her bra. She undid my snap button shirt with one swipe and a giggle. We kissed, and then she undid my belt and pulled my pants off. She tossed them to the floor of the camper. Her skirt was up around her waist as she climbed on top of me. She had taken off her panties or wasn't wearing any to begin with, I wasn't sure. I felt her soft hand grab onto me, and after a bit, she sat down on top of me. She rode me for a few minutes, humming and making little yips. After a while, she flipped onto her back, and I gave her a few solid strokes. Building towards a climax, I slowed a bit and she started to quake all over in her legs. Her chin quivered and her eyes shut. She moaned and licked her top lip, then gently bit her lower lip. The quaking reached a fever; she breathed in deeply and then let out a big blowing exhale. A release of tension took over her face and neck. She sighed as if a large weight had been lifted from her. Another few strokes, and I was finished.

Marisol cooed softly as she laid her head on my chest. The only thing on my mind was how I had never gotten Beatrice off in this way before. Feeling great and also guilty and sad, I was remorseful, as if I had cheated. After a bit, my ego took over, and I was able to focus on having delivered a decisive orgasm to a gorgeous woman. Marisol and I had sex an hour later, and once again when we woke up in the morning. Each time, she became easier to get off, but her orgasms were less devastating and beautiful than the first.

Once we were up and about, Ruiz and I walked Marisol and Linda to breakfast at the Mexican diner two blocks from Ruiz's house. The meal was incredible. Salt and spice lingered on my tongue while I enjoyed cigarettes and coffee. Last night's glory sat heavy on my face; there was no doubt I was beaming. We were that perfect mix of hungover and still drunk. We laughed and told stories from the night before at a high volume, not worrying about the other people at the restaurant who were so clearly annoyed with us.

After breakfast, we drove the girls back to Linda's mom's house and said our goodbyes. As the ladies disappeared into the house, Ruiz and I turned to each other and smiled. Without saying anything, I thanked Ruiz. The warmth of a perfect night between us—a night that could have gone wrong at any moment but didn't.

When we got back to Ruiz's house, we smoked a joint and chilled out. Sleep-deprived, half-drunk, and very stoned, I went to my camper for a nap. When I walked in, I noticed the smell. The stale old camper smell had worn off and was replaced with a familiar scent—mine.

SIXTEEN

Life after Beatrice was spent in two contrasting spaces. Ruiz's house was always on. People in every room, sound blinking out of every speaker and open mouth. Inside the house, it was impossible to be alone. On the other hand, in my home, the camper, there was nothing but solitude. Like a fairy tale, if you go through one door, you will be completely alone, and if you go through the other door, you will never be at rest. When I was in Ruiz's house, I wanted to be in my camper, in the quiet. When I was in the camper, restlessness drew me to Ruiz's house.

One night, while having a beer in my camper, Ruiz sent me a message inviting me to meet up with him at the bar a few blocks from the house. He was with his younger sister Maria and her friends. I had told myself I was going to take the night off, not drink, do some reading, but I was lonely, so I agreed to meet up with them.

They were taking shots and swilling beers when I arrived, and before I could finish my first drink, they were ready to go home. On the way back to the house, we grabbed a case of beer and walked up to the pizza counter at Adriano's. We drank beers outside on the picnic tables, waiting for the window to swing open and our pizza to slide through.

Back at the house, we huddled into the living room. I drank beer while Ruiz and the girls ate pizza. The pizza eaters finished off the pizza and drifted off to a catatonic state on the couch. I made my way to the front porch for a cigarette. Smoking and drinking and watching the street from the front porch was a routine that I had grown to love. Maria came outside looking for a smoke, so I gave her a cigarette and lit it for her.

"You know my brother talks about you?" she said. I wasn't sure if she was asking a question or making a statement.

"Does he? I wouldn't know why," I said, feigning humility.

"He told my parents about how smart you are."

"Yeah? I'm not sure why he would go and do a thing like that."

"They weren't either. My father asked, 'If he is so smart then why does he live in a car?'" Maria laughed in between drags of her cigarette.

Ruiz came out of the house and said to his sister, "Hey, when you're finished, go up to my room. You and your friends are sleeping up there."

"Ok."

"Keep the door locked tonight, ok?"

"We will." Ruiz went inside. Maria took the last drag and stamped out her cigarette. "Good night, Otis."

"Happy Birthday, Maria." She went inside, and I went out to my camper.

I undressed and drank some water before I crawled up into the bunk and got under the covers. A heavy knocking sound echoed around in my head as I slept. Not quite sure what to make of it, I ignored it for a while. Eventually, I came around to the idea that the knocks were coming from outside of my dreams, and I woke up. Maria was at the door of my camper. She didn't say anything, just stood there looking up at me. I let her in.

We didn't speak a word before we started to kiss. She took off her dress and removed her bra before she crawled up into my bunk. I took off my shorts and crawled in after her. As I got into bed, she eased her panties out from under her butt and over her knees. I got on top of her and kissed her. We gently made love out of respect for the delicate nature of the situation, as if Ruiz wouldn't be mad if he knew that I had fucked her softly, carefully.

When I woke up in the morning, I reached for Maria before I could open my eyes, but she wasn't there. The sun was just coming up, and I thought if I woke up early enough, I could have her one more time before she snuck back up to her brother's room. Disappointed, I fell back asleep.

I woke up to my camper door swinging open violently. Down through the opening of the camper doorway, standing in the street with a knife in his hand, was Ruiz. His eyes glowed and his voice was hoarse.

"Get your ass out here," he demanded.

I didn't want to get stabbed, but for some reason, I obeyed. I got out of bed and looked around. A hatchet was laying out, so I grabbed it and jumped down to the sunburnt street. Ruiz saw me with a hatchet in hand and stiffened up like an alley cat. We circled each other in a half-hunched dance in the middle of the street.

Ruiz was a cyclone of rage, his head engorged with blood and anger. We circled a few times, and then Ruiz let out a great scream and ran towards my truck. He thrust the kitchen knife into the side of the camper. The knife sank into the fiberglass, the blade was half-way in when it stopped. As the knife came to rest, Ruiz's hand slipped off the handle and continued onto the blade, slicing his fingers. He looked at his severed fingers, then ran inside the house, leaving the knife stuck into the side of the camper. With the slamming of Ruiz's front door, the neighborhood fell back to the early morning silence.

I grabbed a pair of Buckskin gloves out of my truck and put them on. The knife did not want to come out so easy.

After a series of alternating yanks and wiggles, the knife broke free of the fiberglass shell. The gloves were overkill, but I had just watched Ruiz slice his hand and felt the extra precaution was warranted. Blood and skin were still clinging to the blade as I tossed it into the front yard of the house I knew I was no longer welcomed in.

I started up the old Ford and thought about my next move. The only thing I could think to do was leave Ruiz's neighborhood and head for the mountains. If I now lived in a camper, then why not go camping?

I stopped off and bought a twelve-pack of beer and two packs of cigarettes. The guy who worked the counter at the liquor store also sold weed out of the back, so I bought a big bag from him. I filled up my tank at the gas station across the way from the liquor store. While the gas pumped I cleaned off my windshield with the squeegee. Something about a good squeegee job made me feel like I was taking care of shit, handling my business the right way.

On my way up to the mountains, just after I left the gas station, I almost broke. I thought about calling Beatrice to tell her that I loved her. Thought about calling this whole writing thing off. I considered begging my boss at Ledger Partners to give me my job back. I wondered if it was possible to move into my old apartment and just go back to the way things were. As I continued thinking, I realized Beatrice wasn't going to take me back, neither was my old boss. My old apartment was rented off to someone else, I was sure of it. I lit a cigarette and blew a big puff of smoke onto my dashboard. "Fuck it, I'm gonna take it to the brink," I said out loud to myself. I didn't know what the brink was, but it sounded dramatic and made me feel better.

I smoked cigarette after cigarette on the way up to the Sandias. Stopping off in Tijeras to eat a late breakfast, I took a burrito and some coffee and washed it down with another cigarette. The waitress informed me that there was no smoking on the patio, and I would have to leave if I wanted to smoke, so I did. I headed south on 337 until the turn-off for Otero Canyon. I'd never been out there, but it looked quiet and remote.

After driving dirt roads for ten minutes, I was out there. Not a single car had passed me since I had left the main road. Seeing as I was all alone, I figured if I cracked a beer out on that dirt road, nobody would be there to notice. I pulled off into a turnout and threw the Old Ford into neutral. I kept the engine running and headed for the camper. The twelve-pack I bought was icing down in my little blue and white cooler. I got a beer out of the fresh ice and hopped back into the truck, put it in first, and eased out of the turnout. For the next five minutes, I kept an eye on the rearview mirror, waiting for someone to pull up behind me, but nobody came. It seemed safe enough, so I slowly lifted the tab of my beer until it cracked open, and then I took a sip. The beer tasted good and went down smooth. Drinking beers behind the wheel was way too easy, so I set some mental rules. Not rules, not plural—one rule. The rule was that I would only drink and drive on dirt roads. That's it. No funny business out on the pavement.

The parking lot for the Manzano Overlook was empty when I pulled in—not a single other car. With the whole place to myself, I let loose a little. I rolled up a joint and grabbed a few more beers and scrambled up on top of a rock outcropping. The view was massive. Thick, uniform white pines rolled downhill into sparse pinyon trees and sagebrush, then dropped off into cliffed-out arroyos. The size of the sprawling desert below made me feel alone and small. My insignificance compared to the mountains and vistas hit me so hard that I fell into fractured pieces of myself. The events of the night before, the betrayal of Ruiz, Maria's late-night visit—I couldn't help but pour over every detail like a mirror shattered on the floor.

After finishing my beer, I tried to calm my mind. My breath deepened as I leaned back on the rocks and I shut my eyes. With eyes shut, I fell into windswept dreams. I dreamt that I was in a house and I heard a knock on the door. Through the opened door slithered a gigantic boa constrictor accompanied by a hot wind at its back that blew through the house. A machete lay against a wall so I grabbed it out of fear. The snake came closer and I slammed the machete down on its head, parallel to its outstretched body. The snake writhed and lurched forward, so I hit it again, this time perpendicular to its pulsing body, creating a plus sign wound on its head. After the snake was slain, the local news came to interview me. The reporter greeted me as a hero, but I felt that it wasn't right. I was sad that the snake had died.

When I woke up, the mountain air had blown over me and left me dried out like a piece of jerky. I climbed down to the truck to get some water and to figure out my next move. Back out on the road, I found a secluded place to camp under a stand of pine trees. My stomach was empty, but I didn't have any food, so I started back in on the beers and cigarettes. I rolled a joint and smoked while I looked around my new surroundings. This locale was certainly more scenic than Ruiz's front yard and a whole lot lonelier. I fantasized about building a giant bonfire that would be seen for miles, coaxing all of the other campers in the area to my shady grove. I wondered if Ruiz would ever forgive me.

As soon as all the beer was gone, I went to bed. In the middle of the night, I woke up and went outside to piss. Looking up at the sky, my childhood reflected back at me in the stars above. When I was a kid, I loved lying on my back to gaze up at the West Texas sky. This very well could have been the first time I had seen the stars since I had left Texas. I was a long way from the ranch right then, as far as I had ever been.

In the morning, I was in bad shape. Driving back down the mountain to the city, I could only make it as far as the overlook before I was forced to stop. As soon as I got out of the truck, I vomited in the small parking area, not realizing a car full of early morning site seers was watching me.

"Are you ok?" an old woman asked me, genuinely concerned. She was holding a young kid's hand, and the kid looked scared.

"I'm better now, thanks." I walked off to a thicket of pine trees where nobody would see me. I smoked a joint to ease my stomach, and it went straight to my head. I was paranoid and full of self-doubt. Critiquing my entire existence, I broke myself down and didn't have the strength to build myself back up. My stoned mind was angry and spiteful and didn't possess the ability to propose any actionable solutions. My heartbeat quickened and my mind fluttered; I was left scared like that little kid but without a hand to hold.

Drinking water back at my truck brought me around a little. I splashed some on my face. The water was still cold from the night before and it numbed my cheeks and nose. With a wet, numb face, I smoked a cigarette, and the mixture of cold water and nicotine calmed me down. I started up the old Ford and turned the radio dial to KUNM. The station came in clearer up in the mountains than it did in the city. They were playing a show called, "The Old Standard." The entire ride back to Albuquerque, I was soothed by old-timey blues and folk music, that early Americana stuff you never hear anymore. Music that my father listened to when I was a kid. Strings plucked, and old men sang even older songs, and I found some relief from myself.

SEVENTEEN

When I got back to the city, I called Marisol. By the sound of her voice, I could tell right away she wasn't too pleased to hear from me. Ruiz had told her what had happened with Maria, and she asked me not to call her anymore. Marisol saying Ruiz's name took me back to what had happened the day before. The right thing to do was right in front of me—apologize, ask for his forgiveness, make things right. I decided that I was too chicken shit to show my face back at the house. Imagining all his roommates giving me a whipping was more than enough to keep me from trying to mend fences. Ruiz's bleeding hand flashed through my mind, but I tucked it away and tried to focus on all the other problems I had.

When I went back to the camper, a recent memory came to me in my time of need.

"Yo, man. Where'd you get that camper?" asked Daniel, one of the guys who hung around Ruiz's house.

"Just bought it off an old man. He had it posted on the internet," I told him.

"Cool. It looks nice."

"I don't want to pay rent anymore, figured if I live in it for more than a month, it'll pay for itself."

"Reminds me of California," Daniel said.

"Why's that?"

"When I was in San Diego visiting my cousin, we went to the beach, and I saw a bunch of them like that. All different kinds."

"What were they doing there?"

"My cousin said all the hippies park their campers and RVs and vans and shit at the beach. They, like, live there," Daniel said, then coughed. He handed me a hot pipe while he gasped for air.

"That sounds kinda cool."

"Yeah, I guess so. The weather is nice out there, and the chicks are fuckin' crazy hot."

At the time, I didn't give Daniel's words much thought, but as I drove down through the city, my wheels turned. Lots of books focus on the great American road trip. The longest drive I had ever done was to Albuquerque for school or visiting my aunt in Dallas, but that didn't count. Those trips were too purposeful, there was no leisure or spirit of exploration. Even though I had never been to California, I knew a bit about it. Who grew up in America and didn't dream of going to California? I didn't have a TV or watch movies growing up, but even I knew that California was the land of milk and honey. Escaping Albuquerque was a nice thought, but I pushed it to the back of my mind and went in search of food.

Hunger led me to the drive-thru by my old apartment to grab a burger. In the truck, I ate and thought about how I had fucked everything up. It was so lonely, eating the burger by myself in my truck, that I figured that California couldn't be any lonelier. Was it worth it to try and salvage what I had in Albuquerque, or should I move on and gain more experience? Distractions in New Mexico were everywhere, distractions that I didn't yet have in California. I hadn't been writing at all since I quit my job, and I convinced myself that a move to California would be the jolt I needed to get back on track. A few lonesome hours of kicking around town by myself solidified the decision to hit the road.

I went to the market and bought a bunch of supplies for my trip. Lessons from the previous night pushed me to collect a surplus of goods I could count on. I bought Ramen noodles, breakfast biscuits, cheese and salami, crackers, oatmeal, peanut butter, jam, bread, hot sauce, honey, tortillas, a few cans of beans, instant rice, a little camping pot, a small skillet, a roll of tinfoil, a few apples, a family-sized bag of crinkle cut potato chips, coffee, coffee filters, tortilla chips, and a jar of salsa. I bought a twenty-four pack of cheap beer, a handle of cheap whiskey, and a handle of mid-range tequila. Cheap beer and cheap whiskey posed no problems for me, but I simply could not tolerate bad tequila, so I ponied up an extra ten bucks and got a respectable bottle. I had been rolling joints since college, so when I saw a big can of loose-leaf tobacco, I figured it was a good time to leave behind pre-rolled cigarettes. The drum of rolling tobacco, thin filters, and a dozen packs of rolling papers was still cheaper than a carton and equaled out to much more than ten packs. Hand-rolling cigarettes seemed like a decent way to save money, and I was smoking regular cigarettes at such a rate that I convinced myself that the time it takes to hand roll them would slow my smoking down a bit.

The last step in my preparation was something that I had neglected for a long time. Something I always found a way of avoiding. My family hadn't heard from me in months. The call to the ranch was answered by my mother. She was very glad I was calling but very disappointed to learn that I was headed to California.

"Why don't you come home, pay us a visit before you head west?'

"I don't think I can swing it. I'm just about headed out right now."

"Otis, I hope you know what you're doing. Every step you take that leads you away from home, the harder it's going to be when you come back."

"I guess we'll just have to see how that all works out, I suppose."

"What about Beatrice, I assume she's going with you?"

"No, ma'am. We parted ways." My mother didn't say anything, but I could hear her worry.

I spoke to my father for a minute; he was more somber.

"Son, you're making a mistake carrying on the way you are. What they got in California that's so special?"

"I guess I'll find out."

"You think you got it all figured out, don't you? Well, we'll be here when you fall on your ass. Someday, that window may close, Otis, make sure you know that."

My father handed the phone to Uncle Grant. When I informed Grant of my decision, he told me, "If you aren't living on the ranch, then what difference does it make? California or Calcutta." I was glad to have spoken to my uncle last. He had a way of maintaining his composure in the face of emotions. Calling home lifted a weight off of me, but that weight was replaced by homesickness, and loneliness grew like bamboo from there.

EIGHTEEN

With the supplies gathered, the phone call made, and the truck all gassed up, the only thing left to do was drive out of town. Headed out of Albuquerque, the old Ford pointed due west on I-40. The departure from the city was much less symbolic and emotional than I thought it would be. Too focused on getting on the right highway, before I knew it, I was out of the city and making my way through the desert, nothing ceremonial about it.

I made it to the state border in just two hours. Well into Arizona, I made a stop in Flagstaff, where the pine speckled mountains rise from the desert like a massive, earthen castle. A nice wind was blowing down the mountain, cooling the city at the foot of the San Francisco Peaks. Looking at my road atlas, California was getting close, but what was the point in rushing?

For lunch, the Desert Mountain Diner called out from the side of the road. The only open spot in the restaurant was at the bar, and an old couple sitting next to me was more than eager to chat me up. After hearing about my plans, they suggested taking the scenic route down through Sedona.

"Prettiest drive you can take. Been here my whole life, never seen one better," the old man said, his wife nodding in agreement over his shoulder.

They were right, the drive down from Flagstaff was spellbinding. Opting to stop short of Sedona, I found a nice spot to park for the night in Oak Creek Canyon. I was mesmerized by that perfect crack in the Earth. I drank beers and smoked a joint while I dangled my feet in the surprisingly cold creek that flowed through the floor of the canyon. Red turrets hung over my head, cliffs freckled with green brush, and the creek gently lapped at my feet. That morning, waking up in the mountains outside of Albuquerque felt like a lifetime ago. I ran through all the details of the day and decided it was the most eventful day of my life.

Out of excitement and a feeling of duty, I got my silver pen out and did some writing at the table in my camper. What came out of my hands was this:

> I've left Albuquerque, or, maybe, I've run from my home. Home hasn't felt like a solid place for some time. It's as if I had to throw my life into upheaval just to get closer to something I don't know if I can achieve. This upheaval has taken on many fronts. Beatrice ended things, kicked me out of the house. She was backed into a corner like a hissing cat, and I can't blame her for choosing what must have felt like her only option. Am I heartbroken? Are my actions the actions of a man that is in pain? Or, perhaps I am a man that has been inconvenienced, put out by my own doing, and I am remorseful, only for the situation I am in and nothing more. And Ruiz, he didn't have to take a knife to me, but I'm sure it felt good to do so. At least he did something. I want to be sorry for what I did to Ruiz, but I am not sure that I am. If Maria came to my door tonight, if she showed up here in this red-rocked canyon, would I turn her away? For sure not. How can a man be sorry for something that he'd willingly do again? It feels like a stranger borrowed my body and he's been walking around, carrying on with full sovereignty.

While reading over what I had written, I realized that my shoulders had relaxed and my jaw unclenched just a bit. I took out a book of Roald Dahl's short stories that Beatrice had given me. I read a few pages and then thought about how short stories seemed more tangible than a full novel. Writing a novel was the goal, but at that time, it seemed much too ambitious of a starting place. Short stories were approachable, something to build off of. Practice would be necessary if I was going to write anything longer than a page.

The next morning, I woke up to a saber of pink light slicing through my window curtains. Outside of the camper, my tired eyes took in the sites of my camp. The red rocks illuminated in a salmon hue stirred up visions of another planet. The creek rambling behind me brought me back to Earth. Nobody was around, so I stripped off all of my clothes and eased my stiff body into the creek. I hadn't been in a bathroom that wasn't attached to a gas station in three days, and a thorough washing was in order. Letting the arid breeze dry me off, I lingered naked on the side of the creek while I smoked a cigarette—a native who had lost his tribe.

Continuing through Sedona, marvelous burnt orange towers shaped the walls of the town. Crystal shops and art galleries lined the main street through the bustling village, and I noticed that the word vortex was worked into half the shop names and street signs. Sedona had long held the reputation of being a mysterious place. As I drove through town, I couldn't help but think that it wasn't. Spas and health food restaurants indicated that this was a town for wealthy folks to vacation, no mystery about it. One thing that was not debatable was the beauty of the place. The natural landscape was dramatic and graceful.

In Prescott, I stopped at a roadside cafe for a hot meal, two cups of coffee, and a straw cowboy hat from the gift shop. The cafe's bathroom was spotless, at least it was before I showered in the sink. The road out of Prescott pointed southwest for a long while until it collided with Highway 10 just east of the California border. Expecting California to transform into a tropical paradise as soon as I crossed the border set me up for a letdown; the state line just gave way to more desert.

I drove straight through Palm Springs and then cut down towards San Diego. Entering San Diego, I wasn't exactly greeted by the sleepy surf town that I had imagined. Skyscrapers and sprawl stretched out in front of me as I entered the metropolitan area. Determined to find the sand, I weaved through traffic, one-way streets, and a hectic city center, finally arriving at the beach.

I grabbed a beer out of the cooler, popped my shirt off, and made my way through the crowded sands to the water. My symbolic swim in the ocean was more of a symbolic wade. Growing up in the desert, I had only been swimming a few times as a child. From the deserts of Texas to the deserts of New Mexico, there wasn't a whole bunch of deep water around. Save for a pathetic doggy paddle, I didn't know how to swim. The ocean terrified me, so I walked out into the water until it came up to my belt loops and stayed right there. Eventually, I submerged my entire body, but not without a considerable amount of trepidation.

After I wiped the salty water from my eyes, I had a look around. So much to take in, everything was so new and shiny. The California coast was more impressive than I could have hoped. Marvelous houses hung over the land's edge. Below, people walked around with surfboards and tanned skin. It was warm but not too warm, and the sun felt soft on my face. Holding the ocean in place was a band of sandy cliffs that ran north to south. If I had owned a camera, I would have taken a picture.

Sprawled out on beach towels next to me, a handsome couple chatted and laughed. They were lying on their stomachs with their chests propped up by their elbows like sexy sphinxes. They were smoking from a colorful pipe, blowing the grayish-blue smoke into the breeze. The smoke smelled sweet and bright.

They noticed I was staring at them. "You want to hit it?" the young woman asked, squinting as she looked at me.

I looked around to make sure she was talking to me. "Sure," I said. They passed me the pipe, and I took a long drag and handed it back to them. In a matter of seconds, I became very stoned. "Thanks."

"Where you from?" the guy asked.

"Me? West Texas. But I've just come up from Albuquerque."

"Oh wow. Do you ride horses?" the girl said. Her boyfriend looked at her then back to me.

"Nah. Not in a while," I said. "I'm on a road trip." The couple seemed less impressed by that. "You guys know a good spot to park a camper for a little bit?"

"Not around here. You're going to wanna head up north of the city," the young woman said.

"In between here and Orange County is where you wanna be. There's a few beaches up that way where you can park and chill for a while without anyone bothering you," the boyfriend said.

"Thanks for the smoke." I packed up my things, and the couple waved as I walked off, heading back to the Old Ford.

My stint in San Diego was short-lived. I headed out of the city on the 5, driving north just inland of the coast as the couple had suggested. I drove until beaches lined the road on my left-hand side. My exhaustion coaxed me into stopping as soon as possible, however, the military-owned most of the coast up that way. Eventually, a parking lot called out to me from the side of the road. San Onofre State Park, the sign read. The campground was full, so I parked the camper in the day-use area. I had a couple of beers and thought about how long the days feel when you're alone. The sunset over the Pacific drifted and faded into a deep navy blue, and as soon as the sky was black, I went off to bed.

NINETEEN

Early the next morning, I was pried from my sleep by a hard wrapping—the sound of steel hitting the aluminum door to the camper. Outside of my window, I could see a cop car blocking me into my spot. I got down from my bunk and looked around to make sure there wasn't any weed out. With all incriminating items safely stowed, I cracked the door to my camper. The responding officer was outside, waiting. His muscular forearms stuck out his short sleeves, his hair was bleached out by the sun, and he wasn't wearing a hat. He was in his forties but very handsome, built like the surfers I had seen on the beach the day before.

"Hey there, son. You been camping here?"

"Yes, sir. Just last night, sir." I loaded as many "sirs" into conversations with cops as I could.

"You know you're not allowed to camp here, right?"

"No, sir. I didn't know that."

"Well, you do now. Get a move on before tonight or I'll have to write you a ticket, ok?"

"Yes, sir. Thanks for the warning." The cop walked off, and I watched him get into his car. He pulled out of the parking lot and back out onto the highway, headed south. I waited five minutes, fired up the old Ford, and turned left out of the parking lot, headed north on Highway 5.

The highway led through San Clemente and up to Laguna Beach. Never had I seen such opulence in my life. Looking through my windshield, all I could see was wealth.

Logistically, an entire city of rich people is impossible, but there wasn't any evidence in Laguna to disprove that theory. Where were all the poor people? There weren't even any middle-class homes for miles, just elegant mansions and modern architectural treasures. I parked the truck in a huge parking lot full of cars that belonged in a car show.

The people walking from the parking lot to the beach matched the mansions on the hillside above us. The women looked like the pictures in Beatrice's fashion magazines. They dressed in elegant sheets of silk and wore gilded sandals on their feet. Their hair and skin and nails, all perfectly manicured. Colorful jewels hung down on their freckled chests. Next to my dusty body, they seemed as if they were a different species.

The water was colder than I expected, numbing my legs as I waded out into the hip-high waves. The hot sun felt good on my chest as I laid out to dry, smoking cigarettes and gawking at the beautiful bodies around me. Out in the water, surfers paddled around and sat up on their boards, waiting for waves. This was an incredible place, no doubt about it, but like any good guest, I was worried I would overstay my welcome.

The taco shop next to the beach called out to my hungry belly. When I saw the little menu stapled onto the side of the shack, I was shocked. Three tacos for $15. I had never heard of tacos that were more than two dollars each, let alone $5 apiece. There was a taco shop near campus, and when they changed the price of a taco from $1.25 to $1.75, the students almost rioted.

I bought the tacos, a special treat, I told myself, and I will admit, they were fantastic. They weren't worth what I paid for them, but they were certainly of a high caliber, and you couldn't beat the view from outside the shack. After eating, I smoked a cigarette on the little patio next to the shack and watched the beautiful people line up, one by one, and get their tacos. The people in California were different than what I expected but just as unusual and exotic as I'd hoped. Granted, my assumption before I arrived in Southern California was that everyone there was a movie star, so my expectations weren't exactly calibrated in reality. The clothes, the hairstyles, the sunglasses, and the way people carried themselves were not only different from what I imagined, but they were also different from anything I had ever seen. I finished my cigarette and got back on the road.

On to LA and the endless expansion of human life that covered the valley below the San Gabriel mountains. It took me about three hours to drive from the very south end to the very north end. The highway, which was 5 lanes wide, was stuffed to the gills with cars and trucks, and motorcycles zoomed through the cracks. The air was thick with fumes, and I couldn't get out of there fast enough; however, I was barely crawling through the gridlock. The never-ending sprawl finally petered out into the mountains to the north. I cut over on the 101 and headed towards Ventura.

The northern part of LA reminded me of Laguna Beach. Mountains sloping down into the ocean, fancy houses and stylish cars everywhere you looked. A giant city bookended by beautiful mountains and beaches—I didn't want to be there, but I understood why others did.

The mountains outside of Malibu gave way to Oxnard, and I felt the stress release from my crooked neck. In Ventura, I stopped for a rest. Finding a nice park seemed like too much work, so I parked in a shopping mall parking lot. In the back of the camper, I made some noodles, followed by some chips and salsa. After I ate, I tried to write. The parking lot wasn't all that inspiring, and I couldn't get anything down on the page. I drove on a little further through tired eyes and found a beach in the town of Carpinteria just southeast of Santa Barbara. The sun was making its final descent over the Pacific, and the beach seemed like a good place to stay for the night.

The parking lot at this beach was different from the ones I had been to down south. There were several VW vans. There was a pickup with a camper just like mine, an old RV from the '80s, and myriad old vans. People walked around with surfboards and boogie boards like I had seen up and down the coast, but they had a different shine to them. Carpenteria had the elegance of Laguna Beach with a distinct hippy vibe; the people were just as beautiful but didn't seem to be trying half as hard. As I surveyed the beach, my nose smelled pot smoke and charcoal grills. The mountains were a little bigger and so were the waves. The beach was less crowded and the views more dramatic.

Down on the beach, I found a nice spot to set up shop. I rolled up a joint and a few cigarettes before taking a stroll. Tight-rope walking the line where the water met dry sand before retreating and rolling back into the ocean, the waves lapped at my feet but had the courtesy not to go above the knee. I finished my beer too quickly, so I made my way back to my stuff. When I got back to my cooler to get another beer, two young women had sat down next to my things.

"Hello, ladies," I said, enthusiasm hanging in my voice.

The ladies giggled and said hi back. I cracked a beer and noticed that they were looking at me. Maybe they wanted a beer, I thought, so I offered them one. They nodded yes, and I handed over two cans. "I'm Otis."

"I'm Beth, and this is Liz." They both opened their beers.

"Hi," said Liz before she sipped her beer.

Beth had a confident smile, a smile that couldn't possibly belong to a teenager. Liz held onto her beer with a slender wrist but her cheeks were youthfully plump. The way they drank their beers told me that it wasn't their first drink. For a second, I thought about how maybe I shouldn't be giving these girls beers, then I stopped thinking altogether.

In the ultimate show of my ability as a hunter/gatherer, I sparked up the joint that I had rolled. I took a couple of big pulls and then offered it to the ladies. Liz took the joint, hit it, then passed it to Beth. They gave it back just as the sky was fading into gold. Their hair glowed as they swept it off of their faces and behind their ears.

"Y'all live here?" I asked.

"No. We live down in Ventura. Liz's sister goes to UCSB," Beth said.

"Did I catch a *y'all* in there?" Liz asked as both of them burst out laughing like little girls.

"I believe you did," I said, handing Liz the joint.

"Where are you from?" Beth asked.

"I'm from West Texas," I said and then felt the need to add, "I've been living in Albuquerque for a while, though."

"How long have you been in California?" Liz asked as she passed the joint to Beth.

"About three days or so."

"Wow!" Beth said. "You're brand new."

"Feels like I've been here longer."

"Your sister would love him," Beth told Liz.

"I know, I was just thinking that. My sister totally loves country music and cowboy hats and all that stuff."

"Is that right? We got a lot of that in Texas."

"My mom just bought her a pair of cowboy boots. She, like, has the whole outfit now."

"Really?" Beth said.

"Oh yeah."

"Wow. That's a bit much, but whatever."

"I'm sure I'd love to meet her too," I told them, eager to be involved in the conversation. They both giggled, and then nobody spoke. I looked out at the sunset, which was in full bloom. I lit up a cigarette and, without a word, gave each girl one.

After they finished their cigarettes, the girls brushed the sand off their asses while they got to their feet. The moment seemed to be slipping through my fingers, and I struggled to find a grip.

Before they walked off, Liz said, "Hey, Tex, my sister's friends are having a party up in the mountains tomorrow night. You should come up there." I resisted all my natural urges to celebrate this sweet victory right in front of the ladies who had granted it.

"Cool. Yeah. That sounds alright." I sounded like an idiot, I'm sure, but they seemed unfazed.

"Ok. I'll send you the address. What's your number?" I gave Liz my phone number, and she gave me hers. She sent me a message with the address and told me to call her tomorrow to find out the time of the party because she wouldn't know until she talked to her sister. The girls left me alone with a cooler full of beer, and I seized on the golden liquid in celebration of my fleeting victory over loneliness.

Chain-smoking and staring out onto the vast gray ocean, I watched the day dwindle and disappear. The amount of fear I had for the ocean just three days ago had drastically diminished. Able to look out at the expanse with fondness, I felt as if it were becoming my friend.

A few long-haired, hard-bodied surfers started a fire out on the beach. They played guitar while I watched, and even though they weren't friendly, they didn't seem to mind me being there. I drank until I couldn't remember getting into the camper to sleep. In the morning when I woke up, I was hungover and soaked in sweat, but the glow of recent human interaction still hung a smile on my face. I jumped down from the camper just in time to throw up in the parking lot. The lot was quiet and nobody was around, so I took my time and made sure to get all of it out.

TWENTY

The whole next day, my nerves tried as hard as they could to get the best of me. I smoked cigarettes faster than I could roll them while walking up and down the beach for what seemed like hours, and when I checked my watch, only minutes had gone by. Too restless to enjoy the beach, I fired up the old Ford and made my way up the coast to Santa Barbara. Walking around downtown, I couldn't believe that so many beautiful sun-bathed women were in one place. How could this happen? I imagined that the police officers of Santa Barbara had set up roadblocks, and upon thorough inspection, like bouncers at a nightclub, allowed only good-looking people into this seaside city. But just that morning, the old Ford had made its way into the city limits without encountering any checkpoints, dispelling my theory.

In an ever-present state of defied expectations, these people weren't your traditional attractive people. They almost looked like hippies, but they weren't like any of the hippy men and women of Albuquerque. These people were wealthy and healthy; they wore exotic clothes and sold artwork. The women seemed to float when they walked, and the men rubbed their shaggy beards as they spoke to each other. Everyone was happy, smiling, hugging each other.

I was woozy from all the sun and walking, the cigarettes and women, so I stopped at a shop called Revitalize to see what they had to offer in the way of revitalization. The inside of the store was an ethereal hodgepodge of juice, smoothies, ancient grains, as well as an assortment of magic potions and tonics. I ordered a ten dollar cup of juice full of ingredients I didn't know were meant to go together. Beautiful women floated into the shop, gliding around on the balls of their feet while they smelled little dropper bottles held in their soft hands. My beverage tasted like sweet dirt, but I enjoyed it. I also enjoyed watching the patrons of the shop. Words that I didn't understand were lobbed back and forth, and these women seemed to be in love with everyone within arm's distance. They offered affirmations that seemed so intimate, so personal, and here they were, saying them loud enough for me to hear.

A voyeur in a foreign land, the only thing that kept me from leaving was the cold juice that slurped down my throat, reminding me that I was a paying customer and I was allowed to be there. I finished my drink and returned the glass jar it came in to the lady at the counter. She thanked me, pouring her eyes into mine. Her sincerity almost trumped her beauty in its shocking depth.

As I walked the streets of Santa Barbara, I found a city rich in contrast. Wealthy people looked like beggars, monks, and starving troubadours. The rugged half desert, half tropical mountains struck down into the gentle ocean. Old cars in perfect condition cruised up and down the palm and succulent-lined streets. I walked by a college kid drinking coffee with a man that looked like Leo Tolstoy; they hovered over a beat-up table on a warm patio. Beautiful old Spanish buildings stacked up next to posh hotels and fine dining—the remnants of Colonialism framed by nature and decorated with opulence and casual wealth. In this town, walking around felt like being in love. The kind of love where the individual pieces don't seem to fit, but when you add them all together, they're somehow perfect.

Kicking around town and taking in the sites was almost enough of a distraction to make me forget about the party

Liz had invited me to. I hadn't heard from the ladies, so I figured I'd give Liz a call and see if she had any details. When she picked up the call, she was happy to hear from me, even if she giggled at inappropriate times and seemed distracted. She had such a casual way of speaking, and her lack of urgency relaxed me. My invitation to the party was confirmed, and I was instructed to bring a bunch of beer. When I asked her what time I should show up, she said anytime. The party was all day and wouldn't finish until the morning, if at all. I had never heard of a party that didn't have a start time. I was and am a very prompt person. It was inconceivable that an event didn't have a start time. Thinking through this unusual concept, I conceded that parties were the one scheduled event that I didn't hold myself to promptness. Most people showed up late to parties anyway, so why bother? Even if this was the rationale of the hosts, a specific time was needed in which to ignore when showing up late. Sick of walking around and in need of a beer and some company, I figured I might as well put this *show up whenever* attitude to the test. I bought a thirty rack of beer and iced them down in my trusty cooler. The old Ford rattled through town, nose down like a hound dog on a scent, in search of the mountain hideaway Liz had described.

The city got smaller and smaller in my rearview mirror as I climbed into those rugged peaks above town. I curled up and around the long arm of the mountain, up until the road flattened out into some sort of pass. As per the provided directions, I left the highway for a narrow, shady road that wound through a grove of California live oaks. Out the other side of the grove, I crossed a small bridge over a dried-out creek bed and then passed by a busted-up cabin with a tarped roof. As I drove up a big hill, the addresses on the mailboxes indicated I was getting closer and closer, and then I was there.

A gravel driveway led down to a parking area that was big enough to hold six cars, maybe more. A few beater trucks, a VW van, an old convertible Mercedes, and an Econoline conversion van that stood on blocks were all parked with space for one more. I parked the old Ford and went back into the camper to prepare for my entrance into the mysterious soiree. My routine of rolling a few joints, a few cigarettes, and grabbing the cooler full of iced-down beer had become second nature by this point.

The driveway continued past the parking area and led me to a few small cabins, each one smaller than the last. The cabins were just how you'd want them to be—cedar sided, tin-roofed, each with a stone chimney. The cabins were quiet and appeared to be empty. I loitered on a stone patio for a minute until I heard faint voices and the clinging of metal coming from the other side of the structures. Following my ears, I wound around the cabins until I entered a sandy opening. There was a horseshoe pit bordered on one side by an outcrop of ancient sandstone boulders, and on the other side, a steep ravine. A group of men stood around, nursing beers and tossing shoes. I figured these guys must have just woken up, as three of the four were wearing pajama pants and no shirt. I had to clear my throat two times before they noticed me. A short man with a beer in his hand looked up at me, nodded, and then went back to tossing horseshoes.

"Hi there, y'all. I'm Otis. My friend said there was a party here," I said, hoping to get their attention.

"Who's your friend?" one of the guys said. He looked north of thirty and had a cigarette dangling from his lips.

"Liz. Her sister is friends with you guys, I guess." I sounded less confident by the second.

"I don't know a Liz. Actually, maybe I do," one of them said, as though he was thinking out loud. The other guys laughed and then he did too.

"I don't know any Liz either, man. We're having a party, though, but there's just four of us here now. Not much of a party, I guess," the man with the dangling cigarette said.

"Ok. I guess I could come back later."

"Oh, no. You're fine. I know we don't look like much, but we like to get down. You want a party? Well, shit, you're at one," said a tall black guy with dreadlocks and tattoos all over his arms. "You know what they say, it's not the size of the dog at the party, it's the size of the party in the dog." The other guys sat on these wise words, some of them looking at the ground and the others up at the sky. One of them nodded and then one of them chuckled.

"You play horseshoes?" the guy with the cigarette asked.

"Yes, sir. I do."

"And is that cooler full of ice-cold beers?"

"Yes, sir, it is," I said, looking down at my cooler, nervous to make a wrong move.

"Ok, perfect. Here, give me a beer and take my spot. I need to make a phone call."

"You can have one. Anyone else want one?"

All four of the men scurried towards the cooler, and one by one, they fished beers out of the ice water. Around they went, introducing themselves.

Kenan was first. He was tall and handsome. His chest, back, and arms were decorated with tattoos. He wore camouflage cargo shorts and had a necklace with a shark's tooth on it. He was from LA, and when he was a kid, his parents brought him to Santa Barbara to see the pier, and he had thought to himself, 'One day, I'm going to live here.' He moved up right after high school. He lived in Santa Barbara during his college years, and then it was up to the mountains after graduation. He played bass guitar and keyboard in a hip-hop group and sang in a blues band. He could pretty much play any instrument that fell into his hands.

The older guy with the dangling cigarette who needed to make a phone call was Billy. He grew up in Idaho and had lived in the smallest cabin for the last seven years. The first one to arrive at the property, Billy had recruited all of the other guys, and he also served as the party promoter for all of the social activities on the land. Funny and sharp, his bright personality influenced his music, and his music influenced his personality. He never spoke of his childhood or his parents but maintained a complete air of openness and transparency when it came to any other topic.

The short guy with the heavy beard was Isaiah, and he was the first to sign on to live with Billy. Growing up in Santa Barbara, his early life's ambitions were to become a professional surfer. At fifteen, he discovered the guitar, and now Isaiah was almost professional in both. The only person at the house who didn't smoke anything but drank harder than anyone else, Isaiah seemed to always be spaced out or focused on something other than the present. Occasionally, he would focus in, look you in the eyes, say something profound, then go back to whatever had distracted him in the first place, leaving you to your interpretations. He didn't care for conversations; he was a man of isolated statements.

The last to grab a beer was a shy, quiet fellow by the name of Trey. He grew up on a garlic farm just west of Gilroy, California. Trey was a drummer of many disciplines, techniques, and styles. He moved to Santa Barbara five years prior, and he was the only member of the house that was in a band with Billy. They played improvisational Jazz and went by The Sun Risers. Trey had worked hard his entire childhood, and the incredible amount of free time that mountain life afforded had made him uneasy. He spent his days planting and maintaining pocket gardens hidden around the property. His jeans always had brown stains at the knees, and his shirts were never put to good use.

Billy was a jazz pianist by trade. and that's how he knew Harold, the owner of the property. Harold, a saxophonist who was in his sixties at the time they met, had seen Billy play in LA ten years earlier, and they became friends. Harold was a loner, a widower who had survived a very wealthy wife. When his wife died, she bestowed upon him several properties in Southern California, including the property I was standing on. Harold let Billy and his friends live there for half the normal market rent as long as they all abided by one rule, they had to make music. When Billy first moved to the mountain property, the land and the structures it held were in shambles. With the help of the roommates and the occasional friend, Billy built the property into a beautiful oasis.

These four guys lived in the cabins on the property and were pretty well known for their parties and live jam sessions that often lasted all night. I had never met anyone like them, and within minutes, they had let me in with open arms. My loneliness drifted off into the dusty hills surrounding the property.

After we made introductions, the boys cracked open fresh beers and we took our places next to the rusty stakes. The guys were surprised to find out that I was raised on horseshoes in the sands of West Texas. They weren't bad by any means, but I whipped those boys' asses. I may have been better at throwing horseshoes than them, but they had me beat when it came to drinking. They were throwing back my beer with ease.

We smoked cigarettes one after the other while we laughed and kicked around dust and pebbles. Not only were the boys short on booze, but they were lean on tobacco too. We smoked a few fingers off my can of tobacco before any of the other guests even showed up.

As the day wore on, people infiltrated the property from multiple angles. By the time the sun got heavy in the sky and the breeze moved in, the party was in full swing. The heat, the socializing, my nerves, and most certainly the alcohol left me feeling very drunk. It was too early to be drunk in front of a bunch of people I didn't know, so I sauntered away from the party and out to my truck to collect myself. I drank some water and smoked a handful of cigarettes, and for medicinal reasons, I smoked a joint. As I finished the joint, a car pulled up and parked. Piling out of the car were Liz and Beth, dressed in their finest hippy costumes.

"Tex!" they both shouted and came and hugged me. I wasn't sure why they were so excited to see me, but I didn't ask.

"Shannon, meet Tex!" Liz said to a woman in a lacy crop top. She approached me full of skepticism and sass. Her hair was straight and cut to angles, brushing the tops of her shoulders. She was prettier than the ocean.

"So, you're the boy who's been chatting up my sister?" she said, marching right up to me like a street tough looking for a fight. Her eyes barely came to my clavicle, but I was intimidated nonetheless.

Billy, coming from the house, made his way up the driveway to the parking area. "What's up, babe?" Shannon moved past me and onto Billy. She hugged him and kissed him on the lips.

The three girls walked past Billy toward the cabins and the other party-goers. I followed suit, and Billy stopped me.

"Yo, man, heads up. I don't believe Shannon's sister is of age, ya dig? Tread lightly."

"That's why her sister wanted to put a bullet in me."

Billy laughed, and we both walked past the cabins and up a little hill to a small field full of fruit trees. Billy joined Kenan, Isaiah, and Trey in setting up amplifiers and a drum kit on a homemade plywood stage. Not only did Harold, the property owner, encourage projects like building a stage, he funded them. Once it was sufficiently dark, the boys started playing. Looking around me, I drank in the wide assortment of people that were converging on the orchard. Surfers and hippies, yoga girls and exotic dancers, ravers, musicians, spiritualists, hipsters, greasers, pot farmers, hillbillies, and punk rockers. We listened to the music, smoked cigarettes, some people danced, and almost everyone there was imbibing in some sort of substance.

These folks were passing around jars of dried-up mushrooms, small medicine bottles, tiny bags of powder, a giant mason jar full of something that looked like iced tea, and there were countless cigarettes, joints, and pipes going around in all directions. Smoke signals rose from the limbs of the orchard and danced in the mountain breeze. The air around me seemed to be carrying a subtle electric current.

I felt both out of place and very welcomed. Even with all these different types around, I still stuck out, and people were curious about who I was. They asked me all kinds of questions, and I did my best to answer them.

"What type of boots are those?" a guy with long blond hair and round glasses asked.

"Cowboy boots," I said.

"Oh, yeah, I guess I already knew that."

Another one joined in. "Did you grow up on a farm? Were there cows?"

"I grew up on a ranch, but there weren't any cows. We raised sheep."

"Is it really called a ranch if there aren't any cows?"

"Do you treat the sheep well?"

"Don't they get hot in the summer?"

"What do you do with them?"

The questions came fast and frequently, and I answered them as best I could. I found that this crowd knew a lot about farming fruit and vegetables but not much about raising animals. After a few minutes, the novelty of my existence wore off a bit, and the questions drizzled into regular conversation.

Amid the music and the unusual company, I sobered up enough to the point where I thought another beer would be a good idea. I remembered that my cooler was somewhere on the property, so I gave chase. It wasn't hard to find, laying right where I left it, next to the horseshoe pits.

Inside the cooler, three lonesome beers floated around in iceless water. I grabbed the cooler and returned to the orchard. The chilled-out music washed over me while I drank a beer in the grass in front of the stage. Instead of bringing me back up, the beer left me exhausted. My eyes kept shutting, and keeping them open for more than a few seconds at a time became laborious. It wasn't that I wanted to go to bed, it was more like I had to. After an internal argument, the sleepy side of me won out, and I retired to the camper. The guys were busy playing music, so I didn't bother asking if I could keep my rig parked overnight on the property. Most of the people there were committing serious drug crimes, so I figured they would forgive me for my illegal parking. Tucked into my bed, I fell asleep as soon as I closed my eyes.

TWENTY-ONE

A cool wind blew through the open windows, rustling the little curtain that blocked my eyes from the sun. My body was parched out like a desert wash. It was late morning, and I hadn't moved once during my sleep. When I jumped down from my bed, my foot caught the sheet, and I tumbled face-first onto the ground. I belly smacked the floor of the camper; my lungs let out a wheeze as I hit the laminate. Scrambling off the ground in desperate need of something to drink, I chugged a liter of water without coming up for air.

When I stumbled out of the camper to piss, all of the cars that were parked the night before were still there. I smoked a cigarette as I surveyed the ten-acre parcel. The orchard was littered with sleeping bodies. People were strewn about the stage and out in the grass next to the stage, some of them lying directly in the sun. Billy was the one person who was awake; he was cleaning beer cans off the back porch of one of the cabins. He had a beer in hand and was smoking a cigarette.

"Tex. You're still here?"

"Yes, sir. I'm sorry I didn't ask y'all's permission to park overnight."

"No worries, just asking cause we were wondering where you went. You must have gone to bed early."

"I did. I was dead tired, man. Can't quite drink like the rest of you guys, I guess."

"You should never try to keep up with the boys of La Posada."

"La Posada?"

"It's the name of this property, and me and my roommates, we're its boys," Billy said, puffing his chest up like superman.

"Makes sense."

"When everybody wakes up, we're going to the river. You should come. Cold water'll kill that hangover."

Back at my truck, I ate some eggs, washed up, re-hydrated, put on my swim trunks, smoked three cigarettes and a joint, and still had to wait an hour and a half for everyone to wake up and get ready for the river. Kenan rode in my truck with me so he could show me the way. The river was barely moving, but it was nice and cool.

We set our towels down on the pebble beach, and I peeled off my shirt. Billy, Kenan, and Isaiah took their shirts off and then their shorts, their dicks hanging down for everyone to see. The girls followed suit. Liz and Beth took their tops down and Shannon pulled her dress over her head, revealing nothing at all but a brown triangle of hair above her vagina. Looking around at all the bodies, I realized that I was the only one who wasn't naked. I didn't know what to do, so I took off my shorts. I never liked being the outlier.

Later that day, I found out that Liz was eighteen and Beth was nineteen. But at the river, I was still under the impression that they were both under eighteen. It was hard to relax, thinking I may be committing a crime just being around naked underage girls. I tried not to make eye contact with anyone as I practiced my doggy paddle in water that was shallow enough to stand.

I came to learn that most activities with this crew involved something outside, something musical, cigarettes, beer, pot, and little to no clothing. These common ingredients were often mixed all at once in a cacophony of smoke, harmonies, and fluid dancing laughter. I had never been to a naked party before, and at first, I was nervous I would become erect right there in front of these new friends, but something strange happened. I didn't feel sexual at all. I liked what I saw, but instead of sinful, what I felt was normal. That day was also the day I learned that it was important to put sunscreen on your pecker.

After a few hours, we finished swimming, got dressed, and loaded back into the cars. On the way home, we stopped at a roadside market that had a restaurant attached. We ate expensive sandwiches and bought even more expensive beer. Kenan and I rode back to the cabins in silence, listening to a Hank Williams cassette that had belonged to my father.

As I parked at the property, Kenan stopped me from getting out of the car. "Otis. Wait a second." I sat back in my seat and waited for him to start talking again. "Yo, tonight's Sunday, and Sunday is a little special here at La Posada."

"Ok. If y'all want me to take off, I don't mind. Honestly."

"No, that won't be necessary. You can stay here for as long as you like. Within reason, of course."

"Thanks. You guys have been so generous, I really appreciate it."

"No worries, man. All the cigarettes and beer we can drink. What would we do without you?" We both laughed at this, and Kenan started again, "Sunday is special because we usually take mushrooms on Sunday."

"Ok."

"All of us do." He didn't say it exactly, but I sure got the feeling that if I wanted to stay, I needed to eat their mushrooms.

"Ok. I can live with that."

"You ever done 'em before?"

"Nope. I mean, I've had mushrooms before. In soups and stuff."

"Yeah, but you know what I mean?" He nudged me with his elbow.

"Never tripped before."

"You'll like it. You'll have fun."

"We had a guy on the ranch, Sanchez. He'd come up from Oaxaca. He said they take them all the time down there. For religion and stuff." Sanchez was the only person I could think of who had ever taken magic mushrooms.

"Perfect. I just felt like I should tell you. Things'll get a little strange, but you'll have fun." Kenan smiled a smile that went up half his cheeks.

Before I went inside to join the rest of the crew, I sat in the old Ford and lit a cigarette. I killed the engine but left the radio on. The tape deck was playing Hank's *Lost Highway,* a most fitting track to frame my thoughts. I wasn't thinking about taking mushrooms. I was thinking about La Posada. Traveling for a week or so and living in the camper for about a month, I was ready to park the old Ford and stay put. My hobo instincts were starting to form, and I could sense that this was a place I wanted to stay for a while.

To start the grand ceremony, Isaiah and Trey heated a pot of water on the stove. They turned the flame off as the water came to a rolling boil. Trey dumped half a cup of loose leaf tea into the pot and stirred it around with a cracked wooden spoon. Kenan emptied a cup of ground-up mushrooms into the pot, followed by a few generous scoops of raw honey to finish off the brew. Kenan, Billy, Shannon, Beth, Liz, and Shannon's two friends, Lilian and Erin, stood around in the stone-floored kitchen watching the tea darken. Trey held out a fine tea strainer, and Isaiah poured the steaming tea through the metal mesh and into a wide-mouthed pitcher. The brown concoction was divided out into mugs.

To my surprise, the mixture tasted like the tea my mother made on those cold winter days on the ranch. The steaming liquid went down faster and faster as it cooled and then it was gone. Embarrassed about my lack of experience, I didn't want to ask what to expect. Instead, I watched as the rest of the crew sipped their tea. How long would it take to kick in? What was I supposed to be doing while I was high? How long would it last? I resigned myself to let the mystery play out.

Ten minutes after I finished my tea, I felt a flutter come up from my stomach as if someone was lightly tickling me with a feather from the inside. The flutters came and went. A smile sneaked onto my face followed by an inexplicable giggle. Billy laid out pillows and mats all over the stage in the orchard and we laid down together in what could be described as a pile of people. Isaiah strummed softly on an acoustic guitar with no particular direction. I tricked myself into thinking that nothing was changing, that I wasn't feeling anything and perhaps the drugs weren't going to affect me. A minute went by, and I accepted the reality. I was high. Looking around, it didn't seem like the others felt any different than normal, so I just kept watching. As I watched, champagne bubbles, starting in my feet, rose throughout my body.

Regular, mundane conversation slipped into fits of laughter for no apparent reason. A smile fixed itself on my face and refused to go away. Feeling good completely relieved the anxiety I had going into this experience. My stomach flutter intensified but my muscles relaxed, save for my sphincter, which was working twice as hard as normal to keep my insides separated from the outside world.

As the mushrooms dug their fingers in, I felt a strong swirling of emotions. The feelings that my brain had been locking up and harboring for years, all at once, released like a reservoir breaking through its damn walls during a biblical rain. I felt so happy about having new friends, and I felt so sad that I couldn't be surrounded by every good person I had ever loved. The way I treated Beatrice shattered me, and I realized how much love I had for my parents and my uncle, regardless of who was what. I marveled at the responsibilities of Uncle Grant and wondered why I was unable to sort out my origins. I couldn't believe that the coast of California was a great structure of rock and sand and soil, cemented together by plants until it all fell right into the water. I was in a concurrent state of disbelief and full understanding. An hour in, I felt like I had been high for a lifetime, and somehow, I was still ascending.

The urge to be alone overtook me, so I got up from the pile of lounging humans and walked away from the group without saying anything. I meandered through the property, surveying the land and the plants that lived there, delighted by the geometry of succulents and the way they were placed so perfectly as if they were planted for me to find at that exact moment. I walked all over the grounds of La Posada, examining everything that hit my eye until I realized I wanted to be surrounded by the group again, so I started for the orchard. Riding a wave of electric current, I arrived in the orchard at a moment of stillness and calm. The group was clustered on the stage in a pile of pillows and delicate laughter. As I approached the group, I couldn't help but shoot back up the wave, reaching new heights of my hallucination.

My vision slurred into something similar to a painting come to life. Trees meshed together and swayed, the flowers next to the stage had a soft aura around them. All of the natural elements of the land blended and pulsed in unison. My hands morphed and shifted in front of my face. I noticed every nick, scratch, and scar as if I had never seen them before. The attention of the group shone upon me as I stood above them and asked why they hadn't told me about this feeling sooner?

"We just met you yesterday, we didn't have time. We told you as soon as we could!" Billy said, and we all fell to pieces of laughter.

Searching for my telephone, I decided it was time to call my parents and tell them I loved them. Everybody on stage was adamant that this was a bad idea. In a moment, my urge passed and was replaced by new urges. Deciding against my impulses, I imagined their outcomes instead and found pleasure in doing so.

After a few hours—hours that felt like days—I started on the long, gradual road of the comedown. My tobacco changed hands around the stage and all the little fingers went to work building cigarettes. Lillian, who I had only met a few hours earlier, told me that every single cell in her body had inflated and turned into a bubble, and through the mobility of these bubbles, she had become a liquid. Somehow I knew exactly what she was talking about.

Laying there, coming down from my immense heights, I couldn't stop thinking about how badly I wanted to be close to someone. I was craving affection, human touch, and in my infantile state, I was so jealous of the people around me with their respective partners. This group was very close with one another; the gap in intimacy between myself and the rest of them felt as big as the deserts I had crossed a week earlier. It certainly didn't help that they were all lying in a pile on top of each other, cuddling and massaging one another. On the outside, it seemed that it would be in poor taste to join in—it was too intimate for me to intrude.

Eventually, my emotions balanced and stabilized. A sense of wiseness cascaded through me as I had explored something that made my life infinitely more tolerable. I felt like I had put on a pair of glasses I didn't know I needed. I had learned some sort of truth by looking at the same thing differently.

As profound as this night was for me, it seemed old hat for my new cohort, save for Liz and Beth. At one point during the height of our trip, they announced that they loved each other and cried as they hugged. After that, they fell into each other's arms. They stayed that way all night, Liz playing with Beth's hair.

It was a beautiful night, full of stars and shifting air. When the sun came up, we all went in search of darkness and sleep, like psychedelic vampires. I slept for a few hours and woke up not feeling nearly as bad as I had when I was hungover. My experience lingered inside me, and even though I wasn't high anymore, the mushrooms were still with me. Lying in bed, I saw the bottle of tequila I kept in my camper—it was glistening in a slice of sunlight that shone through the curtains. A shiver went down my body and I thought to myself for the first time in my life, 'I've been drinking too much.'

TWENTY-TWO

My lungs hurt from smoking, but I needed a cigarette. Sitting on the dry-stacked stone wall that encased the parking area, I smoked and looked around at my surroundings. My head was fuzzy and light, and the air around me had a gentle hum to it. Other than the faint whispers of cars on the main road, the property was still and quiet.

The silence was broken when a giant Lincoln pulled into the driveway and parked next to the old Ford, its whitewall tires skidding on the gravel as the behemoth was brought to heel. The driver of the impossibly long Lincoln was Harold, the owner of La Posada. When he paid the guys to do various tasks on the property, he liked to stop by and make progress checks. He got out of his car and looked me up and down. He was wearing a leather jacket and tight jeans, the bottoms of which were tucked into black motorcycle boots. His hair was dyed coal black and slicked straight back. His big boxy sunglasses were so dark that I couldn't see his eyes.

"What are you doing in your shorts?" he asked me.

"I just woke up and haven't dressed quite yet." I didn't know what to say, so I stuck out my hand and said, "I'm Otis. Otis Billings."

"Hi, Otis. Harold." He looked past my outstretched hand and then all around. "I'm sure you're aware that this isn't a campground. How long have you been here?"

"Just a few days, sir. I'm traveling right now."

"I bet you are, Otis. I bet you are." Harold looked as if he had just remembered something and said, "You don't sound like you're from around here."

"Yes, sir. That's right. I'm from West Texas by way of Albuquerque."

"There isn't much in West Texas, is there?"

"No, sir, not really. A bunch of ranches, desert, gas wells. Not much at all."

"Which of those do you come from?" He had perked up and seemed interested all of a sudden.

"I come from a ranch. And the desert, I guess."

"What do you know about horses?"

"What do you mean?"

"What do you know about them?"

"I know how to saddle 'em and feed 'em, know how to keep a barn clean, I guess." I felt like I was talking too much, but he was still listening. "My uncle owns all kinds of horses. Been around 'em my whole life." When I spoke about the ranch and my childhood, I noticed my voice fell into a deeper drawl.

"Excellent," he said, having changed his disposition towards me. "Are the boys around?"

"Yeah, they're here, I think. Might be asleep still."

"I'm going to go see if I can find Billy." Harold walked off towards the cabins, and I put on some clothes. When I jumped out of the camper, newly dressed, Harold's Buick caught my eye. It was a black Town Car that must have been twenty years old, but it was in perfect condition. It was about twenty feet long, maybe longer—the type of car you don't drive but are driven in.

An hour after our initial meeting, Harold came back and knocked on my camper door.

"Ah, there you are," Harold said as I stepped down out of the camper. "I wanted to have a word with you before I take off."

"Yes, sir. What can I help you with?"

"I'm in need, and, from the looks of things, so are you," Harold said, then paused as he searched for the words. "I have an offer for you, an offer to make you."

"Ok."

"I need a barn hand at my stable down in Goleta. My last guy just quit on me, and I need someone who knows what they're doing."

"I'm not exactly job hunting right now," I said.

"I'm not offering you a job per se. I need some help part-time. If you come out to the stables for a few hours a week, I'll let you stay. You can park your truck here free of charge. I already checked with Billy, and he said it's fine."

"How many hours are you thinking?"

"I don't know, maybe eight. It'll depend on the week."

I pretended to think about it for a second and then accepted. A shake of Harold's hand sealed the deal. The old Buick reversed out of its resting place, and Harold put it in drive and punched the gas, spitting up rocks as he gained enough momentum to get up and out of the driveway.

I sat back down on the rock wall where Harold had found me earlier in the day. It dawned on me that Beatrice Sibson was gone from my life. We as a couple were through and had been for some time, but sitting on that rock wall, smoking a cigarette, I realized I hadn't thought about her much over the last few weeks. 'If I had moved on so quickly, surely she had too,' I told myself. The truth was much more complicated, for me and her. With my strong aversion to feelings, I let myself be sad for only a moment, then my memory of her drifted off into some other thought or theory. Preoccupied with the incredible world unfolding in front of me, my life in Albuquerque, even in retrospect, wasn't able to hold my attention.

La Posada was introduced to me as a party house, but during the weekdays, she showed off her quiet side. Days were hot and lazy, and the nights were filled with cool winds blowing off the Santa Ynez Mountains. The boys played music, and I tried to write. We smoked heaps of pot, cooked meals, tossed horseshoes, worked in the garden, and drank beer with the neighbors on Thursdays.

On the weekends, there was almost always a party up at the property, and I got to know a whole slew of characters. Beautiful women, world travelers, aging hippies, hobos, musicians, college kids, yoga teachers, painters, poets, dropouts, burnouts, school teachers, veterans, farmers, acrobats, eastern mystics, and many other people that can't be described in one word all showed up at La Posada to cut loose. The great variety of people shaped the various moods of the evenings. Sometimes you would walk into one of the cabins to find twenty people with their shirts off, giving massages in a big train like a centipede rubbing its own shoulders. Other times, a DJ would set up a booth outside and play Indian prayers and sitar music throughout the night and well into the morning. Faces were painted and costumes were worn, and in general, everybody had a really good time. La Posada was a place of immense pleasure.

With all the good came plenty of bad. This mountain hideaway could be a dangerously indulgent place, especially for the guests who came there to escape their lives. Freeloading and overstaying one's welcome was a weekly occurrence. La Posada attracted a wide assortment of people. Most of them were amazing, but just as many were terrible. Drug addicts, runaways, fugitives, and frenzied freaks trickled into parties and stayed as long as they could, hanging on like a leech on an open wound. The boys at La Posada were so generous with their space, and generous people get taken advantage of. One woman attempted to fuck each and every man on the property in an attempt to secure a permanent spot in one of the cabins. She was sick of the road but ended up right back on it when

Isaiah's girlfriend uncovered her agenda and ran her off the property. The only guy willing to fuck her was me, and she wasn't interested. I guess a camper was much less enticing than an actual house.

In most societies or subcultures, there is an established hierarchy, and La Posada certainly had its own. Billy was king, and the boys of La Posada were his knights. They were revered like celebrities. Every hierarchy has its underlings as well, and I can assure you that the bottom of this food chain was still a pretty good place to be. This wasn't just a place to live, it wasn't just land and cabins—La Posada was a scene. There were rules, norms, traditions, and rituals, all unwritten but practiced nonetheless.

I got along great with the guys. Some of them were peculiar, but we all had similar interests and ideas of how things should be. The women were a bit of a different story. They were all very friendly, and I truly enjoyed talking with them. They just weren't interested in me romantically. Not even a bit. I tried to rationalize this to myself, I tried to be patient, but eventually, I did something I didn't like to do—I expressed my frustrations.

"I wouldn't worry about it too much," Kenan advised.

"You're probably right."

"Whether I'm right or not, doesn't matter," he said, shaking his head. "There isn't shit you can do, might as well not worry about it. When I moved here, I went on a six-month drought. It drove me nuts."

"So you know how it is? It's frustrating."

"Oh for sure," Kenan said. "There's all these beautiful women running around. Half the time, they're naked and high as a kite. I was like, 'What the fuck am I doing wrong?'"

"Right? It seems like they love everyone but me."

"Especially Billy. When I moved up here, there were ten girls in line to date him, and not a single one that wanted me. Things changed though, you just gotta give it a little time. Maybe a lot of time."

"I'm patient, it's just that I don't think I fit in. I'm different than you guys."

"Being different is what runs this place. Being different is celebrated here more than anywhere I've ever been. You just gotta find someone who appreciates your brand of different."

"I guess so."

"We're a tight group, really tight. Shit, I've even used the word incestuous to describe the dating habits around here. You just don't have any clout yet."

"What do you mean?" I had never heard the word clout before, and couldn't contextualize the way Kenan used it. I finished rolling a cigarette and lit it, took a drag, and offered it to Keenan.

"Clout. You know, like rapport. Status. Chicks dig status, however, it happens to manifest. Money and a good job, that's not important to anyone around here. Living in the cabins and playing music gives me some clout, and you best believe I use that shit to curry favor with the ladies that hang out here. Billy ain't the best looking, he doesn't have the biggest dick, but he always gets the top chicks. You ever wonder why?"

"Of course." I had spent a whole heap of time wondering why. Kenan passed the cigarette back to me.

"He's the king around here. He knows everybody. He basically built this place. And the ladies, they know this, man."

Kenan's words were a revelation that forced me into questioning my past relationships. Charm and humor are valuable tools, tools that I often used, but Kenan made me see that there is more to the equation. At Ruiz's house, at house parties in college, in the dorms, at the Tin Star; at first,

I was out of place and uneasy, but after a while, I settled in, and things started to happen.

I decided I just needed to be myself. There were plenty of people around trying to be something they weren't, and I knew exactly how well that worked. I had gone around Albuquerque telling people I was a writer, and the interest it garnered in me wasn't fulfilling. Just like I did in college, I decided to push ladies from my mind. I remembered that I was here to write, after all, not find a wife.

As far as my actual writing went, I wasn't writing a novel, but I was doing a decent job of keeping a journal. It felt good to be doing the thing that I had been telling people, for so long, that I did. The solitude of the mountains was conducive to self-reflection and creativity. The most beautiful part of my journal writing was that I was allowed to be honest. Writing the truth didn't leave any room for grand illusions. I wasn't romanticizing some life I could never have, rather, I was expressing the emotions I experienced in the life I did have.

Being an outsider is a valuable writing tool. I examined the parties and the relationships that took place at La Posada, all the nuance and drama that comes with human interaction. I enjoyed the parties, but oftentimes, that enjoyment came for voyeurism, not participation. Reading back the journal entries that I wrote then, the main theme of my observations was envy. Many pages were devoted to Billy and Shannon, as they were tremendous to watch. They were playful and sharp-tongued with each other, their banter cinematic. Shannon was beautiful and very sexy, but I wasn't jealous of only Billy—I wanted to be both of them equally.

The guys played gigs down in the city most weeknights and sometimes on the weekends. Occasionally I would join them, help them set up their equipment, pass the tip jar around, and help them break down their gear after the shows. When I was a kid, my mother would take me to

Kermit to run errands. The clean clothes and the shiny cars and the many things that seemed to be so important to the people in town were completely lost on me. Living up in the hills of Santa Barbara had restored the mystery of town folk.

Once a week, I went down into Goleta to shovel shit, brush horses, and tidy up around Harold's stables. He worked me pretty good, but I liked being around the horses, and I loved staying at La Posada, so it was worth it. La Posada had a magnetic pull, like the vortex rock towers in Sedona. After each party, a whole host of leftover vans and campers and tents would cling to the property for as long as they possibly could. The boys were welcoming, but about once a week, they would have to have a tough conversation with some drifter who was trying to squat.

The property was like living on an island. We rarely left for anything other than our responsibilities and essentials. We ate what we could find or grow, or we would seize on the food that others brought us. If we got too hungry, we just smoked cigarettes. Pretty much no matter what was happening, we smoked cigarettes. Even though my expenses were protected by my isolation, I had no money coming in, and my self-built trust was diminishing. I wasn't ready to go back to work full-time, but I wanted to stay at La Posada for as long as possible, so I sniffed around to see where I could make a few bucks.

A lot of the hippies that came through La Posada were either coming back from trimming weed or headed to go trim weed. Thousands of people flock to California every year to help with the harvest. Usually, this happens in the late fall, but indoor growers needed help year-round. Trimming seemed to be an obvious avenue to pad my savings, so I asked around, and everyone I asked told me that I should talk to Lillian.

Lillian was a regular at La Posada, a true close friend of the guys, and I knew her pretty well. The next time she was up on the mountain, I asked her if she could help me out with some work. She always needed hands and was happy that I had asked. Before she left to go home, Lillian wrote down an address on an old bookmark and told me to show up the next day for work.

TWENTY-THREE

Early the next morning, I followed a yellowed map down into the St. Ynez valley, the old Ford aimed at the address Lillian had given me. The valley, an open expanse of vineyards, grassland, and chaparral surrounded on all sides by olive drab mountains, was unfamiliar to me. Landmarks were scarce, and the map Billie had given me was not as detailed as I would have liked. After a few wrong turns and a stop at a gas station to ask for directions, I found a sandy dirt road lined with California live oaks and golden bunch grasses. Standing tall next to the sand road was a generic mailbox with the address I was looking for hand-painted across the box. About a mile down the road, I came to a closed aluminum gate. I put the old Ford into park to investigate. The gate opened all by itself just as I got one boot onto the dirt. I was being watched, but I couldn't tell how.

The road ended at a collection of small shacks that were flanked by two greenhouses, each one the size of a small house. A man appeared from inside one of the shacks and walked towards my truck. Before he got to me, Lillian came out of the larger greenhouse and waved to me. I got out of the truck and introduced myself to the man. He introduced himself as Lillian's father but didn't give his name.

Lillian came and hugged me as her dad went back into the shack he had come from. Lillian walked me into a different shack. Inside the clapboard building was an incredible amount of marijuana strung up on the rafters. The pot was still clinging to the branches it had grown on, and there were dried leaves wrapped around the buds like fingers gripping a baseball. My nostrils were painted with the pungent funk of fresh marijuana.

Lillian pulled a few large stalks off the rope and led me out of that shack and into a different one. In there, the walls were lined with giant mason jars, some of them full of weed and some empty. In the middle of the shack was a large drafting table where two women sat. Their scissored hands moved like soft robots, cutting away leaves with incredible efficiency.

Lillian had me sit down at the table across from the two ladies. She handed me a pair of small snippers and told me she'd be back later. The ladies sitting next to me, Jessica and Katrina, introduced themselves as Lillian left the room. Jessica and Katrina looked like extras cast in a movie about a music festival. They chatted with me for a minute, asked me a few questions, all the while, their hands never stopped. Little scissors hooked around their fingers, snipping rapidly, the undesired plant matter falling away in a steady shower.

Jessica gave me a quick tutorial on how to trim a bud. Her hash-stained finger pointed out the mason jars along the wall and told me that they were to be filled up with trimmed buds. Katrina emphasized the importance of labeling the jars, one of them was to bear my name and was to only put weed that I trimmed into that jar.

"If Lillian doesn't know who trimmed it, nobody gets paid for it. I've had it happen before, it sucks," she said. She went on to tell me that the jars would be weighed later on, and my pay was based on the amount that I trimmed. After a few minutes of trimming, the ladies showed me what I was doing right and what I needed to improve on. The work was easy and mindless, tedious as peeling an endless bag of potatoes.

Jessica lit a joint the size of my pointer finger and passed it around. As we worked, we talked a little bit, but most of the time, we just worked. The ladies played their music on a little speaker and the day crawled by. After my eight hours were through, Lillian weighed out all of the pot I had trimmed and paid me $120 cash for my labor. She assured me that as I got faster, I would make more money. She paid out $250 per pound of trimmed weed, and once I was up to speed, the expectation was that I would be able to trim a pound in a day.

Between my hours at the stables and my three days a week in the trim shack, I was almost working full-time. I wrote my journal entries less and less until I wasn't writing anymore. My drinking picked back up, and I settled into a rhythm not too dissimilar to the one I'd left in Albuquerque. Financial stability was nice, but in the back of my mind, I knew that I was getting farther away from where I was supposed to be going.

TWENTY-FOUR

In the morning, I liked to have my coffee on the back deck of the largest cabin. One of these mornings, Billy strolled by and found me looking out over the madrone trees trying not to think. He had a seat at the picnic table and rolled up a cigarette from my can.

"You know, I was wondering, what it is that you do?" he asked.

His question landed on my ears like a fist. In the absence of a fully formed answer, I asked him, "How do you mean?"

"We're musicians. We live up here because it's conducive to creating music. I haven't seen you pick up an instrument or sing any songs."

"Harold told me that you were ok with me staying here. Did you guys not agree to that?"

"Of course we did. That isn't what I'm getting at. Not at all," he said in a softer tone. "There's two kinds of people that are attracted to this place. You know the types. Party people and creatives. The partiers stick around for a few days, and then we ask them to leave. The creators often end up living here or they become our close friends, and they visit the property whenever they like. They become a part of this thing that we've built. You don't need to make music to live here. But it seems silly to live here and just work a nine to five, drink beer, and watch the calendar turn. Don't you think? I'm not accusing you of anything, I assure you, but that's the basis of my question. What is it that you do?"

Billy was so calm, so stoic as he smoked his cigarette. I wanted to cry.

"I haven't been talking about it much, but I'm a writer. I write."

"Why haven't you been talking about it?"

"Cause I haven't been doing it enough, I guess."

"Why not?"

I cleared my throat of flem and licked the cigarette paper in my hand, closing it tight. The cigarette cracked and popped as I pulled deeply from it, exhaling a thick stream of smoke before I attempted an answer. "I've been asking myself that same question. I started cleaning stables so I could live here, and for other reasons, I started trimming weed. I'm happy to have the work, cause I like staying here. It's nice to not be out on the road. But I'm starting to feel like maybe I need the road to write. I don't write too much when I'm comfortable."

"What do you write?"

"Uh, different stuff."

"Like poems? Short stories? Essays? What are we talking about?"

"I am trying to write a novel. Nothing's coming out though. I've been journaling mostly, when I do write, that is."

"Ok."

Billy seemed to be done with his questioning. I expected some sage advice, some great proclamation on creativity, but nothing came out of him except cigarette smoke and hot breath.

"You don't have any advice for me?"

"I don't know. I guess not," he said. He took a sip of his beer and looked me in the eyes and said, "You need to figure it out for yourself. Nobody will teach you how to live the way you want to live your life."

"I need some inspiration. You know where I can find some?" I laughed at this to show him I was joking.

"There's honesty in that question. Inspiration, on its face, looks like an external factor, some situation or event, that presents itself. I don't think I believe that, though. Inspiration is internal—it's how you view the event that matters, not that the event happened. What I'm getting at, I think, is that you will find inspiration in any number of things, if you are looking at it the right way."

"And what if I'm not looking at it the right way?"

"Then you should keep those jobs you got."

Billy left me to my coffee, my thoughts, and my view of the landscaping. I was restless but afraid to stand up. Feeling like I had forgotten something, I wracked my brain, but there was nothing. Back in my camper, I tried to take a siesta but settled for reading and staring out the window.

The next morning, I was slow to get out of bed. I wanted coffee, but I was too lazy to get up and make it. I wanted to eat doughnuts, but nothing like that existed on this land. Just before I was able to get myself up to make coffee, I heard gravel crunching underfoot.

"You busy?" Billy asked me. He was standing outside my camper, shirtless, looking in the open door.

"No," I said and hopped down from my bed.

"I want to show you something."

I dressed and put my boots on. I followed Billy up through the orchard and down the other side to the back road that straddled the property. We walked the shady backroad for a little while until we came to a gravel driveway that looked like it went back a ways into the trees.

"From here on out, no talking until I say so, ok?"

I nodded in agreement and followed him up the long driveway. The gravel road crossed through a cedar grove and past a house set up on the hill above the road. Eventually, we made it to a trail that broke away from the endless driveway and headed down towards a small gorge. A little way down the trail, Billy stopped off in a clearing. We had a view of the gorge below us and the hills above.

"You can talk now, we're far enough away." He lit a cigarette and so did I.

We started back walking, and in a few minutes, we were at the base of the small gorge. The water in the creek bed was still and stank of rotting leaves. The creek bed narrowed into a coin slot formed by fifteen-foot tall gray boulders. We climbed and scooted, hoisting ourselves through the sections of tight stone. We came to a scooped-out room in the rock and stopped. I looked up and could see a sliver of sky.

"Neat spot," I said and re-lit my cigarette.

"Check this out." Billy pointed to a drawing on the wall of the room. It did not look like any kind of graffiti I had ever seen. "It's a petroglyph," he said.

"What's that?"

"A fancy word for a drawing. I think the Chumash made it a long time ago."

"What is it?" I asked.

"You see that?" Billy pointed to a bug on the water. The bug had four thin legs sprawled out wide. The legs pressed down on the surface of the water, creating a circular indentation. I looked up at the drawing and connected the bug to the wall. I must have made an epiphanic face because Billy started to laugh.

"Cool, right?"

"Yeah, it's really cool," I said.

We crawled out of the slot canyon and marched up the trail until we got to the gravel. We slid by the house and through the cedar grove. When we made it back to the road, we both exhaled at the same time. We didn't say anything, even though we were far from the house. There was nothing to say.

Around the house, at parties, I watched how women looked at Billy. I noticed how men looked at him. Most days, he was quiet and aloof, and if he didn't like you or if he wasn't in the mood for conversation, it was easy to tell.

"If Billy says something funny, it's twice as funny because Billy said it," one of Lillian's friends told me. At the time, I had thought it was strange that she told me this. Strange, not because it wasn't true, but because it was.

TWENTY-FIVE

The days got hotter and hotter, and the land La Posada sat on turned into fine-grain sand. Our gardens flourished in the late spring with minimal attention. In the summer, they demanded large doses of water to keep upright and green. The summer not only brought heat and arid winds, but it brought an influx of guests to La Posada. The university had let out, and foreign travelers flocked to the California coast. The combination created an explosion of partying and socializing, the shrapnel of which peppered our property. We hung Japanese lanterns in the orchard and people were drawn in like moths.

The highest point on La Posada was atop a giant boulder. The boulder, known affectionately as "The Rock," was shrouded by trees and draped on one side by a forty-foot cliff that landed on the neighbor's property. During the summer months, we were entertaining so often that socializing became a chore, and The Rock became my refuge. Up there, the stars were bright, and you could see the lights coming up from the coast. I smoked cigarettes and drank beer and listened to the faint sounds of music as it streamed out of the orchard.

On a particularly warm night, during a rather crowded party, the orchard overflowed with dressed-down hippies, and smoke billowed through the trees like a choking fog. Billy and Kenan were holed up in Billy's cabin. When I walked in, they were sitting at Billy's desk, both of them squeezed into the corner of the bedroom. A woman I had never seen before was lying on the bed, looking up at the ceiling. Billy snorted skinny lines of cocaine off of the wood desk in front of him. He disappeared three of the lines and handed the straw off to Kenan, who then took a turn.

"Otis?" Kenan said, holding out the straw.

"No thanks. Never done it before."

Billy wiggled his nose with his index finger and said, "If you've never done it, might as well keep it that way."

"Where's Shannon?" I asked, looking at the woman on the bed.

"Not sure," Billy said.

"Hasn't been around in a while, has she?" I asked.

Billy looked at Kenan, waiting to see if Kenan would answer first. "Haven't seen her in a week or two, I suppose," Billy said, licking a cigarette closed.

Kenan made a face at me that suggested I change the subject.

"Did you meet Lauren B?" Billy looked over to the bed. "We've been hanging out lately, she's a good one." If Lauren B was the woman on the bed, she must not have heard her name called, because she didn't move, her eyes stayed fixed on the ceiling.

"What happened to Shannon?" At that moment, for some reason I couldn't grab ahold of, I felt loyal to Shannon and not Billy.

"She's been with Tommy," Billy said, chopping at his cocaine with a credit card. "I believe they are seeing each other now."

"Is that right?" Kenan asked.

"It is," Billy said matter of fact, looking at Kenan. No one said anything for a while, and I studied Billy. I wanted to see if he felt pain, jealousy, or hurt of any kind.

I excused myself, telling them I needed a beer. Up on The Rock, I escaped the noise and the small talk. For some time, I sat there by myself until I heard a stick break underfoot. Piercing my quiet, two little voices came up through the trees below me.

"It's easier than it looks," a woman said.

"Easy to get up, maybe. How about coming down?"

"It's not bad at all. I promise. I've been up and down it before, much drunker than I am now."

One head popped up through the darkness. After a moment's pause, the head came towards me and another head popped up behind it.

"Oh. Sorry. I didn't think anyone was up here," said a young woman. Her hair was black in the night, but as she got closer, I realized it was brown and curled up in coils. The next girl came and stopped behind the first. She had straw blonde hair that stopped abruptly at her shoulder. I couldn't see their faces, but I could sense they were beautiful.

"No worries, I don't mind. Come on up." The ladies stepped forward and out of the shadows, their faces illuminated in moonbeams and light pollution. They walked out onto the rock and took in the 360-degree view.

"I'm Otis."

"I know who you are. You're the cowboy. You live here, right?" the blonde asked.

"Yeah. I do. I'm sure I'd remember you if I could see you in the light."

"No worries," she said. "I'm Polly. This is Sandy."

"Nice to meet you two. I'm glad you made it up here. It was getting a little lonely."

"I hate to ask, but do you have a cigarette?" Polly asked.

"I do. Would you like one?" I handed my pouch over to her in an inviting gesture.

"Can I have one too?" Sandy asked.

"Of course," I said. Polly fumbled with the paper in her hand, tobacco spilling out the sides, her untrained fingers struggling to keep it all together. "You want some help with that?" She handed the pouch and the unfinished cigarette over to me, and I twisted two cigarettes up as quickly as I could.

They thanked me as I sparked my lighter and held it out to them. They trained their cigarettes onto the flame.

"What are you ladies up to this summer?"

They looked at each other and laughed. "Nothing," Sandy said.

"Nothing, huh? That sounds like a good summer."

"So far, so good," Polly said.

"You girls in school?"

"Yeah, we just got out. We go to Santa Barbara City."

"I've seen more than a few of your classmates up here. Seems like the city college is a fun bunch."

The girls giggled and Polly said, "Yeah, this place is legendary. Everybody knows about your parties."

"Why aren't you down at the party?" Sandy asked me.

"Needed a breather, I guess."

"I'm gonna head back down, wanna come?" Polly said, looking at Sandy. Polly got to her feet, and Sandy took a long draw from her cigarette and thought about it.

"I'm gonna chill up here for a bit. I'll be down in a minute," Sandy said, looking at me. Polly didn't hesitate or protest as she climbed down into the darkness. Sandy finished her cigarette and laid back on The Rock, face up to the stars. We stayed quiet for a while, on our backs, a few feet apart from each other. Without moving her body, Sandy asked, "Are you really a cowboy?"

"Not really. I don't know why everybody says that."

"If everybody says it, it's probably true."

"That's pretty sound logic, I suppose."

"I think it's cool."

"What's cool?"

"Cowboys. That you're a cowboy."

We kissed for a little while up on The Rock, then Sandy pulled away to leave. She had work in the morning. We exchanged phone numbers, and she told me that she wanted to hang out two days later. "It's a date," I said, thinking I sounded suave.

Two days later, Sandy rang my phone. I was a little surprised. My experiences had led me to believe that plans made on top of a rock rarely came to fruition. Her friend's band was playing at a brewery in town, and she wanted me to meet her there. In a business-like fashion, she gave me the details, said goodbye, and hung up.

I'd be lying if I said I didn't purposely dress in a western fashion. The young lady thought cowboys were cool, and I would have been a fool to not play into my obvious strength. I fired up the old Ford and made my way into town with a two-part plan. Plan A was to sleep over at Sandy's. Plain and simple, that was my goal, no-brainer. Plan B was a contingency plan, in case Sandy wasn't keen on me sleeping over. Since I had to work the stables the next morning, Plan B was to go to the stables after my date and park the camper there for the night. I liked going into situations with multiple options, made me feel like I had my shit together.

It sounded like the band was already on as I walked up to the brewery. Just before I opened the door to walk inside, I remembered a most crucial detail. I didn't know what Sandy looked like all that well. I had a good idea but wasn't confident in my memory, having never seen her in the full light. It was too late to worry about it now; I opened the door and made my way inside. The place was empty save for four older folks sitting at a table and a lady on the dance floor dancing with herself. Sitting at a table near the bar, alone, was a pretty girl who looked to be on the young side of twenty-one. Her hair hung down in ringlets and she had freckles on her nose.

She watched me walk towards her table, and just before I arrived, smiled, and said, "Otis!" She got out of her seat and hugged me. I suggested we get a drink, so we walked up to the bar.

While we waited for our beers to pour, Sandy told me that the band on stage wasn't her friend's, but a different band, just the opener. She assured me that the place would fill up before her friend's band went on.

"What are they called?" I asked as our beers were being delivered.

"Who?"

"Your friend's band. What's their name?"

"The Wild Ponies."

"They a country-western band?" As soon as the words left my mouth, I felt as though the question was a stupid one.

"I wouldn't say country. I don't really know how to describe them."

We sat back down at our table and made small talk. Uncomfortable at first, the conversation smoothed out, and the Wild Ponies hit the stage. Sandy and I danced for the first few songs until I got tired and thirsty. I ordered another beer at the bar while Sandy twisted and twirled around the dance floor, oblivious to her surroundings.

The beer came, and I made for the patio out back to have a smoke. To my surprise, the only people back there were two cooks, fresh from the kitchen. The sound of my lighter sparking caught their attention; they both looked over at me.

"Hi," I said. They nodded their heads and went back to their cigarettes and conversation. In less than a minute, they stamped out their smokes and disappeared. I was by myself out on the patio; it was peaceful. When I finished my cigarette, I smoked another.

I ordered two beers and brought one out to Sandy on the dance floor. She had worked herself up into a fever and gladly gulped at the beer.

"Thanks!" she said before taking another sip. "You got any cigs?" she asked, looking up at me. I hadn't realized how tiny she was until that moment.

"Yes. I do. They got a patio out back—wanna have a smoke?"

"Let's do it."

When we walked out of the back door, the cool air hit Sandy's sweaty body and she let out a little gasp. "Ah, fresh air. It's so nice out here." Sandy opened her arms up and embraced the night. We sat down at a picnic table, and I rolled her a cigarette and lit it for her. We sipped our beers and I enjoyed the silence.

"I forgot to ask you," Sandy said, remembering something, "You wanna trip?" She pulled a rolled-up plastic bag out of her pocket. She grasped one end of the bag in her fingers and held it up. The bag unraveled itself. I looked closely to see what it was, even though I had a pretty good idea. "Mushrooms," she said. Sandy's casual nature gave me pause. We were all alone, but I looked around just in case to see if anyone might be watching.

By the time my head swiveled around the patio and then settled back on Sandy, she had fished a mushroom cap out of the bag and put it in her mouth. She chewed it, gagged a little bit, and then chased it down with a swill of beer. She offered the bag to me.

"I'm ok for now. Maybe later," I said with no intention of eating any of her mushrooms. She shrugged off my soft refusal, and we went inside.

We danced and we drank beers, and we had a nice time together. Going into this date, I had high hopes of making a solid connection with Sandy. My wish was that we would have enough chemistry to build a bomb. Halfway through the night, we had about enough chemistry to bake a cake. Luckily, she felt it was enough to invite me over to her place when we left the brewery.

Sandy guided me through a residential neighborhood full of beautiful houses that were artfully landscaped. "Park wherever you see a spot, we're basically here," she said, unbuckling her seatbelt.

I pulled over and put the old Ford in rest. We got out, and Sandy led me through the front yard of a Spanish Colonial house—a fine example of Santa Barbara architecture. The house and landscaping were manicured to perfection. I couldn't comprehend how a college student could live in a house this nice. "I live out back," she said as I followed her through the driveway and around the side of the house.

The house was backed up by a pool, and on the other side of that was a casita designed in the same fashion as the main house. We walked through a large arch-shaped door and into the tile-floored cottage.

"Can you roll me another one of those cigarettes?"

I broke out my pouch and got to work.

"Beer?"

"Absolutely. This is a beautiful place you got here. Your rent must be insane."

"Nah, I don't pay anything. My parents own the place and let me stay for free because I'm in school."

I finished rolling up the cigarettes and Sandy handed me a bottle of beer. "Don't light that in here, we'll smoke by the pool in a second," she said as she unraveled her bag of mushrooms, took out a pinch of stem and dust, and placed it in her mouth. Again, she grimaced and chased the sour fungus down with a sip of beer.

We sat by the pool and smoked our cigarettes. The backyard landscaping, the glistening pool, and the slate patios all made for a peaceful venue for a smoke. I looked over at Sandy, who was hypnotized by the shimmer of the pool. She stared through the glittery surface, through the blue tiles on the bottom. She was gazing into the earth, using the pool as some sort of lense.

"Wanna swim?" she asked without taking her eyes off the pool.

"You don't think your parents will mind. It's pretty late?"

"They don't care if I have friends over."

"I could go for a swim."

Sandy stood up and pulled her shirt off. She had no bra on. Next, she dropped her shorts; she had no underwear on either. She dove in headfirst, breaking through the glass top of the pool. She swam around on the bottom for an unnatural amount of time. Finally, she surfaced and waved me in. I pulled off all of my clothes and hurried into the pool so that Sandy's parents wouldn't see a naked man scurrying around in their backyard.

The water felt amazing on my body. Sandy slipped through the water and into my arms. We kissed and splashed around, and she had little regard for the potential sleep being had in the main house. She squealed as she ran around the edge of the pool, her breasts bouncing and water pouring off her sides. Like a child at a birthday party, her face flashed with a primitive joy.

The swim came to an end when Sandy splashed me, hopped out of the pool, and ran into the carriage house. She didn't dry off before she entered the house, and she didn't return once inside. After a few minutes, I realized I was by myself, in someone else's pool, naked as a dolphin. I too got out of the pool and fled to the casita.

The welcome rug just inside the front door seemed to be a good place to drip dry. I looked around, but Sandy was nowhere to be found. 'Maybe she is getting towels,' I thought.

Sandy burst through her bedroom door and back into the main room of the cottage. She was still naked, and instead of towels, she was holding a leather belt.

"On the floor," she commanded, standing in the middle of the room. Sandy did not appear to be the same human I was just swimming with—she didn't appear to be human at all. A psychedelic madog, her eyes sparkled with demented thoughts. I had no choice but to obey her commands.

Still wet, I went and sat down on the cold Spanish tile floor.

"On your hands and knees," she said like she was ordering around a dog.

I did as she said. Just as I settled into my new position, I heard a tremendous crack and then felt a hot line across my ass. Sandy let out a sinister laugh. I turned my head only to see her rear back and swing again. Crack! This second lashing was twice as hard as the first. She swung again, and then one more time, laughing like a maniac all the while.

Much to my surprise, after the first lash, I didn't feel the belt at all. Instead of pain, I felt a surge of energy in my heart that left my eyes tingling.

Sandy's laughter subsided. I stood up and she dropped to the floor. Excitement shot through my body as she took me into her mouth. After a nice long go at me, she stood back up and went over to the couch. Her movements had a robotic effect to them, arousing me while also making me uneasy. She dug her knees into the cushions and put her hands on the back of the couch, pushing her ass out and arching her back. She looked over at me, still standing on the tile, and smiled.

Taking her from behind, she squirmed back and forth, gasping and groaning. I looked back to the front door of the cottage and saw that the door was wide open. Ignoring our openness, I regained my focus on the task at hand, picking up speed with each pass.

"Don't come inside me," she said. "Let me know when you are about to go."

"I'm about to go," I said.

Her timing was impeccable. Before I evacuated, she flipped around on the couch and took me back up in her mouth in one fluid motion. After five minutes of quiet panting, we went back outside and laid on her parents' pool chaises while smoking cigarettes in silence.

Sandy finished her cigarette and said, "I have to work tomorrow, you can't stay over." Her tone led me to believe that this was an invite to leave.

"I guess I'm good to drive home," I said.

Back in the cottage, I gathered my clothes and suited back up. "This was a blast," I said before I headed for the door.

"It was fun."

"I'd love to do it again."

Sandy thought about it for a minute and said, "No thanks."

At first, I didn't understand, and by the time I had asked, "What?" I had fully processed her words.

"I had fun, but I don't want to hang out again. I just wanted to fuck you. Ok?"

"Any reason why you don't want to see me again?"

"I just told you."

I didn't inquire further, as I had already asked one too many questions, possibly two too many. I drove back to La Posada, too distracted to remember my Plan B. The lights were on in the cabins, but I didn't go inside. I opted to smoke cigarettes in bed, replaying the events of an eventful night. Where had I gone wrong? It was hard to say. The hardest part about having sex with a beautiful woman is that once is never enough. I wanted to have sex with Sandy until her beauty morphed and faded away and I was done with her. I wanted to be the one who said quit. The truth was hard to accept; there would be no winning her over, no getting her back, and it wasn't going to happen ever again. I fell asleep as soon as I accepted that reality, just before the sun came up.

TWENTY-SIX

The next day I woke up to find the sun high up in the sky. I drove down to the stables in a hurry, hours late for work. When I pulled into the parking lot, I saw something I hadn't ever seen there before—Harold's Buick. He was waiting for me inside when I walked in.

"Where have you been? You're late," he said.

"I'm sorry, I overslept. I'll just stay late today."

"The fuck you will. I'm going to hire someone who gives a shit. I should have never trusted a drifter," he said as if he were talking about me to somebody else. "You've been relieved of your duties, stable boy. Oh yeah, and I want you off my property."

"What do you mean?"

"Just what I said. You're out. You can go back out on the road where you belong."

"But it was just this once, it won't happen again."

"Ah, horseshit. Once is too many times."

Harold didn't seem to have an appetite for any more of my pleading, so I turned around and walked straight back to my truck. Speeding up the mountain, I drove as if I could somehow outrun the news, get there before Harold's words did. I was convinced that La Posada could still be mine.

News of my banishment had already reached Billy by the time I made it up there, and he had already agreed to Harold's orders. Billy loved La Posada more than he loved me, and it wasn't even close. I felt a stab in my chest, but I tried to keep a positive facade in front of the boys.

I told Lillian the news and let her know that I was going to be leaving town soon. She assured me that I could work a few days in a row so that I could stash a bit of cash for the road. On my last day in the trim shack, she gave me a jar with well over an ounce of pot in it. A parting gift, she told me.

That night, the guys invited a bunch of people over for a proper send-off. At the party, I realized that I had come to know quite a few people, and most of them showed up to the party. The entire time I was in California, I had felt like a stranger, but at my send-off, I didn't feel strange anymore. That night, we drank too much, listened to music, and smoked all kinds, just like the other parties we had, but at this party, it felt like everyone was there to see me. The party would go on without me, of course, but it was nice to know that I had been a part of it.

The night ended when I went to my truck and cried in my bed. The camper was all packed up, everything in its place, like a Uhaul ready to move someone's life to a new spot. The next morning, I took off before anyone woke up because I didn't want to see their faces.

With no idea where the fuck I was going to go, I started up the old Ford and drove out towards the main road. Looking out onto the road, I knew that if I turned right, I would go down into Santa Barbara. If I turned left, I would go down into the Santa Ynez Valley, into the famed Santa Barbara wine country. The old Ford sat idle while I tried to come up with a place and a plan.

The only place that jumped out to me was the mysterious Big Sur. Just the night before, at the party, I was talking to one of Kenan's bandmates, and he told me I ought to head out that way. I didn't know anything about Big Sur other than that it was up north of San Luis Obispo. I'd been told,

"It's a place, more like an area than an actual town." This did nothing to clear up the ambiguity, but I was intrigued. The old Ford let out a great cough as I shifted into drive and gassed out across the Southbound lane, swinging a big left towards the Santa Ynez Valley, headed north.

I stopped in Santa Maria for gas, groceries, and a burrito. I bought a can of rolling tobacco and two cases of cheap beer. As much as I had been drinking, I somehow still had a bunch of whiskey left and about five fingers of tequila, so I didn't stock up on the hard stuff.

I drove north through Pismo Beach where I met up with US Highway 1. I took the 1 up the coast to San Simeon. I stopped to use the bathroom and asked the lady at the gas station if I was close to Big Sur.

She told me, "Honey, if you drive any further north, you'll be there." She laughed and went on, "San Simeon's the last stop."

As I drove north of San Simeon, the land made a dramatic change. The mountains got closer and closer to the coast until they spilled right into the sea. The road became a cross-section of the coastal range, curving around the great flank of the mountains. I stopped at salmon creek falls to eat some lunch by the falling water. Tourists gathered around the falls on both sides. An older couple in leather chaps and black leather vests were stretching their legs as they viewed the small cascade. A family with two kids sat at a picnic table eating their lunch in silence. The kids seemed to be sick of the parents, and the parents seemed to be sick of each other. I couldn't take my eyes off of them. So much drama in their chewing faces. Anger, sadness, fear—it was all over them and I had no idea why. A snapshot of their life, completely out of context. I would never know a beginning or an end to their story, but I had a view of that moment. They finished their lunch and made their way back to their RV, and I followed suit.

After an hour of driving up the coast, I stopped at Sand Dollar Beach to take in the landscapes and go for a swim. I grabbed a beer, rolled up two joints, and rolled a handful of cigarettes. The massive beach was almost empty. A bit of fog hung onto the coast, and a chilly breeze blew off the choppy ocean that pushed up against the weathered cliffs. The few beachcombers that walked up and down the sand wore parkas instead of swimsuits. I headed to the north end of the beach and found some caves to explore. I drank a beer and smoked one of my joints in the natural caverns carved out by the surf. A small man with a big camera entered the cave. He was snapping pictures, so I left and walked back towards the parking lot. Not ready to leave, I decided to head to the south end of the beach just to see what was down there and because I didn't have anything else to do. When I got there, I came upon an old man with a bucket in his hand. He was dressed in shabby jeans and a yellow rain jacket. His feet were covered in shin-high rain boots; a Greek fisherman's cap sat on top of his greasy head.

"What's the bucket for?" I asked him, too curious not to.

"I'm headed over to the cove to see if I can find some jade."

"How do you find it? It's just laying on the beach?"

"Sometimes. Usually, you gotta dig around a bit and look carefully to find it." He started to walk away but stopped. "You wanna come? I can teach you."

I had nothing better to do so I joined him. The old man scampered over rocks like one of those iguanas in the Galapagos Islands. He seemed to be following a path in his mind, and I had to push to keep up with him. We made our way into a rugged, slick rock cove, and the old man began to scour the ground, kicking and clawing at the small rocks in the foam of expired waves. After a while, he picked up a small rock and washed it in the surf. He held it up to my face and said, "This is what we're looking for." The rock was a milky green color with slashes of black throughout. It was about the size of a golf ball, maybe a little smaller.

I took out a cigarette and lit it. I offered the old man one, and he gladly accepted. "I'm Doyle," he said and offered to shake as he exhaled smoke from his hairy nostrils.

"I'm Otis," I said to him while I shook his hand. "This jade worth much?"

"Not really. It's worth something, I guess. I just like to spend time outside and have something to do while I'm out here." He went back to staring at the ground and then looked up again. "I get antsy just sitting on the sand, ya know?"

I shook my head in agreement. "You live out here?"

"Big Sur's overrun with tourists, but I'm local. I live up north of here."

Doyle found a couple more pieces of jade, and I found nothing but rocks that weren't jade. After an hour or so, Doyle and I hiked back towards the parking lot, passing a joint back and forth. I had never smoked weed with an old person before, and I enjoyed the novelty of it. When we got to the lot, I invited Doyle to have a beer. He was happy to oblige.

"Camper's pretty nice. You been traveling?" he asked as if his definition of traveling was different from mine.

"Yes, sir. I've been on the road for a few months now. I was staying down in the mountains outside of Santa Barbara for a while. Had a nice arrangement down there, but it fell apart," I said, the sting of my exile still fresh.

"That's life, man. I'm sixty-three. Guess how much I've had fall apart on me?" He looked out into the waves as he spoke.

"I reckon a whole bunch," I said. Doyle had a good laugh.

"It shows, huh?" he laughed again. "Where you camping?"

"I don't know yet. Figured I'd just drive around till I found something."

"You're going to be driving for a while," he said, sneering.

"You think?"

"There isn't as much camping as you'd think out here. There's some paid campsites, but they fill up quick. If you want to, you can camp out on the property I stay at. I'm a caretaker. There's plenty of room."

I didn't stop to think about the invitation, I just accepted. We finished our beers, and I pulled my rig over to where he was parked. He told me to follow him to a place called Palo Colorado. Before he got in his car, he said, "Keep close. If you get lost, you'll never find it."

He drove an old Nissan pickup truck with dents on the inside and the outside of the bed. I followed closely behind as he zoomed up the highway. After an hour of driving, he turned off the highway and led me through a redwood grove speckled with mossy cabins. We rose up out of the redwoods and the road turned from packed mud to sand and gravel. The higher we climbed on the road, the dryer the land got. By the time we got to Doyle's property, we were almost on top of the sun-scorched mountain. The land was made up of hard-packed rock and dust, held together by tinder-dry brush.

Doyle was caretaking something, but what it was, I couldn't tell. Raw, untamed earth, steep mountainside, and not much else made up the property that Doyle was looking after. The only building in sight was a dilapidated shack that he had made a home out of. He showed me around the inside. A camp stove on a table made up his kitchen. He had a toilet in his bathroom, but it was only strong enough to flush piss.

After the grand tour, he climbed into my truck and had me drive about a quarter-mile on an overgrown road cut out of the side of the mountain. Eventually, the road led to a flattened-out area where Doyle told me to stop. We got out of the truck and walked up to a natural ledge on the slope that Doyle called 'The Lookout.' It was the best view I had ever seen in my life. The mountain fell away from the lookout and down into the ocean thousands of feet below us. Looking to the south, the jagged peaks of Big Sur sawtoothed across the skyline. Due north, the mountains that separated Carmel from Big Sur rolled and swept. East of us, you could almost see the top of the mountain that we clung to, and looking west, we could see miles and miles of the Persian blue Pacific. The horizon wasn't quite flat; the view was so expansive that you could see the Earth's subtle curve. Doyle said that the shelf of land we were standing on was the best camping spot on the property. I took the hint and positioned my truck to rest on an even section of ground with the back of the truck pointed out towards the view.

We each opened beers while we passed a joint back and forth. For dinner, I cooked up a few hot dogs. Doyle and I ate steamed weiners wrapped in white bread and smeared with yellow mustard. Doyle asked for ketchup, but I didn't have any. We chewed quietly and looked out on the beaming ocean. La Posada came to mind, and I pushed the memory away. I focused on where I was. All around me was empty property—from the looks of things, nothing but solitude. The quiet part of La Posada, with none of the insanity, beautiful women, and friendship.

Doyle invited me to stay the night, that night, but I persisted. He didn't come out and say that I could stay, but he didn't protest when I did. It took me a while to understand the nuances of La Posada, but the property out in Big Sur wasn't like that. There wasn't much to settle into outside of the challenges of my own mind. La Posada had a system to it. A complex, dynamic, ever-changing system. Doyle's property was more of a, 'What you see is what you get,' kind of place.

On my first full day on the property, I was awash in time. I woke up, smoked a joint, walked around for a while, took in the view, cleaned up around the camper, ate some breakfast, wrote a journal entry, smoked a cigarette, organized the camper a bit, read a short story, took in the view again, and when I checked the dashboard clock in the truck, it was 11:13 a.m. Time passed at least half as quickly when I was alone compared to being with others. Every week in Big Sur went like two weeks everywhere else.

TWENTY-SEVEN

Doyle and I got along well. Seemed like the old hermit even enjoyed having me there some of the time. I was sure to give him a wide berth, and he was sure to stay in his shack. The first week I was on the property, I only saw him once. We had a cigarette together, shared a few words, looked out on the view, and then he parted ways. Most of my interactions with Doyle went like that. Even though it wasn't possible, he seemed to be a man with no past, no personal history. Like one of the many varieties of manzanita on the property, I imagined Doyle had sprouted from the ground and spent his life clinging to the mountain.

Whenever Doyle came to my side of the mountain, I assumed it was to talk over some logistics or ask a favor of me. So when he came just to talk, it was surprising.

"What are you doing up here?" Doyle asked me. He passed me a joint while we stood side by side, looking out on the vast view that we were both so familiar with.

"Supposed to be writing."

"What're you writing?"

"Not much."

"Then what are you doing up here?" he asked, perhaps a bit more aggressively than he meant to. "Look, I don't blame you, I'm up here, ain't I? Took me a long time to realize this is where I belong. You're a young man, though. Didn't take you long to figure out that everything is shit down there," he said, looking down the mountain to the ocean. Without a single man-made structure in sight, I inferred that Doyle thought all of mankind was hiding down at the bottom of the mountain we stood on.

"Sometimes, I think my life is predestined. It's like I start up the old Ford, put her in drive, and she does the rest. The situations I get into, the places I end up—they've all been written by someone else. I didn't plan it this way, it just happened, and now here I am."

"Figured you were running from something. Didn't know why you'd want to be up here all by yourself. No women to chase, no partying or nothing."

"I like it up here. Things move slow, you know?"

"I know it. Sometimes they don't move at all. Things down there, they're always moving fast. They never fucking stop. I hate it. I ain't one of these old folks who say, 'Things have changed, society has gone to hell.' Things have changed, but society is just as shitty as it ever was. Maybe less so than when I was your age. Get a education, get a job, get a wife. None of that ever made sense to me, ya' know? Nowadays, I don't think there's so much pressure on young folks like there was when I was a young man."

"Maybe not out here, in California, but where I grew up, those pressures, they still exist. Out here, the old pressures probably got replaced with new ones."

"Life works that way, don't it?" Doyle looked sad as I shook my head in agreement with him. "What do your folks think about this life you got yourself? Living on top of a mountain with a crusty old man." Doyle laughed.

"Not sure, haven't talked to them in a while," I said. Doyle went quiet.

He finished his beer and lit up a cigarette. "You're smart, Otis. Down there, it's all turmoil. Guys like you and me, we're better off up here on this mountain. Society, it'll work you hard, wear you down, it'll take all it can from you, and then when you got nothing left to give, it'll leave you to die. Fuck, I know it's depressing, but it's the truth. What's that old saying? Cog in a wheel. You know what happens to a cog once it's wore out? It gets tossed in the trash, that's what." Doyle looked out at the ocean and shook his head as if he was continuing the conversation in his mind.

"You get lonely ever?"

"Haven't been with a woman in years. Not afraid to admit it. This life ain't for everyone. That's why so many people are down there, and so few are up here."

I opened another beer and lit a cigarette, and standing at the edge of a massive drop, I looked out below me. Out over the mountains, I looked for things that I had never noticed before. For weeks, I looked out at that view, and each time, I spotted something I hadn't noticed before and made a game out of it. Doyle went back to his cabin and left me all alone with my mind.

Marijuana smoke and the solitude of Big Sur were a terrific combination, and as one vice ramped up, another fell off. The benefits of trading heavy drinking for heavy pot smoking were especially evident in the mornings. My body felt better, my mind clearer. After a quiet few weeks in Big Sur, I had all but smoked through the weed Lillian had given me. Doyle smoked throughout the day, so I asked him if he knew anyone that sold weed. Without saying anything, he led me into the small greenhouse tent next to his shack and unzipped the entrance. Inside were a few marijuana plants almost ready to be harvested. He took out a knife and chopped a small branch off of one of the plants and handed it to me. I thanked him and complimented his green thumb. He thought for a second while he looked at the ground.

After a while, he said, "If you're going to stay here, I could use some help on the field."

"Yeah?"

"The owners of this property have a whole lot of plants out there. We're about to harvest, and we'll need more hands than we got." He thought about it some more. "I'll talk to the owners and see what they say. You ever trim before?"

"I did quite a bit down in Santa Barbara."

"Good."

Later that week, Doyle came to my camp and told me that I was in. The owners were coming soon to cut all the plants down and start the process of trimming, drying, and curing the harvest. They agreed to Doyle's plea to add more hands—on the condition they would pay me in weed, not cash. I agreed, even though it meant I would have to sell the weed to get paid, and selling a ton of weed made me nervous. Putting my anxiety on the back burner, I focused on the incredible amount of work we had ahead of us.

Doyle wasn't sure when the owners of the property would show up, but he said it would be soon. The waiting game lasted a few days, and then one morning while I was finishing up my coffee, a black Cadillac SUV pulled onto the property and stopped at Doyle's shack. Twenty minutes later, three men carrying chainsaws arrived with Doyle at my camp. They had thick accents, but from where those accents had come, I didn't know and didn't ask.

The five of us hiked down a clandestine path to what Doyle called the "Field of Dreams." A clearing in the forest with about fifty pot plants, each the size of a Christmas tree, all planted in perfect rows. The men with chainsaws went to work sawing through the woody stalks, felling fifty marijuana trees in a short time. As the plants hit the ground, Doyle and I collected them and laid them out on big tarps. After fifteen minutes, the field of dreams was turned into a field of stumps. We wrapped the tarps up, and with one person on each end, and one guy flanking to make sure we didn't drop anything, we drug all that pot up to Doyle's shack over several trips.

Doyle pitched a tent near my camper and emptied the shack of his few possessions. We filled every square inch of the plywood cabin with hanging plants, strung up on fishing line. Doyle gave me a full, untrimmed plant. "Here's your cut. Spend it wisely," he told me with a chuckle. I was to dry, trim and cure the plant on my own time. I chopped the bush into manageable branches and hung most of them to dry in the cab of my truck. The remaining few sprigs decorated the camper.

The drying process went on for a full week before Doyle and I started in on trimming the plants. We chipped away at the massive harvest, little by little, but after three days, we had barely made a dent. Doyle called the owners and told them we needed help. The next day, the three men who had cut the plants down returned to the property. With their help, we trimmed all of the remaining plants over the next five days, working from sunrise to sunset, only stopping to sleep and eat dinner. We placed all of the trimmed buds in large white plastic buckets to cure. After all the work was finished and the only thing left to do was wait, the chainsaw crew left. Doyle and I decided to head down the mountain to find some drinks and real food. We had been living on hotdogs for what seemed like weeks, and I jumped at the chance to enjoy a real meal and some human interaction. We burped all the buckets, swept out the shack, and put on the nicest clothes we had, ready for a night out.

Part campground, part restaurant, and part cottages for rent, the Redwood Inn was the only slice of civilization near us, and it wasn't all that civilized. The restaurant was empty when we arrived. We sat at the bar and chatted with the retired San Francisco cocktail waitress, Betty, who tended the bar. Doyle ordered chicken fried steak and I ordered a steak straight up. After we stuffed ourselves with beef, we stuffed ourselves with booze, drinking until Betty wouldn't serve us anymore. When the bar shut us down, I wasn't in any kind of shape to drive, so Doyle and I went to my camper and parked in the lot out front of the Redwood Inn to sleep.

"Come stay in the camper with us," Doyle yelled out to Betty as she opened the driver-side door of her car, done with her shift.

"Get the fuck outta here. I got a man at home who's only half as drunk as you two."

"Well then, it's settled, you're staying with us!"

"Last thing I need is another boozehound trying to get on top of me. Night, Doyle." Betty got in her car and drove off. We went to bed.

The next morning, we woke up to an irate man knocking on the camper. "You know this is a campground right? You need to pay for a spot to camp," he said loud enough that his words permeated the walls of the camper and bounced around in our aching heads.

"Yessir. We know you have to pay, but you guys were full last night," I said after I opened the door to the red-faced man wearing a hunting cap and fleece jacket.

Doyle lashed out, "Fuck you, Mark. We're not tourists."

Mark, dumbfounded, looked into the camper and saw Doyle lying down on the floor. "Just 'cause you're not a tourist don't mean you can do whatever you want." Mark gave up and walked back into the inn.

I smoked a cigarette in the parking area while Doyle went inside and took a shit in their bathroom. When he finished, he filled up a six-gallon jug of water off their hose, and then we headed back up to the property. After dropping Doyle off at his shack, I put my camper back in its place of rest, laid down, and closed my eyes. As I drifted off to somewhere sweet, Doyle's cries rang out over the mountain.

"Otis! Otis! Come out here!"

When I got outside, Doyle was keeled over with his hands on his knees; his pursed, wrinkled lips sucked air like a vacuum hose. "It's gone. They're all gone."

I had a strong sense of what he was talking about, but I asked him to clarify. "What's gone?"

"The buckets." He inhaled deeply and let out a big wheezing cough. "The weed. Man, it's all gone." Walking toward Doyle's shack, he followed and said, "Something bad's happening."

"What do you mean it's gone? It can't be."

"The whole fucking place is empty. There's nothing there."

The door of the shack was hanging open when we arrived. I didn't need to go inside to tell that the whole place was hollow, but I walked in and looked around anyway. We had neatly stacked about sixty white plastic buckets in that plywood hovel over the past week, and now it was completely empty. All of it, 137 pounds of weed, just up and vanished.

"They're going to kill me." Doyle knew the owners of the property better than I did, so I took his words literally. I needed him to calm down, so I tried reasoning with him.

"What do you think the chances are that they came back and collected all the weed? Did they tell you when they were coming to get it?" I asked. Doyle thought for a second while his heartbeat reached a sustainable level.

"I don't know. They didn't say when they'd come back." Doyle began to catch his breath. "They didn't say anything when they left. You met them, they don't talk much."

"I'm sure they came back and got it. Just call and make sure."

"Fuck, man. I don't want to call them."

"If they took the buckets, then you're fine. If they didn't, they're going to find out sooner or later. Might as well be sooner."

"Fuck. You're right. Fuck, fuck, fuck." He sat down and settled in on the plan. "Goddamnit."

Doyle lit a cigarette, breathed in the first of the smoke, and exhaled it out all at once. He put his cigarette hand down by his hip and took a deep breath while shaking his head from side to side. He picked up the phone that was mounted on the wall inside the shack. He pressed the necessary buttons and waited. After a lifetime went by, someone picked up the other line.

"Dmitry, that you? It's me, Doyle, up at the property." Doyle listened to the man on the other line ask a question. "Well, I'm not sure if something's wrong. That's why I'm calling. Did you guys come back up here and get all those buckets?" Doyle took a drag of his cigarette and listened carefully. "It's gone. All of it," he said as smoke streamed out of his nose.

The sounds coming through the earpiece on the phone got louder. Dmitry must have talked for a full minute.

"He was with me the entire time." Dmitry asked another question, and Doyle answered, "I don't know, maybe twelve hours all in all." Doyle stopped and listened carefully. "Nobody knows. I didn't tell anyone. Otis didn't tell anyone. Nobody knows anything." Doyle listened for a second, then, with a terrible resignation in his voice, he said, "Right here." As he said this, his eyes crept over to me. Doyle went quiet for a minute and then hung up the phone without another word.

"What did they say?" I was burning to know what was about to happen.

"They're real mad." Doyle stubbed out his cigarette and immediately lit another.

"They're coming, and if I were you, I wouldn't want to be here when they get

here."

"Do they think I stole the buckets?" I asked. I knew the answer to this question, but I wanted to hear what Doyle had heard on the other line.

"They just asked where you were."

"When the buckets got stolen?"

"I told him you were with me, but he wanted to know where you are right now." Doyle looked me in the eye. "They're coming up here."

I didn't say goodbye, I just went and packed up. I felt sick leaving Doyle in the mess he was in. I didn't steal the buckets, and I didn't know who did, and I sure as shit wasn't going to take the punishment the owners were about to dole out. Sticking around and explaining my side of the story wasn't going to do me much good, and I'm sure Doyle knew that.

I spilled down the dirt roads that led out of Palo Colorado. My mind shuffled through the scenarios of what could have happened to all that pot. I didn't notice how fast I was driving or that my tires were slipping a little as I took the rutted-out turns at high speed. I was so distracted that it took me a full second to realize I was coming head to head with a black Cadillac SUV. The behemoth stuck out against the dusty road, being that it was so shiny and clean in a place where nothing was new. I got closer and closer to the SUV, and fear began to spill out of my eyes. I couldn't let the Cadillac see my eyes, so I closed them as I passed by.

We passed each other, and my attention honed in on the rearview mirror. Certainly, the Cadillac was about to stop and turn around any second. I wondered if the old Ford could handle a chase with the camper on the back. Rolling off the side of a mountain trying to evade the angry men inside the Cadillac seemed to be the most obvious conclusion if and when they turned around.

Their brake lights never flicked on, and as far as my rearview mirror could tell, the SUV never turned around. I exhaled when I made it to the bottom of the canyon. I stopped where the road t-boned the highway, and I rolled a cigarette. Before I started driving again, I lit my cigarette

and breathed the gray smoke deep down into my lungs.
My mind slowed down and my heart rate began to fall as
I moved south on Highway 1, headed straight for the only
place I knew to go.

TWENTY-EIGHT

On my way down south, I went through my options and found that I didn't have many. In my possession, tucked safely in the back of the camper, was a big white bucket full of the only weed that didn't get stolen. It was tough to gauge exactly how much pot was in that bucket, but if I had to guess, I would say it was a shit load. Enough to put my ass in prison, I reckoned. Touring the country with that bucket in tow sure didn't seem like a good idea, so before I could plan for the future, I knew I needed to offload it.

After a few hours, I started to get close to Santa Barbara, but I didn't have a fully formed plan. I drove up to La Posada because I couldn't think of anywhere else to go. Trey and Kenan were home and happy to see me but also confused. I had to answer a lot of questions, and some of them I answered not so honestly. The guys didn't pry, they just said the obvious, "You need to call Lillian."

I called Lillian up at her house and arranged to meet with her the next day. With permission from the guys, I parked my rig and stayed overnight. Being back at La Posada was like running into an ex-girlfriend. The beauty and excitement were still there, but I knew I couldn't partake in its intimacies.

I left early in the morning to meet with Lillian. She gave me a hug and invited me into the main house, a part of the property I had never seen before. I brought the bucket with me, and she sat me down at an old farm table.

"Where's your dad?" I asked, just making conversation.

"He's not around right now." Lillian folded one leg over the other and looked at me sternly. "Before we get down to business, which is why you're here, I assume, it's important that you know that my dad has nothing to do with this. This is a favor from me, and only me."

"Noted. I really appreciate it." The importance of Lillian's distinction was not lost on me.

Lillian took a handful of buds out of the bucket and laid them on the table. She broke up one of the nuggets to see how well dried the product was. She operated with the skill and professionalism of a fishmonger examining a freshly caught tuna. Out of the pantry, Lillian returned with a kitchen scale. She carefully weighed out all of the ganja in the bucket. All in all, I had just over two pounds.

"I'll give you two grand for it," she said. "And that's a friend price, I assure you."

I trusted Lillian as much as I trusted anyone, so without any questions, I accepted the offer. She handed me twenty new one-hundred dollar bills. Lillian walked me to my car. and I stashed the money in the camper. A massive weight had been lifted, the stress and fear of the previous day receded, as if I had just arrived on vacation after a hectic voyage. When I hopped out of the camper, Lillian was still there.

"What are you up to today?" Lillian asked.

"Not much. How bout you?"

"We just finished up a big harvest, and I was thinking about going on a celebratory hike."

"Nice. Just around the property?"

"There's a hot spring about five miles from here. Out in the National Forest. Wanna come?"

I thought about it just long enough to remember that I had absolutely nothing to do. "Sure."

"I'm going to go change real quick, be right back." Lillian went into the house for a few minutes and came back out wearing hiking boots, carrying a little pack. "You ready?"

From the driveway, we hiked for a mile through the tall grass and oak trees that dotted Lillian's property. As we got higher up, the land hardened and cracked. The khaki grasses and gray oaks gave way to sharp-toothed shrubs and manzanitas. We came to a viewpoint that looked back on the valley below that we had just walked through. We drank water and caught our breath. The grasses and bushes below us quaked in unison as a hot wind passed over them.

Lillian fumbled around in her backpack for a few seconds before she produced a small vial with a rubber dropper for a cap. "I wasn't going to bring this, but since you came along, I figured what the heck."

"What's in there?"

"LSD," she said matter of factly and screwed off the cap. "Do you want to?"

"Sure."

"Open your mouth and stick out your tongue." Lillian dropped a single drop of clear, flavorless liquid on my tongue, and then she dropped two on her narrow, delicate tongue. Her tongue was so small, the size of a child's. I swallowed my drop and then looked at her as she closed her eyes and savored the tasteless liquid.

"What's it like?"

"It's best to ask questions first, take drugs second," she said, laughing. "It's pretty similar to mushrooms but it can be more intense, more electric, if that makes sense. Don't worry, we're in the right place," she assured me.

We hiked down from the overlook on a windy path that led us into a garden of massive boulders. Out the other side, we walked for about two miles on flat ground through a much heavier forest of oaks, pines, and manzanita. Hiking quickly, we came to a thin clear creek. Beige-colored sand and rocks made up the creek bed, giving the water the appearance of briefly steeped tea. Upstream a ways, on the side of the creek, a pool had been formed out of masoned rock. The bottom of the pool was lined with cobblestones and filled with crystal clear water the temperature of a very hot bath.

I had been feeling the drugs for a little while, but seeing the hot spring and the beauty surrounding me made me fully realize. Sitting down next to the hot spring, I shared a cigarette with Lillian. I slipped off my boots and Lillian took off her sweaty t-shirt, revealing her beautiful teacup breasts. She then dropped her shorts and looked at me as I examined her naked body. The hair on her vagina, the hair under her arms, and the hair on her legs were ungroomed. Her beauty was raw and wild. Her slender body slipped into the spring without a noise.

Lillian and I had worked together in the same trim shack for many hours, and during that time, I had fantasized about her. She had dark, curly brown hair and an oversized nose that framed her small face. The more time I spent with her, the more attracted to her I had become, but never as much as I was at that moment in the hot spring. My vision was fuzzy, my whole body was fuzzy, carbonation bubbled and rose from my belly. Lillian glowed in the pool like a firefly fluttering bioluminescence in short spurts. I wanted to be next to her.

Stripping down naked, I eased my body down into the pool. Sitting across from Lillian, an invisible force drew us together. Inch by inch, we scooted until our hips touched so delicately that I thought it was my imagination.

Lillian was chatty, her words landed on my ears like a warm massage. She explained the science behind the warm water we were bathing in. "The groundwater is heated by magma from the Earth's core, then it seeps out of the spring for us to enjoy," she said, cupping water in her hands, staring at her reflection in the tiny reservoir she had created.

She told me about the mountains of California and other hot springs she had visited. I listened to her intently while the flow of LSD coursed through my head and pulsed behind my eyes. The drug was not as powerful as I had imagined; instead of being overwhelmed as I had anticipated, I felt pleasant and comfortable. Lillian asked me how I was feeling, and I told her in a few words, my mouth moving timid and slow. She explained that the acid she had given me was not very strong and I was welcome to another hit. I declined, and then we fell back to silence. I watched my hand move from the surface of the water to a submerged state and back up again. Ripples fell away from my palms and lapped at the shore of my torso.

When I looked up from the water, Lillian and I made a most dangerous eye contact. I wanted to look away, to break the stare and retreat from the possible awkward aftermath, but my carnal desires overruled, and I locked deep into Lillian's light brown eyes. We wrapped each other up in arms and soft kissing. I held her narrow weightless body, my legs and feet grasping the pool for traction.

We made slow love in the hot spring as if we were afraid of creating waves. I was so grateful to Lillian at that moment. It was probably the drugs, but I felt like we were connecting on some level I had never reached. A sexual and mental fourth dimension, where a lifetime of my feelings and all of Lillian's emotions could be felt at the same time in unison. The sadness and excitement brought on by the past year, the fear from my childhood, and my anxieties about the near future swirled into the love that Lillian had for her father and the deep sorrow she felt about her mother. We climaxed together and woke up in the third dimension; she was resting her back on my chest as I rubbed her shoulders and neck.

We held each other for a long time in that hot bath that never cooled. Lillian asked me about my relationship with my parents, and I told her about the nuances of my life. "I don't really know who they are in so many ways. And they certainly don't know who I am, anymore," I said, feeling exposed.

I told her about my insecurity around traveling and living on the road, how much I feared loneliness. She talked about her mother dying and the way it affected her view on life and relationships. While she spoke, Lilian crumbled weed into tobacco, her boney fingers building a spliff.

On our way back, Lillian lit our path down from the mountains and into the valley. Her flashlight bobbed and swayed with each step. She gave me permission to park on her property for a day or two if I needed to, and I thanked her for her help, for everything she had done for me. As we neared her house, she asked me a question that I had forgotten to think about.

"What's your next move?"

"Good question," I said. The thought of my future sobered me up a bit. "Not sure as of right now."

"I would let you stay here longer, but I'm trying to leave town."

"Where ya headed?" My curiosity was beyond piqued.

"Mexico, hopefully. My dad won't have a harvest for another six weeks or so. I wanna go chill on the beach for a while."

"Who ya' going with?"

"Nobody yet. Usually, there's a bunch of trimmers headed down there. For some reason, I can't find anyone going south. I'll figure something out, I'm sure."

"I'd love to go down to Mexico. Never actually been."

"Really?"

"Yeah." I waited for her invitation.

"If you drive, I'll pay for gas."

We worked out the details with a plan to leave in two days. Lillian went into the house, and I went to my camper. I was still pretty high, and if I had a choice, I would have chosen to spend the night with Lillian, but she didn't offer. I wanted to come down with her in my arms. Being alone wasn't a bad second option. I spent the rest of the night writing down everything that had happened in the past few days; a most productive journal session. Spliffs, a few beers, and a bunch of writing brought me all the way down. Laying in my bed was a revelation when I decided to finally fall asleep.

TWENTY-NINE

The next morning I drove into Santa Barbara to stock up on food and booze for the trip. La Posada was halfway in between Lillian's place and Santa Barbara, so I stopped off to say hi and get stoned with the boys. My excitement overran my discretion, and I told the guys about the previous night.

The boys of La Posada didn't seem all that enthused with my story. When I told them that Lillian and I were going to Mexico together, they told me about Taylor. Taylor was Lillian's long-time boyfriend. The boys told me that he was down in Ensenada and most likely the reason that Lillian wanted to go to Mexico.

The day rolled into night, and instead of going back to Lillian's, I stayed on the mountain to party with the boys. Horseshoes clanked and beers cracked open, music played and people laughed all around me. Trying to drink away my conflicted feelings, I had trouble staying present. I wasn't quite sure how I felt about Lillian, but I didn't like the idea of her being with someone else. Rolling all the possible scenarios over in my mind, predicting outcomes, and practicing for conversations I might have in the future, I was very good at getting lost in the theoretical. When I cut through all the bullshit, all the predictions and pontifications, when I was honest about my true intentions, I knew I just wanted her to want me, if for no reason other than my desire to have sex with her again. By acknowledging this truth, I was able to calm my wild mind to a manageable speed.

With the waning of one anxiety came the blossoming of another. The ranch was normally kept far from the front of my mind, but with another move coming, my family wore heavy on my conscience. Feeling compelled to reach out to my mother, I decided on the most non-confrontational medium of communication—email. I wrote:

> Dear Mom,
>
> I miss you very much, but I will not be able to come home for a while. California has been great to me, but it is time for me to move on again, this time to Mexico. I've been trying to figure out where I need to be in life, and the only place that speaks to me is the road. I want to come clean with you and tell you something I think you already know; I'm avoiding the ranch. A few years ago, Uncle Grant told me the truth, that he is my real father. At the time, I didn't know what to do with that information, so I hid from it, went back to Albuquerque, and stayed away from home. Years later, I still don't know what to do with the information; I'm still hiding from it. I have so many questions, so many things I need to know but I'm not ready to ask. When I'm ready, I know that I will come home and fix things, but I don't know when that will be. Don't worry about me, please. I will be careful and safe.
>
> Love, Otis

Instead of hitting send, I hit the delete button and erased my ambitions to communicate with my parents. Even through the veil of the computer, I was too scared to wade into the waters of openness. At that moment, I understood the objective truth—that I needed to go home and fix things. But that meant breaking off plans with Lillian and ending my voyage. That just wasn't going to happen.

The next morning, I made my way down to Lillian's property. She was waiting for me when I got there, a duffel bag sitting at her feet, a book in her hand.

"Hi there. Are you all ready?" she asked me.

"Yes, ma'am. I need to use the restroom real quick, then I'm all set." She went around to the back of the camper and put her bag just inside the door. I took a piss behind the closest trim shack.

The 101 southbound was wide open when we got on it, allowing us to make our way through LA with much less traffic than either of us had anticipated. Within a few hours, we skirted down around San Diego and queued up at the border. Without any protest, the Mexican border agents let us pass with an ounce of pot hidden in a pillow that Lillian had made specifically for the occasion. Lillian gave me an, 'I told you so,' look as we waved to the armed border agents.

The end goal, at least for Lillian, was to get to Ensenada, but she didn't want to go straight there. Some of her friends had rented a surf house just outside of Rosarito, essentially the halfway point between Tijuana and Ensenada. Lillian arranged for us to stay with them for a few days before we continued on down south. Thankful to have some extra time with her, I set a goal of convincing her that I was worthy of her love.

We made it to the surf house before sunset. Lillian's friends showed us down to the beach where we enjoyed beers under the blushing sky. The sun dropped down over the Pacific Ocean in a silent symphony of color. Tired from driving all day, Lillian and I headed to the camper early. She crawled into bed in nothing but a t-shirt. We kissed for a while, and then I mounted her. A few minutes in, I couldn't find the kind of passion that had blistered my skin at the hot spring. Just a few days earlier, I had enjoyed Lillian so much that I thought I might be in love. That night in my camper, it felt like I was fucking a stranger. The intimacy was all gone, and what was left in its place was mechanized sex with a woman that I liked but certainly wasn't in love with.

Lillian fell asleep right away but I didn't. Lying awake, I pivoted on my plans and shifted my agenda. Did I want to win Lillian's love? After thinking for a bit, I decided I wasn't going to quit her just yet. The magical love that had been conjured at the hot spring was real, and I wasn't ready to give up on its resurrection. The next morning, we fucked again right after we woke up. The sex wasn't mechanical at all this time, but it wasn't Earth-shattering either. We didn't make love, we fucked. I thrust into Lillian as she worked herself into a climax—two individuals, each with their own agenda. We lay panting on my bed, sweaty from the warm Baja air.

"What are you thinking about?" I said as I held her with as little contact as possible.

"Taylor," she said.

"Who's Taylor?"

"My boyfriend. You don't know Taylor?"

"I don't think so."

"Oh. He's good friends with the guys at La Posada. He must have been in Australia when you lived there, but I thought you may have met him before he left."

"I didn't know you had a boyfriend," I lied.

"I thought you did." She looked at me caringly and put her hand in mine. "I feel bad that you didn't know. Are you ok with that?"

"Sure. I am. Is he ok with this?"

"Yeah. Of course. We're in an open relationship. We have an agreement."

"How does that work?"

"It's not really any of your business. But, we have an agreement. Taylor spends a lot of time traveling, so when we're together, we're together, and then when we're apart, we do what we want to do."

"Does it work?"

"It works ok."

I lit a cigarette, got out of bed, and put my swim trunks on so that I could wash off in the ocean.

After Lillian's divulgence, things changed between us, in a good way. I was able to return to a friendship mindset, which was nice. In Rosarito, we fucked every night, but we kept a certain distance during the day that allowed both of us to relax and have fun.

After a few days, we made our way down the coast to Ensenada. Lillian and Taylor reunited. I felt out of place at first, but Taylor and his friends were very nice guys. They invited me to stay for a few days, so I did. Without any real plans, I wasn't in a rush to take off. The scenery was beautiful, the beaches were quiet, and the weather was perfect.

Out of the blue, happiness came to me—instead of the loneliness I had prepared myself for. Hoping that I wouldn't have any hard feelings when Lillian and Taylor reunited, to my surprise, I didn't. I was able to take my ego out of it and see the situation for what it was. Taylor and Lillian were in love, and that had nothing to do with me. I knew what I felt, but I didn't know how I got there or how to replicate it. Regardless of that, I felt good.

After a few days I organized the camper and formulated a plan for my coming departure. When I first started living in the truck full time, the loneliness and lack of security drove me into human interaction. At this point, my fear of the road was hard to distinguish between a high. So many unwritten stories laid out in front of me, waiting. Embracing the mystery, I readied myself to move on.

On my last night at the Ensenada house, Lillian snuck away from the group and came out to find me in my camper. "Can I talk to you?" she asked as if she had a serious matter to discuss.

"Sure, what's up?" I said, a bit suspicious.

"I just want to check in with you. See how you are feeling, ya know?"

I thought for a minute. "I don't know what you mean."

"You aren't very emotional. Or, I mean, you aren't used to expressing your emotions, right?"

"Oh. No. I suppose I'm not. Not something I've done much of."

"I figured. That's why I came out here. No telling what you'll get into out there. Might be good for you to talk to someone. May be your last chance for a while," she said and let out a giggle to let me know she was trying to cut the tension.

I nodded my head and let my guard down. "I've been going at it alone for a while now."

"I'm sure that's been hard."

"It can be. It's liberating too. And lonely, and confusing. Feel like I'm breaking ground in fresh snow sometimes." I sat back and relaxed. Lillian crawled into bed with me. Laying next to me, she put her hand on my chest.

"Takes bravery to do what you're doing. I've really enjoyed being with you. You make me feel safe."

"Thank you. I like being with you too. I've never met someone who's so easy to talk to."

"It's really hard navigating this whole friends who fuck each other thing, but you've done a solid job at it. I mean, I never know what you're thinking, so it's kind of hard to say, but I get the feeling you're able to keep things in perspective. Since Taylor and I opened things up, I find most of the guys I spend time with grow jealous and resentful or they get hurt. Takes a big man not to, I think."

"Thanks for saying that. It hasn't always been easy. The guys up at La Posada told me about Taylor. Before you did." She smiled a half-smile. "I was a little hurt when I found that out. Probably why I took it so well when you told me."

"Makes sense."

"But you've been great. You're honest and caring, and you didn't do anything you shouldn't have done. At least not in my opinion. All the emotions I felt around this situation, I was able to take care of them myself."

"You didn't have to, you know that, right? You could have told me. We could have talked about it."

"Yeah, I guess I never thought about that option," I said. Lillian laughed and smiled, showing her teeth. She was very charming when she smiled.

"You're a tough guy, aren't you? Just never thought about sharing your feelings?" she asked, laughing. "You might want to try it sometime, you might be surprised as to what comes out."

"What will come out?"

"Vulnerability. Intimacy. Maybe you'll share something with someone that will bring you closer to them."

"That's terrifying. I can't be doing that." I smiled and looked into Lillian's eyes. She had that look in her eyes, the look she had given me at the hot spring. We made love slowly, with an incredible amount of heat trapped between our chests. A warmth that we both indulged in. We rekindled the magic from the hot spring, but this time, it was conjured by pure intimacy and not drugs.

"I love you, Lillian," I told her when we finished; she was laying her head on my chest.

"I love you too," she said as she snuggled her face into my neck, up under my chin.

I loved Lillian in the way that people loved each other at La Posada. The love that was so difficult for me to understand when I first arrived in California—I had figured out how to possess it.

The next morning, I thanked Taylor and his friends for their genuine hospitality. Instead of making impromptu decisions, I left Ensenada with a plan and a destination. Taylor had spent a lot of time in Mexico and encouraged me to drive down to the bottom of Baja. In La Paz, he told me I could catch the ferry to the mainland. He assured me I would have no problem finding camping all the way down the Baja Peninsula, and then once I was on the mainland, I would find beach towns full of people. Lillian gave me a handful of weed and told me to be careful at the checkpoints. I hugged everyone goodbye and set off southbound on the sun-cracked highway.

THIRTY

Being on the road alone was akin to that sensation you get when you turn to a friend to tell them something and realize they are no longer sitting there. The beauty of Baja through my windshield, and nobody with me to marvel along. And it was beautiful. Tinder dry agave mountains, rugged as broken teeth. Endless coastline pushed up against the dark blue sea. Baja was the drier, less developed cousin of the California coast.

The further I drove, the thinner society got, until the only proof of humanity were dirt-stained shantytowns full of hungry children and skinny mules. Despite the poverty and the harsh climate, the people were spirited. Men smiled through their cigars and old women pressed tortillas, awash in laughter and music. During the day, I drove the crusted-over highway, stopping in each settlement for tacos and tortas, freshwater and agua fresca.

Before sunset each day, I followed dirt roads west to the ocean. Each night that I was in Baja, I was able to camp with a view of the ocean, sometimes up on an agave bluff, oftentimes right on the beach. A mix of hardscrabble Mexican fishermen and aimless American surfers welcomed me into their world. I smoked pot with the surfers and listened to their stories of migration between California and Baja. They gave me suggestions on where to camp along the coast. I used their word-of-mouth map to make my way down the peninsula. The fishermen were less talkative but just as helpful. I traded them cigarettes and alcohol for fish, mostly Dorado and Red Snapper. These seamen had me eating better than I had on any of my extended road stays.

After a few days of driving, the road emptied out even more. Cars became scarce and the small towns became smaller and smaller until they ran dry. Half-way down the peninsula, the road crossed into a nature reserve, Reserva de la Biosfera El Vizcaíno. I drove through the Reserva and out to Bahia Tortugas, a little town on a bay of the same name. A little lady working a tortas stand just outside of the Reserva had told me that they had whales out on the coast, and if I drove to Bahia Tortugas, I would see them. There weren't any whales, but I did see some pronghorn on the drive. They reminded me of home.

The long road out from Bahia Tortugas led me back to the main highway, which turned east through the mountains and out to the Sea of Cortez. I remember thinking that it was strange to name a body of water after a man that had brought so much pain to the natives of Mexico. Maybe that's why it has two names—the Gulf of California being the other, which I think sounds more peaceful.

The deep blues of the Pacific Ocean were swapped out for the turquoise green on the other side of the peninsula. Unlike the Pacific side, the waters of the Gulf were tranquil and warm. The visions of Mexican paradise that I had conjured my whole life were there, on the eastern side of Baja. Around the southern end of the Bahia Concepcion, I left the highway for the sandy peninsular roads that straddled the most beautiful white beaches I'd ever seen.

The next three days were spent smoking pot and drinking beer while I walked naked on the beach. I laid about, reading books and writing about my travels. With the beauty around me, my loneliness was a terrific muse. There wasn't another person or another car, nor any signs of civilization at all except for the dirt road I had driven in on.

The entire time I was away from the highway, I didn't speak to another human being.

Eventually, driven by my desire for conversation, I drove down to La Paz, the biggest city, by a large margin, that I had seen since I left Ensenada. Old churches, crowded town squares, taco shops, markets stuffed with produce and people—I welcomed it all. I was in La Paz for forty-eight hours, and when I wasn't sleeping, I was on my feet, zigzagging through the city. I had so much fun taking in the sites of La Paz that I had almost forgotten the reason I was there, to catch the ferry to the mainland.

I queued up for the ferry early in the morning, and before long, it was hot as hell. Sitting in my truck, I thought about how I had never been on a ferry boat before. Not knowing what to expect, I guessed this would be a rinky-dink operation. I pictured an old boat that could hold a dozen cars or so.

The ferry attendants sold me a ticket for the trip and directed me into a parking lot for loading. When I pulled into the lot, I was confused as to why the lot was so big. Cars were lined up by the dozen in six different rows. It couldn't be possible that all of these cars were getting on the same boat. When the ferry landed, I thought it was a cruise ship at first; it was so big and fancy. At least a hundred cars came spilling out of the hull of this great ship. I was terrified. For some reason, a small boat seemed more manageable, less intimidating. Scared out of my mind, I drove into the belly of the enormous vessel as directed by the men in yellow vests.

The other cars squeezed into the ship, and I followed the flow of traffic. Once parked, the people from the cars around me got out and climbed the various staircases that flanked the parking area. None of them seemed scared, so I relaxed a bit and made my way up the stairs and into the sitting area of the boat. Through the large glass windows, I could see men standing in a group, smoking cigars and cigarettes on the front deck. I joined them as they made small talk and looked out over the deck onto the azure water that ran to the horizon on each side of the ship.

The men asked me where I was headed, and I told them that I was going to Puerto Escondido. The men saw my light skin and issued strict warnings, not unlike the warnings Taylor had sent me off with. One man stepped forward and spoke for the group. He instructed me to get down to Oaxaca as quickly as possible and warned me to never go to Acapulco. As he said this, the other men in the group shook their heads in agreement. I listened to their advice and thanked them for the tips.

I made it down the coast in a few short days, but I ignored the advice of the men on the boat when I drove right through Acapulco. After a day or two of driving without incident, I got confident and probably a little stupid. Sinaloa is one of the most violent regions of Mexico, but I only met nice people who seemed harmless enough.

By the time I arrived in Puerto Escondido, I was ready to find a party town with hotels and modern amenities. I had enjoyed my long drive through rural Mexico, but that didn't mean I wasn't enamored by the international flavors of the resort town. The first night, I drank beers with a group of guys from Denmark and ate tacos with a couple from Argentina. I sat at a coffee shop and had a cup of good Mexican coffee while German, French, and English conversations bounced around.

Even though I had met some foreign travelers in Santa Barbara, people from other countries were still novel to me. Their childhoods, education, life experiences, the food they ate at home were all drastically different from the world I had been reared in. Chain-smoking cigarettes with strangers and diving into conversation was how I spent my first week in Puerto Escondido. Europeans seemed to like their conversations almost as much as they liked their cigarettes, so they were happy to oblige me.

After a few days of drinking on the beach and talking over coffee, I moved out of Escondido, settling into a smaller town just south, Brisas de Zicatela. Zicatela had a hippy vibe similar to La Posada with a down and out in Mexico feel that made me feel right at home. I found a beach in town that had a few resident RVs and parked the old Ford so that my camper door faced the water.

I ate tacos, lay on the beach, and drank beer all day. There was always a party and plenty of interesting people to meet. Camped out in vans and station wagons next to me were a bunch of trimmers who had spent the harvest season in Grass Valley or Mendocino or the mountains outside of Santa Cruz. After they cashed out, they came down to Mexico to spend the winter. They weren't just Americans. Brits, French, Belgians, Italians, Canadians, and many others did the annual migration from the pot fields of California to the beaches and leisure spots of Mexico. Their money went further down in Mexico, and the parties were seven days a week.

Out on the beach, I met a group of girls that were spending their vacation surfing. They were nice, so I stuck around and made conversation. After chatting for a bit, a few of them went into the waves and one stayed behind and had a beer with me.

"What are you doing in Mexico?" I asked her.

"I'm going to grad school next fall, so I'm traveling around Mexico until then."

"Seems to be a lot of you in Escondido."

"A lot of us?" she asked.

"Grad students. I guess it's a good time to travel."

"I got the time off, so I figured I should maximize it."

"Makes sense."

"What hostel are you staying in?" she asked.

"I'm not staying in a hostel. I drove down here, I'm parked up there," I gestured to the parking lot.

"That's awesome. I'd love to do something like that."

"It's been fun." I stubbed out my cigarette and laid down on my side, facing the young woman. "Where're you staying?"

"I'm staying at a hostel. About a mile down the beach."

"I've never been to a hostel? I guess they're pretty cheap?"

"Yeah, they're cheap, but I'm down here for a month, so I'm volunteering."

"For what?"

"For the hostel." She could tell I wasn't putting it together, so she went on. "They let you stay for free and feed you a little bit as long as you do some bartending and cleaning."

"Sounds like a good deal."

I drove the ladies home after they were done surfing, two of the girls in the cab with me and three more stuffed into the camper for the short drive through town. I parked the old Ford in a small sandy lot overgrown with brown weeds, and the girls took me to the bar in the back of the hostel. The owner wasn't there, so I had a few drinks on the patio until he was. Beautiful young people from all over drinking beers, smoking cigarettes, and wearing very little. Seemed like heaven. I got the girls high on Lillian's weed and we watched the ocean.

The owner of the hostel, Johnny Melrose, was a Canadian guy not too much older than me. He was born and raised in Calgary and dropped out of high school when he was sixteen to go work in the oil fields. He saved his money up through his early twenties and then moved down to Mexico with the direct intention of starting a hostel. He bought an old house, which now made up the main building of the hostel, and with the help of some locals, built out the property to its current glory. Johnny added additional buildings and a big bar area on the beachside of the house. He was somewhere in his thirties when I met him, and he had been partying hard for at least the last decade.

Johnny didn't need much convincing to bring me on as a volunteer. Since I was living in the camper, he would be able to keep a bed free, and since he had more empty parking spots than he had empty beds, we had a deal. One minor roadblock was that he already had enough volunteers. This was a minor setback, as one of the volunteers was leaving at the end of the week, and all I had to do was hang out and wait for my turn. He said I could keep the old Ford parked right where it was in the meantime if I paid him fifty pesos a day. Once I came on as a volunteer, I got to park for free, all my meals were comped, and I had access to the facilities. Since I wasn't taking up a bed, he threw in two beers and a cocktail of my choice each day that I worked. On the days I was off, I was not entitled to booze, but I was able to stay for free, and I still got meals. We shook hands on the deal, and I settled in on the patio—a spot that I would become very familiar with.

THIRTY-ONE

El Crocodillo Hostel, or Croco for short, was similar to La Posada in that they both had Spanish names, parties were frequent, and both seemed to attract gorgeous women from all walks of life. The major difference was that La Posada had a great balance between chaos and silence. El Croco did not. The mornings were the quietest time of the day, and they weren't all that quiet. Booze breath snores filled the dorm rooms as the last of the yipped-up drunks went to bed. There was always someone yanking a big suitcase through a hallway or arguing over a bill at the front desk. Voices and music, footsteps, laughter, and lighters flicking on; sound was omnipresent like the ringing that comes with tinnitus of the ear.

I was so glad to have the refuge of the camper. I could still hear the faint sounds of European techno music in my dreams, but I slept better than most. Living in a camper in America was low rent, a step above homelessness. In the hostel scene, owning a camper was some kind of status symbol. People were always curious to see what was on the inside, envious of my mobile domicile. Most were interested in having little parties in the camper, isolated soirees that allowed the hostel residents to do their drugs in privacy. I never did any cocaine, but a whole bunch of it got done in the safe confines of my camper. My generosity was often rewarded with a fresh pack of cigarettes, a beer, or even a bag of weed.

The miscellaneous drugs that went through the hostel didn't interest me much outside of an occasional psychedelic experience. The locals searched the rainforest for hallucinogenic mushrooms and would bring them down to the beach to sell to tourists. Guests sometimes brought me mushrooms as an offering. Just like every other place I had lived, the hostel had a hierarchy, and the volunteers who had been around awhile were at the top. Some of the guests thought that if they made friends with me, then they would make friends with everyone at the hostel. Bribing me didn't pay the dividends they desired. As soon as the mushrooms took effect, I didn't want to socialize. More often than not, I would strip off my clothes and wade into the ocean. I could sit for hours watching the horizon, waiting for it to change shape.

I made all kinds of friends at the hostel, but I realized that I mostly preferred the company of women. As friends, as lovers, as partners in conversation. Most of the volunteers were women, and I spent my free time with them. Not only did I enjoy the company of the female volunteers, but I found the volunteers, in general, to be much more tolerable than the regular guests. The same old 'getting to know each other' conversations were so abundant at the hostel. 'Where you from?' 'What's it like there?' 'Where have you been traveling?' It didn't take long before I dreaded these banal conversations. With the other volunteers, I had already done the introductory small talk, gotten it out of the way, and we could talk like friends rather than two people on a blind date.

I wasn't completely impervious to mundane chit-chat, however. When I tended bar, I had to interact with the guests, and engaging in idle conversation was inevitable. Most of the time, the conversations were predictable, like reading from a script. Every once in a while, a guest would stray from the norm.

"What do you do?" a small, bright German girl asked me as she sipped her beer.

"I volunteer here."

"No, what do you do? With your life?"

My reflex was to tell her I was a writer. That I was writing a novel. But I didn't feel like lying to her, so I told her the truth instead. "Nothing much. I've been traveling for a while. I don't do a whole lot more than that." Right away, I got the feeling that she loathed me. She said something like, "Ok," or "Cool," or some other dismissive word, and the conversation ended there. In her eyes, I gathered, I was just another party boy, one amongst many. And the reason a party boy travels is to find a new place to get drunk. If this was what she thought of me, she wasn't wrong, but I didn't enjoy being made to say it out loud.

The next day, I didn't have to work, so I didn't leave my camper until late in the day. I smoked cigarettes in bed and thought about my shortcomings, realizing that, by most measurements, I was a failure. I forced myself into writing, but the only thing that came out was frustration; my mind and focus drifted to more critiques of myself, truths that I didn't dare write down. I decided that drinking tequila out on the patio was a better use of my time than fighting the pen in my camper.

In the morning, I got up early to sweep the patio. As I swept, I watched a German couple smoke cigarettes and slice up fruit at a picnic table. Too enamored with them, I was unable to sweep. Something about the way they smoked cigarettes while they ate made me hungry. They were nice to look at. Nice hairstyles, clean clothes, and they both wore expensive sunglasses. They left a mark on me that lasted all day.

Annoyed by the mental intrusion, I got drunk and tried to forget about them. Out on the patio by myself, sipping on a beer, a group of ladies sat down next to me. They lit cigarettes and ordered a round of Tecates. I left my stuff at the table and asked them to watch it for me. I went to the camper and grabbed a bottle of Cazadores from my cooler. I returned to the table with the bottle and rolled a cigarette. Before I lit the cigarette, I took a big pull from the tequila bottle. The ladies watched as I grimaced and set the bottle back on the table. As if it hadn't been my plan the whole time, I offered the bottle up to the group of women sitting next to me. They looked around at each other and collectively nodded their heads and shrugged their shoulders. They passed the tequila to one another, each one taking a small pull straight from the bottle.

I took a drag from my cigarette and exhaled a big puff of silver smoke. "I'm Otis," I said.

The ladies went cigarette for cigarette and beer for beer with me, however, that first pull of tequila was the last that any of them took. They asked me questions about growing up in Texas and if I had ever shot a gun. Europeans always asked me about guns when they found out I grew up in Texas. I both got used to it and dreaded the inevitable turn. On this particular night, I was lonely enough to overlook the less than appealing small-talk.

After many beers, I took one of them, a stubby Dutch girl, back to my camper. She was built like a baker's wife but very sweet, and she was a generous lover. Afterward she lingered in my bed while I smoked cigarettes and stared at the ceiling. I fired off one-word answers to her questions until she got the picture and went to sleep in her dorm bed.

Sex didn't make me any less lonely, in fact, I was more lonely than before, and I now had a heavy dose of guilt. Taking the day on seemed unfathomable, so I finished the bottle of Cazadores off before lunchtime. All day, I smoked like a wet stick, mixing Mexican weed into my cigarettes.

Women didn't make me feel better, neither did booze or weed, so I tried to write my feelings away. The idea of starting a novel was too overwhelming, and the introspective nature of journaling was too depressing, so I settled on poetry. I wanted to get my emotions out as soon as possible and leave them on the page. The words I wrote and the meaning behind them were trite. It seemed like there was no medicine for what ailed me, and anything that I took just made me worse.

THIRTY-TWO

During my hostel days, I didn't eat much. I found other means of sustenance. Smoking weed as if it were food, drinking alcohol as if it were water, and smoking cigarettes as if they filled my lungs with oxygen. Cigarettes filled a deep recess that had always been inside me since I was a kid. Cigarettes made sense; they fit into my life like a puzzle piece. I got a little high just getting the pouch out of my pocket to roll one. By the time I had licked the paper closed and put the stick in my mouth, I was edging on orgasm. When I lit the cigarette and exhaled my first puff, everything went away, and what I was left with was just me—no errant thoughts, no more impulses, just my mind in its clearest state. The only time I lived in the present was between those fifteen drags.

When I wasn't smoking, I wanted to be. When I finished smoking one cigarette, I wanted another. Cigarettes were incredible after a meal and perfect with coffee. Getting out of bed in the mornings was a treat because the first cigarette of the day was my favorite. When I drank, I couldn't even taste the smoke. Not that I didn't like the taste of smoke, I loved it, but when I was drinking, the cigarettes were so integral that I barely noticed I was smoking them. I smoked when I was drunk, I smoked when I was hungover, I smoked like a brush fire when I was tripping, and I loved a cigarette when I was stoned. Weed mixed with tobacco when I was stressed out was exactly what I needed, also when I was anxious and when I wanted to relax. My pointer finger and my middle finger got so used to holding cigarettes that when they weren't holding one, they thought they were. All day, my thumb would flick the butt of a phantom cigarette, unless, of course, there was a real cigarette to flick, and usually there was.

Through the smoke, my moods shifted, rose, and fell. Surrounded by people who were excited by life, I basked in their conversation, hoping that I would become happy through osmosis. But happiness can't be leached from others, I learned.

Every day, I went to the ocean. My fear had diminished to the point that I was comfortable swimming out to where I could no longer touch. I had let my body go to shit over the last few months, and swimming every day helped me get back to a somewhat respectable shape.

In my search for happiness, I decided to be more observational. The people around me were full of joy, so I watched them. The other volunteers, I noticed, didn't seem to party nearly as often as the short-term guests, especially the females. They weren't plagued by hangovers, and they were able to wake up early to do interesting things during the day. They ate healthily, exercised, and in general, took care of themselves. Back in my college days, I knew that I needed to slow down on the booze, but this was the first time I had connected the cause and effect of my drinking to my state of mind. With empirical evidence in front of me, I followed the lead of my fellow volunteers, governed my intake of booze, and replaced tacos with fresh fruit and vegetables. The positive effects didn't take long to hit.

The sunrise was a welcomed sight, perhaps for the first time since my childhood. The singing of birds no longer bothered me. Cool air off of the ocean, Mexican coffee, and writing on the patio with nobody around—little by little I developed a routine that brought me out of the shadows of shame.

One morning, Sami, a hippy girl from somewhere in Orange County, invited me to go hiking with her. Since I wasn't hungover, I was up early to receive and accept the invite. Sami and a few of her friends had borrowed Johnny's Jeep, so we drove out to Cascada La Reforma, just north of town. We hiked up to some nice waterfalls and swam in the large blue pools that formed below. Just me and four women swimming in paradise, what an inflating experience. Then they were jumping off a fifteen-foot cliff that hung over one of the pools. Too scared to jump, I watched and lay in the sun, pretending to not be interested.

The ladies got tired of the cliff and laid out towels next to me on the side of the stream. I rolled a large joint, and Sami cut up some mangoes and passed the pieces around. I watched the women smoke from the joint and eat slices of mango, and I remembered that I didn't know the other three girls very well, if at all. Over the afternoon, I parsed their stories and placed them in my memory.

The woman I recognized most was Evelyn; I knew that she was from Alberta, Canada. She had just done some trimming in Mendocino and was waiting for Alberta to thaw out before she went home. She was sleeping with Johnny Melrose, which was the reason why we were able to borrow his Jeep. Sitting next to her was Anja, a Danish girl, eighteen, who was taking a year off before going to university. Sami, Evelyn, and Anja were very nice people, and all of them were attractive in their own way, but I couldn't help but be enamored over the other woman who had tagged along. Sitting by the river, she couldn't be bothered to look at me.

Her name was Clemence Arnaud, and she was from Valence, France. She was giggly stoned and her chin dripped mango juice onto the nape of her neck as she sucked at the skins. That day was the first day I had met her because she had just come on as a volunteer that week. She had long curly brown hair and lustrous, buckeye nut eyes. Her bright blue bikini top didn't match her reddish-brown bottom, but she was perfectly put together. Watching Clemence eat a slice of mango made me regret not jumping off the cliff.

After a few hours of sun and swimming, we made our way back down the trail and sat our wet butts on the beige leather seats of Johnny's hunter-green Jeep. We bounced down the washboard road towards town in a bit of a hurry to get Anja and me back to El Croco for our bartending shift. Evelyn drove while I nodded off in the passenger seat. I woke up in the driveway of El Croco, Evelyn nudging me awake. Half asleep, I stumbled off to my camper to change out of my swimsuit. I hadn't bought an article of clothing since I left Albuquerque, and my wardrobe had gotten pretty shabby. For some reason, on that day, I noticed how worn down my clothes had become.

When I showed up to my bartending shift, I was greeted by a surprise. Anja had given her shift away to Clemence. Clemence showed up wearing the same bikini top from earlier and a pair of wrinkled pajama pants, her demeanor akin to having just woken up from a nap. I wanted to know everything about her, but instead of conversation, I gave her space, figuring it best to not let my eagerness show.

The night flew by as we popped open beer bottles, mixed up margaritas and rum punches, and poured out rows of shots. Clemence played music over the bar stereo, songs I had never heard before. She danced between orders and smiled when she caught me looking. Before I knew it, the bar quieted down and the party moved to a bonfire out on the beach. My excitement softened and I became more comfortable around Clemence, at least enough to start a conversation.

"Where ya' coming from?" I asked, starting with an old standard.

"The south." Her accent was nice. "I started in Brazil. Then over to Columbia and up through Central America. You?"

"I guess I started in California. I drove through Baja and then took a ferry to the mainland. Been here for a while."

"You drove here? Are you the man with that truck?"

"Yep. That's my truck out back."

"With the little, uh, the little house on the back?" Her search for words was very charming.

"Yes. With the little house."

"No, what do you call it?" she asked.

"It's a little house."

"No," she said and smiled.

"Yes. It's where I live. It's my house," I said, trying to coax out some laughter.

She laughed and I ached a bit as the beauty in her smile set in on me. She was too much for me, but I was undeterred.

"You are making fun of me." She giggled again and put her eyes on mine. I broke a smile.

"It's called a camper."

"A camper. Yes, this is right. Like the boy that sleeps in the wood," she said, seeming pleased to have the image in her mind.

"Yes. Just like that." We both laughed. I was engorged.

"I don't know why they call you camper. You are more like… I don't know the word in English, escargot."

I thought for a second and realized I knew this word. "You mean a snail?"

"Yes, you are the snail, this camper, it's your shell." She laughed and I laughed, and then I couldn't think of anything else to say.

Our shift ended, and I went to bed, but I didn't sleep easy. I was awash in Clemence. The waterfall, the mango skins, and my life as a snail played through my head. I thought about how my camper had become my home—not overnight, but a gradual shift had happened. A shift that was so slow, I hadn't realized it, but there I was, at home.

I woke up refreshed, still glowing from the night before, but Clemence was nowhere to be found that day or that night. Smoking away at my cigarettes, hoping she would appear in the common area, I waited for hours. She never came into sight. Giving up, I went to bed agitated.

The next morning, I was early for breakfast. Clemence was sitting by herself reading a book over a plate of toast. In my excitement, I lost my tact and plopped down next to her without second-guessing myself. She looked up at me and half-smiled.

"Good morning. How are you doing?" I asked, hoping to spark a conversation.

"I'm reading," she said and continued to do so. Wishful thinking pushed me to wait to see if she was just finishing the page she was on before stopping to chat with me. She finished the page, turned to the next, and continued reading. I finished my fruit plate and slinked off to my camper like a maimed dog. I smoked a thousand cigarettes while punishing myself for my carelessness. Rewinding, in my mind, every single movement of muscle that I made, playing back to the moment she dismissed me in favor of her book.

Later on, I saw Sami on the patio and filled her in on the situation.

"You interrupted her while she was reading," Sami said.

Out of all the scenarios I had pushed through my brain, the most obvious was the one I hadn't considered. She didn't hate me, she just wasn't interested in talking to me at that moment.

Sami put my mind at ease until I realized that in my desperate search for answers, I had disclosed to her that I was infatuated with Clemence. My brain swelled and pulsed with thoughts of grade school dances and high school crushes, cementing the fact that I had been reduced to a schoolboy. This little curly-haired French girl stripped me of my manhood. I stepped outside of myself, outside all of the excitement, and became aware of how foolish I was being. Where had my rational brain gone?

I went in search of the bottle of Cazadores stashed in my camper. I pulled a long draw from the bottle and lit a joint. When I smoked through half of the joint, I took another pull from the bottle of tequila and then finished the joint. Smoke filled the camper so thick that I couldn't see to the other side. A change of scenery was in order if I wanted to change the fortunes of my day. With a cigarette dangling from my lips, I walked out to the beach. After a few miles of walking, I came upon a little taco stand, so I sat down for lunch. I ate a few tacos and knocked back a few beers, and I tried to shoot the shit with the man who owned the stand. He didn't have much to say. I complimented him on his cowboy hat; he thanked me and went back to listening to the radio.

Back at the hostel, I decided I was going to let things play out with Clemence however they may. Que sera, sera. Worrying and stressing wasn't doing me any good, so I forced my brain to stop with the nonsense. Two guys playing dominoes on a plastic table asked me to join their game. The last time I had played dominoes was when I was a kid, and it was a pleasant discovery to find that cigarettes, tequila, and Mexican beer went well with the game of tiles. As each game came to an end, I pleaded with the guys for one more. Eventually, they got too tired to count and refused my pleadings. They said their goodnights and went off to sleep.

All alone on the patio, I felt a little strange. Quiet didn't suit El Croco, and it didn't suit me. I felt like I was being watched. Resisting the urge to sleep, I rolled a cigarette and opened one last beer. The ocean was a charcoal mass sprawled out in front of me, almost indistinguishable from the black sky draped above it. The sound of shuffling feet behind me wasn't enough to break my gaze away from the void. Clemence sat down next to me, and I perked up a bit, as if the bottom of my foot had been shocked by a low voltage taser.

"Can you build me one of those?" she asked. I didn't answer her with words, rather, I went to work rolling. Handing the cigarette over to her, she placed it in her kissing lips and waited for me to light it, which I did.

"How was your night?" I asked as she blew a puff of smoke from her red mouth.

"It was nice. I went dancing in the town," she said. "What about you?"

"Didn't do much. Just shot the breeze with some of the boys here."

I tried to think of something else to say, something clever. Nothing came, so I just smoked, exhaling little clouds out towards the ocean. The smoke danced in the sky before it dissipated.

"I heard about you," she said, breaking away from the quiet.

"Oh yeah?" I asked, fearing that Sami had sold me out.

"I heard that you are a cowboy. A real Texas cowboy." She smiled and then giggled a little bit before putting her cigarette to her lips.

"Me? Naw. I'm not a cowboy," I said, pretending to be humble.

"No? You didn't grow up on a cow farm?"

"Nope. I grew up on a sheep ranch."

"Oh! You are a sheep boy!" She laughed and I shot her a smile. We finished our cigarettes and went to our separate beds. I was back on the emotional mountain top. Clemence had a pull on me, the strength of which I had never experienced before. For the second night in a row, I had trouble sleeping. I tossed around in my loft until I was restless enough to give up on sleep and get down from my bed. I wrote a poem full of flowered images of love. Reading it back to myself, I felt embarrassed for having written it.

THIRTY-THREE

Over the next week, I saw Clemence much less than I would have liked. I tried to engineer chance encounters with her, but I didn't have much luck. Forced to wait for our work schedules to align, eventually, we shared a night-time bartending shift. When our shift came, we were greeted with an abundance of quiet. Some kind of party at another hostel had sucked the life out of El Croco, which suited me just fine. Clemence and I talked all night, mostly about music and books. I hadn't read a book cover to cover since I was living with Beatrice, but I lied and told her that I had recently read a book by Tom Robbins called *Jitterbug Perfume*. I had actually read it, and I knew Tom Robbins was well regarded by other travelers, and I hoped she would be impressed.

"I have read that one also. It is an ok story, but this Tom Robbins, I don't like him. He tries too hard. He should just get to his point. I like Kurt Vonnegut better."

"I haven't read any Vonnegut."

"Really? He is my favorite American writer. You should read him. What are you reading right now?"

I couldn't think of a lie quick enough, so I told the truth. "Nothing right now."

"I have a book for you that you must read."

"What is it?"

"One Hundred Years of Solitude."

"I've heard of that." She gave me a copy of the book after our shift. She told me that she had just finished reading it and was curious to see what I thought. Reading made her lonely. After she finished a book, she wanted to talk about it, but it was so hard to find anyone who had just read the same book.

That night, I stayed up and read for a few hours, getting through the first hundred pages of the book. I was completely lost; the story was all over the place, and I had no idea what was going on. The narrative unfolded in disjointed anecdotes, and I couldn't piece any of it together. I couldn't keep the characters straight, let alone identify with any of them. How was I supposed to talk about a book that I couldn't make sense of? Worried that Clemence would think I was an idiot for not being able to understand the book, I woke up early the next morning and read on, hoping to catch on to some sort of meaning. Nothing took; I couldn't follow the story, and I became convinced that this wasn't even a story. Two hundred pages in, and I didn't want to read anymore. I brainstormed for what I would tell Clemence, and came up with nothing but the truth. If she asked, I would have to come clean.

A few days later, I was eating breakfast by myself when she sat down at my table. She hadn't forgotten the book and asked me about it straight away.

"Well, it's ok, I guess, but I have to be honest, I don't understand it."

"Do you like it?"

"No. Not really." I hoped she wouldn't make me defend my reasoning any further, so I offered up an explanation. "It's hard for me to like a book that I don't understand."

"It takes a lot of courage to admit you don't like this book."

"Thanks. I was a little worried I'd offend you."

"You don't offend me. I don't like this book either. It doesn't make sense."

"Really? I thought it was just me. Seems like everybody loves it."

"I think people are too afraid to say they don't understand it. This is the only explanation I have for this book. Everybody say to me, 'Clemence you must read this,' but this book is not good. How can anyone like it?"

"I like your theory. People can be that way sometimes. It's intimidating to admit you don't like something that everyone else likes."

"I like being different. I don't like what the group likes, I never have." Clemence lit a cigarette and looked out at the ocean. "When I was a girl, I had to always wear strange clothes so that nobody would be the same as me." Without looking at me, she said, "Now that you have passed my test, I want you to read a book that I like."

"You tested me?" I was so flattered that I worried I would go erect.

"I wanted to see what you say. I didn't want to be the only one at the hostel that hate this book."

"I guess I'll be your guinea pig. What will you have me read next?"

"Why are you my pig?" We both laughed again.

"What's the next book?"

"I will look and see what I have in my bag."

Clemence had me read several books over the next few weeks, and my lust for her evolved into what I could only describe as love. I wasn't sure that you could be in love with someone before you had even touched them, but I didn't know what else to call it. I adored her. Days were planned with the sole intent to keep her in close proximity. I walked the line of obsession. She was friendly with me, seemed to enjoy my company but always kept me at arm's length. She had many suitors at the hostel, constantly getting pestered by horny short-term guests. Never budging, she ignored their advances and their conversation in general. She was blunt and honest with them, telling the other boys straight away that she wasn't interested in giving her time to anyone she didn't see fit.

THIRTY-FOUR

A scenario in which Clemence and I were together was hard to imagine; however, that didn't stop my pursuit. In place of reciprocal love, a fantasy established roots. A fantasy that was equal parts delightful and equal parts frustrating. During the day, we were close enough to each other that I was able to blur the line between fact and fiction. At night, the reality was impossible to ignore, as my bed remained empty.

Clemence, in her professorial way, had taken to giving me books she thought were worth reading. The books made me feel close to her. One assignment was a book about George Orwell's experiences as a poor man, a book that I, for many reasons, really related to. One night, alone in my camper while reading Orwell, I was interrupted by an unexpected knock. Annoyance turned to elation when I discovered Clemence standing on the other side of the door. With one foot crossed in front of the other, she looked small and vulnerable.

"Are you sleeping?" she asked, showing a side of her I had never seen.

"Just doing some reading. What's up?"

"I was wondering if I could sleep in there tonight?" Before I could say yes, she explained her reasoning. "I'm so tired. I didn't sleep last night, and the dorm is very loud. I can't go another night with bad sleeping." She spoke as if she was expecting to be met with protest.

"I don't mind."

"Thank you." She stepped up into the camper and climbed right into my bed. I turned off the light and went to the bathroom to brush my teeth and take a piss. Clemence was asleep by the time I got back. I crawled into bed as if I was crawling across a lake covered with paper-thin ice. She lay on her side, facing away from me. Slowly, she scooted backward until her butt fit perfectly into the crux of my hips.

"Aren't you going to hold me?" she asked.

I slid my right arm under her neck and draped my left arm over her ribcage. After a few minutes, her rhythmic breathing indicated that she was asleep. We stayed like that until morning. I slid my arm out from under her neck and left her to sleep. Outside, with a cigarette in hand, I was smiling like a jack-a-lantern. Sleeping next to Clemence was more fulfilling than sex with a stranger.

The next night, Clemence didn't knock before she entered my camper. She didn't need permission for what was already hers. She slid in under the blanket and cozied her ass into me without any exchange of words. I wrapped her up from behind in the same embrace as the night before and waited for her to fall asleep. When sleep didn't come, she squirmed her ass into my erect cock and then let out a slight chuckle. Frozen in embarrassment, I pretended to be asleep.

"You are afraid to kiss me," she said. This felt like a challenge, and I decided I had to make a move or my opportunity would be gone forever. She turned her face up to meet my plunging lips. As we kissed, she turned her body to face me. We kissed for a long time, so long that I don't remember the moment that the kissing ended and the sleeping began. The next morning was sweet and lazy; a nice breeze blew through the camper window, gently lapping the curtain.

From there on out, Clemence slept in the camper with me. There was no spoken agreement, it just became reality. As with everything Clemence did, she flowed right in like a seasonal creek.

Patience thrived in the absence of sex. I was left with no other choice. This was unknown territory, delicate ground, and I couldn't let my thirst for Clemence's love push me into making a mistake. Discipline was not an attribute that I felt I had in great reserves; however, for Clemence, I developed new versions of myself. Deep inside, I found that I was capable of suffering in pursuit of nirvana.

It wasn't until well after Clemence moved in that the sex came, like a much-needed rain, a happy reprieve from the beautiful sunny days that came before. Although the sex was amazing, I found that it was secondary to the release I got from just being in her presence.

Clemence was unlike anyone I had ever met, a true revelation. Her words were carefully chosen, and when she spoke, people listened to her with interest. Clemence was like a movie come to real life—people sat quietly and watched her, captivated.

Growing up, I hadn't noticed how isolated and sheltered we were on the ranch. Since I hit the road for California, since I moved to Albuquerque, experiences, ideas, and perspectives came at me fast. But the speed at which I was exposed to new ideas was never faster than with Clemence. The breadth of her intellect dwarfed mine. She was an expert in Christianity, Islam, Judaism, Hinduism, and Buddhism, however, she wasn't a religious person, herself. She spoke French, her native tongue, she was nearly fluent in English and Spanish, and she could hold a conversation in German and Italian. Geography was one of her many hobbies, and she was an encyclopedia of world history.

To this day, many of my beliefs and closely held ideas were introduced to me by her, and if they weren't from her, they had to be defended against her. The world my parents created for me on the ranch was shattered by her reasoning and practicality. She could deconstruct novels, philosophy, theories, poetry, and reconstruct them in her image. I was so easily converted by her. She was a way of life, and I was a willful young man brought to his knees at the altar of Clemence.

We spent two months at El Croco together before we went on the road in the old Ford. We took to the rainforest, spending a week swimming in cascading turquoise rivers and eating mushrooms fresh from the jungle. I was her private driver and her personal cigarette roller; she had never done either despite her love for nicotine and the open road. When she needed a smoke, she'd have me pull over and roll her one. She made French food with Mexican ingredients on a propane camp stove. We lived on the road for a month and a half, moving at whatever pace we wanted. As with all borrowed time, the moments we shared never felt like they were enough. Never satiated, never quenched, I was always wanting more.

THIRTY-FIVE

With the constant moving and the saturation of experiences, Clemence and I were spending more money than what we had originally budgeted for. I was prepared for this, Clemence was not. She asked me if we could volunteer at a hostel for a bit. Like the junky that I was, I felt as though my stash was in danger of being compromised. There was a lot of hesitation on my part, deflections, and in the end, silence.

Sensing my fear, she pounced on me. "You're afraid, aren't you?"

"Of what?" I asked, although I, of course, knew damn well what I was afraid of.

"You are afraid to share me. You want to keep me in your world only. You don't want me to leave the truck, do you?"

"I don't know why you say that. I didn't say I didn't want to go to a hostel. You're putting words in my mouth."

"I have to put words in your mouth. You don't put them in there." She looked out the window as I drove, then continued, "Why don't you ever tell me what you want? We never talk."

"I don't know what you're talking about."

"Bullshit. You know. You're doing it right now," she said, happy that I walked into her trap. "You want to know? You want to know what I'm talking about?"

"Yes, I do." I didn't.

"You follow me around like a little puppy dog. A sad little puppy. You do whatever I say, and you don't stand up for yourself. I took all your fire. I liked it at first, but now you drive me crazy."

"You took my fire?"

When a car hits a patch of ice, the driver can hit the brakes, they can turn the wheel, but with no traction, nothing happens, and the driver is left waiting for the crash to come.

"You are so cautious around me. It makes me insane." She lit up a cigarette that I had rolled for her before we started driving. She rolled down the window and exhaled a cloud of smoke. "Why are you so afraid of me?"

"I'm not." We both knew I was lying; I feared her like a god. The conversation ended without a resolution. She possessed me—a marionette on a string and she was the puppeteer. And now, the puppeteer had become enraged that the marionette couldn't move on its own.

Her expectations of me were fair, I knew this, yet, for some reason, I was unable to meet them. All she wanted was the real me, but all I could offer was the puppy dog. The puppy dog was too scared to lose its owner, too scared that an awkward pause or a bad time or a difficult conversation would break apart the whole thing. I walked on eggshells for months, and when she allowed me to step away from them and take to solid footing, I couldn't do it. Walking on eggshells was all I knew, and solid footing was too scary for me to accept. I never told Clemence that I loved her because it was apparent she didn't feel as strongly about me as I did about her.

I didn't want to share her with the rest of the world, but what choice did I have? We took residence at Playa Blanca hostel in Sayulita. Clemence had a friend at the hostel who had been volunteering with her boyfriend, and they were moving on, so we moved in. The hostel paid us fifty bucks a week plus meals. I gave my share of the money to Clemence since I was still in solid financial shape. Things went ok for a while, but the conversation we had in the truck before we got to Sayulita lingered.

When we arrived at Playa Blanca, we were both in a social mood, her more so than me. The volunteers at this hostel weren't too different from the crew at El Croco. We drank and smoked and got acquainted with all of the new faces. Among the volunteers was this good guy named Didier, a handsome Frenchman. Clemence was very excited that a French speaker was staying at the hostel. Didier seemed like a friendly guy, a nice guy. He had been volunteering for a month and knew the place well. He was better looking than me, his skin was darker, and he had a face full of pleasant angles. A bit taller, a year older, and his first language was French. I held on as long as I could.

Didier and Clemence became fast friends. Those first few days, they spoke for hours, all in French, stopping occasionally to apologize to me for not speaking in English. "It's just, it's been so long since I didn't have to think to speak. You understand?" Clemence said. I shook my head in agreement. I understood. My lack of language comprehension was irrelevant; I could see what was happening even if I didn't understand their words. Plans and scheming and endless thought about how to keep Clemence were futile, and in the end, the only thing I could muster was to cling to her side like the puppy she had made me into. Rather, I had made myself into.

Didier and Clemence spent more and more time together, and Clemence and I spent more and more time apart. Their bartending shifts aligned almost every night. Such a cruel coincidence, I thought. Later, it came to light that Didier was in charge of creating the schedule. Hatred for Didier would have manifested if it weren't for the fact that it was so easy to fall in love with Clemence, I couldn't blame him.

I walked into my camper one afternoon before my bartending shift, and Clemence was gathering her things.

"Hi." She stopped her organizing hands and sat down.

"Hi."

"I'm just getting some things." She looked away from me, breaking eye contact. "I will stay in the dorm from now on."

"What happened?"

"Nothing happened. I just don't feel like myself anymore. I need time to think," she said, looking away from me.

The normal gist of our interactions was as if Clemence was a hummingbird and I was always trying hard not to startle her into flight. The months of being careful piled on top of each other and weighed on me. Burying your feelings, your wants, your fears, your excitement, and your insecurity is, of course, a temporary solution. Eventually, they dig themselves up and pour out with volcanic strength and heat.

"Tell me, and don't give me some generic bullshit," I demanded.

"Tell you what?"

"You have never spared anyone's feelings. You look people in the eye and you tell them the truth. That's who you are."

"What do you want me to say?" She took her eyes from the floor and looked at me straight.

"I want you to tell me that you don't love me."

"Why would you want this?"

"Just fucking say it!" I raised my voice at her for the first and only time.

"I don't love you." Maintaining eye contact with me, she was so powerful looking.

"Do you love him?"

"Who?"

"Do you? Do you love him?"

"No, I don't love him either. Why are you so dramatic? We are travelers. This is how it happens. Don't try to make me a villain, Otis. I'm not your villain."

The hardest part was that she was right. She owed me nothing; my love for her was mine and she wasn't responsible for it. She hugged me as I cried, and then I left the camper. She finished packing her things and moved into the dorms.

A week later, she sat me down and told me she was leaving Playa Blanca, headed for Chiapas. There's a church there, she told me, where the indigenous people perform ceremonies with flowers and chickens and bottles of Coca-Cola. She didn't invite me to come, and out of desperation, I asked if I could.

"No. I don't think that would be right," she said, as if her words, said softly enough, wouldn't inflict pain.

"Are you going alone?" My dignity waned then disappeared.

"Yes, I am going alone." She paused, then added, "But Didier will go too. I don't think I will come back. Chiapas is close to Guatemala, and I will go back there next."

During our travels together, when Clemence rode in the passenger seat of the truck, more often than not, she slept. The road put her to sleep. She would ask me to wake her up when I saw that she was sleeping, but I never did. Alone with my thoughts, I wondered about her, mostly about what she thought of me. What label did she have for me? Clemence considered me a traveling partner that she happened to fuck, it's obvious now, but then, it was a surprise to find this out. When you live in denial, everything is a surprise—one that you live in constant fear of.

The morning that Clemence left was like the first day after the apocalypse. Life would go on, but it was difficult to see the point. There was nobody I could talk to. How could anybody else relate to being the last man left on Earth? The other volunteers knew exactly what had happened. They were nice about it and only talked about Clemence and me when I wasn't around.

When Beatrice broke up with me, she was the one who seemed heartbroken. I too was sad, but I was also relieved. Exactly how Beatrice dealt with our break remains a mystery, but if I had to guess, I bet she leaned on her parents and friends. She probably discussed the events leading up to the split and probably told them about me moving out. Maybe she told them about all of the selfish things I had done. Or, maybe Beatrice told them I was a good person but I needed to do some growing. Her friends probably told her that I took her for granted, and her parents probably told her that she could find someone who is a better match for her. All of that support and love would have been helpful in the days that followed Clemence's departure.

The hardest part about getting your heart broken is you don't know what the other person is thinking and feeling. Are they sad too? Do they regret what they did? Are they happy? Relieved? There's no way to tell, but that doesn't stop one's incessant conjecture. My brain found new life as a computer, a computer programmed to run a series of painful simulations. One of them was a scenario in which Clemence was heartbroken. In this scenario, she stopped the bus halfway to its destination and got off. She would apologize to Didier and tell him she must go, and he would understand. She was in love, after all.

There was also a scenario in which she fucked Didier on the back of the bus while an excited indigenous man sneaked quick peeks. There was the simulation of the bus crashing. There was one where she was sad and regretful but hesitant to come back to me, thinking that I would be too mad to take her back. I thought about a scenario in which she and Didier really were friends. Old Didier would tell her that she was leaving something special. She would come back to Sayulita after she had an epiphany brought about by seeing an ancient Mexican woman lay her salt and pepper head on her sun-blasted husband's shoulder. All of the simulations centered around her being on a bus, which was funny because I didn't even know that she was on a bus. That's how little I knew about this new version of Clemence.

Not sure what to do with my pain, I tried to wash it away with beer and tequila. In the morning, it was beer and cigarettes until it was time to work my shift. Sometimes I stopped drinking while I worked, and sometimes I didn't. It didn't take long for the folks at the hostel to realize that I was up to my eyes in booze and piss. The owners, a trust fund hippy couple from San Diego, sat me down after an especially drunk bartending shift.

"Otis, we're worried about what's been going on," the wife started.

"We don't like what you're doing to yourself," the husband said, taking a stern tone.

"I get it. I'm not doing so well."

"You haven't been for a while. The other volunteers are worried, we're worried," the wife said.

"We've been talking about it, and we don't think a hostel is the right environment for you," the man said.

"What do you think is the right environment for me?"

"I don't know, man. Where's home?"

"I don't have one," I said.

They let me sober up for a few days before they expected me to leave. The condition I was in wasn't a hangover, I was withdrawing. My heartbreak stung worse than ever. The booze had partially numbed me from the pain. Instead of the pain passing, it just hid out, waiting for me to sober up. The shivers and the shakes came in waves, and in a way, I enjoyed them. The fever and the sweats forced me to live in my misery, a strangely consoling place. Left for dead, by my own doing, my suffering felt like some sort of sacrifice. A bloodletting; at least, that's how my sick mind justified what I was doing to myself.

An Argentinian guy, a volunteer at the hostel named Diego, brought me fruit smoothies and tortillas to help me recover. The first few smoothies didn't stay down, but eventually, I was able to keep them inside. Once the smoothies took root, I was able to eat the tortillas, and I turned a corner towards a return to normalcy. I smoked a cigarette with Diego, and he told me about his father, who was a drunk. Diego used smoothies and bread to help him get through his withdrawals. His story came with a warning. "They will make you feel better, but they can't save you," he said.

After thanking Diego for his help, he asked me not to kill myself. Before I hit the road, I took a look inside the camper. It was a mess and smelled of sour sweat and vomit. A guest from the hostel presented a sage bundle from her bag. She said it would do more than just cover up the smell. She lit one end on fire and walked through the camper with all the windows open. The smoke stuck to the walls of my camper and the smell reminded me of the rainstorms in New Mexico.

Figuring I would be out on the road for a while, I decided to use the computer at the hostel. In my email inbox sat a message from my mother, dated just ten days earlier.

> Dear Otis,
>
> I called your phone, but the message says your number has been disconnected. With no other way to reach you, I have resorted to this. Your Uncle Grant is sick, and we aren't sure if he will get better. The doctors think he will pull through, but I think you ought to get home to see your uncle.

I know that he told you. I'm so sorry, Otis. I'll explain everything when you get here.

Love, Mom

When I left California for Mexico, there was a part of me that knew I ought to have headed to Texas instead. That little part of me fired back up and pushed the same buttons. I tried to think about the right decision, but when the choice was between home and pushing on, pushing on was easier, so I chose that. I set my sights on the interior of Mexico.

Before I left, I said my goodbyes to all the folks at the hostel. Saying goodbye was a strange thing for me, considering the circumstances. They had seen me at my worst, my most vulnerable—a level of intimacy that I wasn't used to reaching with relative strangers, let alone my closest confidants. They were still strangers to me, but I felt that they knew me better than that, and the fact that they were scared for me kind of scared me. With no destination other than the open road, I left the hostel. My body was still too ravaged to allow me to buy any booze, but I had a fresh can of tobacco and a big bag of Mexican shit weed. I was on my way.

THIRTY-SIX

Based on no reasoning at all, I headed east until I ran into Guadalajara, Jalisco. A city built on tequila, full of weathered sandstone buildings, and rough cobbled streets seemed like the perfect spot for a freshly dried-out drunk. Walking around, my only aim was to sightsee and distract myself. I checked into a hostel so I could meet some people and take a shower, plus I had this persistent urge to sleep in a different bed. Checking into the hostel, there was a group of German guys inhabiting the common area, and they were quick to make conversation.

"Hey friend, how are you?" a tall blonde man asked. I wasn't sure if he was talking to me, but I answered him.

"I'm alright, partner, how about you?"

"I am good. Just getting ready for tonight." He looked around at his friends and they all smiled. "Have you been in Guadalajara for a long time?"

"Just got here. How about yourselves?"

"We came yesterday. We want to find a party, do you know?"

"Suppose if you look hard enough, you'll find one."

"Maybe you join us? Find some ladies, have some drinks."

"I just may. I've been trying to lay low, getting a bit antsy, though." They didn't seem to understand all the words but they didn't ask to clarify, so we left things at maybe.

After a day or two, the boredom and loneliness caught up with me. Turns out the tequila capital of the world is a shitty place to get away from booze. I started by drinking a beer, then I had some tequila, and then I woke up a couple of days later with a busted face.

I ate breakfast alone; my jaw was so sore that I could barely chew. Juice and cigarettes were the only things that would go down without an ordeal. The German boys entered the common area, freshly showered and looking chipper. They saw me, and the five of them sat down around me. They told me that they had seen me the night before and filled me in on the details of how I acquired my bumpy face. At a nightclub in town, they saw me sitting at the bar, by myself. They tried to say hi, but I was too drunk to know who they were. Focused on two Canadian girls on the dance floor, I had little interest in chatting with the gang. The Canadian girls were good sports—they danced with me and let me buy them a beer—but after a while, they got annoyed with me and left. Some of the local gentlemen at the club felt that I had spoiled their chances with the ladies. They surrounded me in the bar and walked me outside to discuss. The German guys didn't see what happened after that, but it wasn't too hard to see it on my face.

I didn't need to see any more of Guadalajara, so I moved on. The old Ford was right where I had left it. Baking in the sun for a few days didn't help the smell of the old rig. When I sat down into the driver's seat, my butt fit to the grooves, and I was flushed with something almost like nostalgia.

The natural progress of my aimless voyage took me to the insanity that was Mexico City. The outskirts of the massive city were gridlocked, keeping me at a near standstill for hours. I stopped and asked a woman where the tourists hang out, and she pointed me to La Roma barrio. La Roma was a beautiful part of town, full of life and fancier than I had expected of a Mexican city. The streets were lined with restaurants and bars, chic hotels, and trendy boutiques. People were everywhere, in every shop, on every street corner, the noise as thick as paste. I parked the old Ford a few blocks away from the main strip and went for a walk. Drinking beer as I walked, I found a stand selling tacos the size of a cardboard bar coasters for a few pesos apiece. Little kids played on the sidewalk, a young woman strummed an acoustic guitar and sang sad songs, two old men argued over a broken watch. Humans swam against each other, against an invisible current that was so abrasive, the constant rubbing could have started a fire at any second.

THIRTY-SEVEN

After walking all day, I sat down on a bench in front of a decaying church. People took pictures in front of the ancient building, their arms wrapped around each other, big smiles on their faces. The church looked sad, like it had seen hard times and a lot of bad weather.

Two women, about the same age as me, approached and asked me to take a picture of them. I agreed and they got in position. One of the women was a real stunner; the other was short and squat. They looked funny standing next to each other.

"Are you visiting?" the beautiful one asked.

"I guess so."

"You want us to show you around?" the short one asked.

"Ok," I said, happy to have company.

They took me to a little stand that served mixed fruit in a cup. The old man behind the counter sliced up watermelon and mangoes with the grace of a true swordsman. After we ate the fruit, there was more walking. I followed the girls around, ignoring their conversation, smoking cigarettes and sipping from old bottles filled with new beer. They seemed to enjoy the novelty of me, and I was happy to be around someone other than myself.

When the girls led me into a shopping mall, my brain hesitated but my body followed. The bright lights mixed with the odor of perfume and made my head spin. I thanked the two ladies for their kind hospitality and made my way towards the exit. They gave chase, begging me not to leave them. We walked outside, back into the streets.

"I don't really like shopping much," I told them.

"We are done with shopping," the beautiful one assured me. "Let us talk," she said, walking me away from her friend. In a low voice, she said, "My friend, she likes you."

"She seems awful nice," I said as I looked over at the friend. She was smiling and looking at me, the edge of her lips poked into her chubby cheeks, leaving big dimples.

"She wants to go to a love hotel with you. She likes you."

"Love hotel?"

"Yes, she likes you." She looked back at her friend and leaned into me. "She likes Americanos."

I had never heard of a love hotel before, but I had a guess as to what it might be. The ladies led me off the main drag and through some side streets. We arrived at a shabby motel, not too dissimilar from the ones along the highway in Albuquerque, and the three of us walked inside. The girls negotiated an hour's occupancy and paid the man behind the counter. He smiled and shot a wink over my way.

The room was basic, bordering on rudimentary. I had to go to the bathroom and was pleased to find that it was attached to the bedroom and not the hallway. The bathroom was nothing more than a toilet with a shower head up above it and a large rusty drain in the middle of the concrete floor. There was nothing in the room except for a bed and a single folding chair set up against the wall. The beautiful girl sat down in the chair and took a magazine from her purse. She thumbed through it while her friend, the short one, stood next to the bed and unbuttoned her blouse. After the blouse was off, she pulled her sheer tank top up and over her head. Then she took her jeans down around her ankles, stepping out of them and leaving them where they lay. She looked at me as if to signal it was my turn.

I took off my shirt. The short one was out of her panties and bra and had climbed up on the bed. The beautiful one looked up from her magazine, and with her head and eyes, she motioned for me to get on the bed. Her patience appeared to be wearing thin. I took down my pants and my boxer shorts and sat on the bed.

"Go," the beautiful one said. She went back to her magazine and I climbed up onto the short one. She took my cock into her little hands and stroked me until I was hard, then guided me into her.

I pumped and pumped and she moaned and closed her eyes. I looked at the beautiful one and she looked up from her magazine, smiling at me. An enticing smile that almost convinced me that she would be next up. I stared at her, imagining that I was inside of her instead of her friend. Her short friend was in the throws, her eyes still closed. I kept going, harder and harder, and her moans grew louder and faster.

My eyes were locked on the beautiful one, not noticing the short one's legs wrapping around me. At my pinnacle, I tried to pull away, but the short one's legs squeezed around my hips and pulled me into her. I came inside her as she squeezed me in tighter with her dense legs.

She lay on the bed, looking exhausted, and the beautiful one kept thumbing through her magazine. I got dressed and pulled my boots on, then headed for the door.

"Nice to meet you," the beautiful one said as I opened the door. She was smiling, and her friend on the bed was smiling, her legs still spread and open. I shut the door and walked to the lobby of the motel. The man behind the counter perked up as I neared. He had been waiting.

"Te divertiste ahi?" he asked.

"Fue bueno," I said to him and pushed my way out the door.

Walking outside, the city looked alien, like it had changed in some way. The sky was darker, the buildings grittier than before. I hailed a cab and told him to take me back to La Roma. The cab driver was antsy and excited. His hair was salt and pepper and his trim mustache was dyed jet black. Not a single one of his buttons were fastened on his shirt and his potbelly hung over his lap as he drove. He giggled every time we hit a rough patch in the road. The road was full of rough patches.

After we drove a few blocks, he looked me over and started in with his hustle. "Cocaina?" he asked. At first, I wasn't sure why he said this, so I said nothing. "Cocaina?" he asked again.

"No, señor. No gracias."

He thought for a second, and a light bulb went off. "Chicas!"

"No, señor. No chicas."

"No cocaina?" he asked, and I, again, shook my head no. "No chicas?"

"Si. No chicas y no cocaína."

He let out a big belly laugh, seeming shocked that I just wanted a ride. He started in on the hotel routine, asking me over and over which hotel I was staying in. I just kept saying no thanks, and he kept asking which hotel I was staying in. Finally, I arrived in La Roma, and the cab driver stuck his fat greasy hand out.

"Tip. Americano, give tip!"

"Por tu? Ese es tu consejo. Conduce, sin hablar."

"Fuck you, amigo." He laughed and shook his head. I walked into the nearest bar and ordered a beer and a shot. My buzz was pretty much gone at that point, and the beer and shot only made me tired. I made my way back to my camper and went to bed amongst the car horns and screeching tires.

Early the next morning, I awoke to the sounds of traffic and the smell of diesel fumes. I didn't know what to do with myself in a city like this, so I went walking. Walking past a hip-looking coffee shop, I took a peek inside. There were a few travelers scattered around the tables, so I ordered a cup of coffee. Having a seat and sipping my strong brew, I couldn't help but notice the two women sitting next to me were speaking French.

"Excuse me, ladies," I started. "Do you speak English?"

"I do. Hers is only a little," said one of the women. She had big eyes and short brown hair; she wore a white cutoff t-shirt and black jean shorts.

"I'm looking to leave the city. Any recommendations for where I should go?"

"I don't know what you like," she said, smiling.

"What's the best idea you got?"

"You're in Mexico, go to the beach." She laughed and blew on her coffee.

"Any other ideas? I'm a little sick of the beach."

"Hmm. I am not so sure."

"What's your favorite place you've been to?"

"Here in Mexico? Oh. It's nice. I just come from there, but you need a car to go."

"That's perfect. I have a car. I drove here."

"Drove here? Or to Mexico?"

"Both."

"I see. Then you should go to Sierra Gorda."

"Yeah? Where is it?"

"Pretty far north of here. It's a nice drive." She lit up a cigarette. "It's very beautiful. How do you say… uh, cascada?"

"Waterfall?"

"Yes! There are many waterfall there. It's quiet, very few people."

"That's what I'm looking for." I finished rolling a cigarette and felt my empty pockets. The short-haired woman lit my cigarette for me. "Thanks." I took a deep drag and tried as best I could to give her a look of gratitude.

The bookstore next to the coffee shop had a terrific road atlas of Mexico. Sierra Gorda was on the map and didn't seem too hard to get to. I decided to leave the next morning, so I stocked up on supplies, including beer and tequila, as my thirst for alcohol had fully returned.

THIRTY-EIGHT

Relief from the chaos didn't come quickly. Driving away from Mexico City and its endless sprawl was a chore, but eventually, the city gave way to suburbs and slums, which relented to farms and countryside. I drove through emptiness and thread-bare farms until tree-draped mountains rose from the desert. The air began to moisten and cool, and I could smell life in the wind that blew through the cab of my truck.

The lights of Jalpan de Serra came into view just after the sun went down and the sky turned to a dark blue. The restaurant I stopped into only had one thing on the menu—thinly sliced beef simmered in a spicy red sauce with onions and peppers, served with black beans and rice. After dinner, I went to sleep while parked in the middle of town. The next morning, the air inside the camper was sticky in the early heat. I was glad to be out of bed and onto the streets.

Taco stands, juice pressers, and fruit vendors lined the square in front of one of the town's two missions. I ate watermelon and walked around aimlessly in the sun. Jalpan was different from other Mexican towns in its prominent topographic features. Surrounded by dark green mountains, the southern end of the city was bookmarked by a large lake. Seeking nature and solitude, yet there I was, in a crowded little city square. Nature was so close to me, but I couldn't touch it just yet. I finished my watermelon and started for my truck, ready to move on.

As I walked through town, I felt a set of eyes on me. When I looked, the people all around me were focused on all things other than me; however, the feeling of being watched persisted. A man with a donkey passed by me, revealing a set of almond eyes that locked into mine. I stopped walking, maintaining eye contact the entire time.

This woman, she didn't look away either—it was as if she were daring me to go my separate way, knowing full well that I wouldn't. She had corkscrew rivulets of rosewood hair and her skin looked like liquid. She was dressed in a silk tank top and baggy linen pants. Sitting on a concrete wall that was barely taller than my knees, she patted the empty spot next to her, and I walked over and sat down. Once I sat down, she took her gaze from me and looked off straight ahead.

"Hello," she said in an American-sounding accent. "Can you roll one of those cigarettes for me?" she asked, looking down at the cigarette burning in my hand. I rolled a cigarette and handed it to her. She took the freshly rolled cigarette into her plump maroon lips and waited for me to light it.

"What are you doing here?" she asked, exhaling a thin stream of smoke from her pursed lips.

"Just stopping through. I was about to leave before you called me over."

"I didn't call you over."

"You sure did." My cigarette had gone out while I rolled one for this stranger, so I relit it and took a nice deep drag. "What are you doing here? You fit here about as well as I do."

She ignored my question and smoked her cigarette. "Did you come to see the magician?"

"I came here to see the mountains. Get a little peace and quiet."

"The locals call him La Fantasma. They are very afraid of him, but they shouldn't worry so much. He never leaves his mountain." She spoke with complete indifference toward me, as if she was having a conversation with herself. "You're here to see him, aren't you?"

She broke her forward stare and looked at me. Her eyes were swirling tide pools of cacao. I was interested in what she was saying even though it made no sense to me. She took a drag off of her cigarette and blew the smoke directly in my face. Compelled to pull her wrinkled pants off and fuck her right there, I restrained myself.

"I know where he lives."

"Who?" I was rolling another cigarette for myself. When I finished, I rolled another for her.

"The Phantom. He will see you if I take you there." I knew she wasn't going to answer any of my questions, so I didn't ask any. I thought about leaving her and going to the mountains by myself, but I thought that this woman might be the reason I was in this town. Plus, I wanted to know what her maroon lips tasted like.

As we drove through the mountains, she told me one thing about herself. Her name was Esila. She smoked my cigarettes the entire time we drove, ordering me to pull over and roll another as soon as she finished one. The road went from gravel to sand and then to rock. The further we drove, the rougher the road got until we came to the base of a small but steep mountain. The dirt trailed up the mountain. I could see from below, it switched back and forth more than a dozen times before it reached the top. Before I started up the switchbacks, Esila had me stop the truck. Without any explanation, she opened the door and got out.

"Hey! What are you doing?"

"I'm not going up there," she said. She walked off the road and onto a small path that led into the shrubs that surrounded the base of the mountain. In a few seconds, she was gone from visibility. I got out of my truck and walked to the edge of the road. She was nowhere.

The switchbacks cut back and forth across the northern face of the mountain then topped out at a collection of casitas on the summit. It was so still and quiet, everything appeared to be asleep. There wasn't anybody to greet me other than an old dog that didn't seem interested in my arrival. I got out of the old Ford and started to poke around a little. The casitas weren't scary; they were quite ordinary, but I felt a strange little rush searching through them.

I called out, "Hola," hoping someone would answer me back. As I called out, I wondered who I should even be asking for. Would I tell them I'm there to see La Fantasma? Maybe Esila had been lying and this place was abandoned, and she just needed a ride out to this empty mountain for no particular reason. I pictured myself showing up in someone's home, asking for a phantom of which they knew nothing about. I knew before I got out of my truck that this was an unnatural situation and walking through the hacienda had pushed into the absurd. Yet there I was, perusing a stranger's home, calling out to them.

Searching the property turned up nothing. Headed back to my truck, from behind me, I heard a loud whistle. When I flipped around, a tall man was standing in the driveway, his thumb and middle finger resting on the edges of his mouth. He had coal-black hair and no shirt on, his sinewy muscles stretched over his long thin arms, and his ribs showed through his skin as if his sides were smiling.

"Hello," he said. "Have you come to see La Fantasma?" He laughed as if he had just told a joke. I laughed with him.

"Are you him?"

"I guess so," he said.

"I'm Otis. Otis Billings."

"Hi, Otis." The Phantom shook my hand and smiled. "Why have you come here?"

"I'm not sure."

"Who brought you?"

"A woman that I met in Jalpan. Esila." Her name didn't seem to resonate with him.

"If you don't know why you're here, then what will we do?"

"I'm not sure."

"Don't you find it strange? To show up to a person's home, that you don't know, and you don't have any idea of why you're there?"

"Yes, sir, it's strange. I don't normally do stuff like this. I thought I might find something here."

The Phantom looked at me and nodded his head. "You don't make no sense, but I think I understand." He looked over his shoulder at the dog walking behind him. "Often when people come here, they're looking for something, and more often than not, they don't know what that thing is."

"What do you do with them?"

"Drink beer. Did you bring any?"

I went and got two beers out of my cooler and handed one of them to the Phantom. We drank our beers in silence. I sat looking around the property and the mountains that surrounded us. I hadn't taken the time to admire the beauty of my surroundings until then. Below us, we could see the arm of the mountain reach out and follow along the ridge of another mountain. Never touching, only running parallel, these two great arms cradled a steep river gorge. The emerald walls of the gorge led down to a turquoise river that curved out to the horizon.

"Let me show you some magic, ok?" I looked up at the Phantom; he had his hand out. "Didn't you come here to see magic?" He motioned with his hand to give him my newly opened beer. I handed it over and watched as he took the can and set it upright in his palm, wrapping his fingers around the sides. The can started to quake as a stream of cold white smoke came up from the opened mouth. The Phantom laughed and handed the beer back to me.

"Is it safe to drink?" I asked in the tone of a joke, but I really did want to know. The Phantom laughed and dropped his head without an answer. Reluctant, I took a sip. The flavor was unmolested. After a while, the Phantom stood up and began to fiddle with a pile of sticks. He built a fire in a cinder block fire ring. Not an actual fire, rather, he set up paper and kindling and logs in the shape of a fire, but he didn't light it. The sun was beginning to set and the heat of the day was getting blown off the mountain by an aimless wind.

With the fire built, the Phantom lit up a pre-rolled cigarette that he pulled from a foreign-looking package. He sat down on an old bench next to the fire ring. He invited me to sit next to him. The Phantom became friendly and talkative as he spoke about the land and the way his family had come to own the property. The Phantom didn't say how he got his name or give any clues as to why people feared him.

The topic of conversation the Phantom was most passionate about, the one he wanted to discuss more than any other, was the subject of growing coffee. How it's grown, how many plants he had going, where he sells it, the process the beans underwent from plant all the way to roasted beans, and to the final resting place, your cup.

"Have you had a good cup of coffee before?" he asked me.

"Yeah, I guess so."

"If you had a good cup, you would know. I promise you."

"I guess I've just had regular coffee then."

"That's right. The coffee they have in the city, it's bullshit. You must come to the source, to get the finest cup."

"Alright."

"Out here, we grow good coffee. I will admit that it is not as good as the coffee they grow in the south, but almost."

We both lit cigarettes and I waited for the Phantom to offer me some of this miracle coffee, but he never did. The sky grew dark, which caught his attention, as he had been waiting for darkness. He bent over next to the fire ring and set a lit match into the center of the pile of sticks he had set up two hours earlier. The fire was the culmination of a day that didn't answer any questions but only created new ones.

I sat on the ground and leaned back onto the bench that the Phantom had pulled up to the fire ring. He smoked a joint, choosing not to pass it to me, his eyes flickering orange. Our conversation picked up steam, and I realized that I wasn't drunk but I was under some kind of influence. The influence of the Phantom. I looked at him with great fondness as he spoke. I was aware of the grasp he had on me, but I could do nothing to break the spell—I wasn't even sure that I wanted to. The stars above us fell away from the sky, down towards the horizon. That mountain top felt like the coldest place in Mexico. We huddled ever closer to the fire as the night wore on.

The Phantom's light tone shifted away from humor and towards sincerity. His face was well suited to serious conversation.

"What are you still doing here?" he asked me.

"Here? On this property?"

"In Mexico. You've been here a long time, right?"

"Yep. A long time."

"Why?"

"I like it here. It's beautiful. Good food, nice people. It's cheap to live."

"That's it? You came here because it's easy to live?" he asked with a laugh stuck in his throat.

"That's why I stayed, I think. I came here to write a book. Can you believe that?" I asked myself. "I never got around to writing that book. It never came to me."

"It never came? Books don't come, they are created. Nobody gives you a book, the writer gives the book to everyone else," he said.

"I failed to create a book. I came to Mexico to write, and before that, I went to California to write. And I'm on this mountain with nothing to show." The words I feared the worst felt really good to say aloud.

The Phantom sat quietly, thinking, and then he perked up. An idea had lit up his black eyes.

"Are you familiar with Shiva?" he asked.

"Shiva? I don't think so."

"Shiva is a god. A Hindu god."

"I don't know much about Hinduism." I knew very little about religions other than Christianity.

"That's ok. You don't need to know everything. Do you know where the Hindus live?"

"Is it India?"

"That's right. You're very smart, Otis. Aren't you?"

I felt as though I could be completely honest with the Phantom, and I answered him, "Yes. I think I am." Then, I qualified my statement, "I've been told my whole life that I'm smart. Don't always act that way, though. I'm selfish. I treat people like they're inferior to me. I manipulate people." Telling these truths to fire was much easier than saying them directly to a person.

"I'm sure you do. You're smart. I can tell." The fire put a sheen on the Phantom's brown skin, his cheeks glowing like a stage. "Since you don't know who Shiva is, I will tell you. He is one of the three most important gods in Hinduism. Shiva, along with Brahma and Vishnu, make up the Trimurti, which means the three forms of god."

I smoked my cigarette while I listened to his oration. Transformed from a playful trickster into the chief of a two-man tribe, the Phantom was most captivating.

"It could be argued that Shiva is the most popular god in India. There are many cities dedicated to him and many holidays celebrated in his honor. Each of the three forms, Brahma, Vishnu, and Shiva, have jobs or roles in this life. Actually, it's more of a role in the universe. Shiva's job is the great destroyer. In order for Brahma to create the universe, and for Vishnu to protect the universe, first Shiva must destroy it. Shiva must destroy the entire universe."

"Ok," I said. I wasn't following his line of thinking.

The Phantom opened another beer. He reached his arm behind his head and scratched his back while he yawned. I sat in silence, pouring over his movements, waiting for him to go on.

"We view destruction as an ending. But that's not Shiva's job. He creates by destroying. Destruction is the beginning."

"Sounds nice. Life and death is a cycle, not a beginning and an end."

"See, you *are* smart. And you need to destroy something, don't you? You won't be able to create anything until you destroy." I nodded in agreement. The Phantom stood up, setting his beer down where he had been sitting. He put his cigarette into his mouth and held it there with his clenched lips. The Phantom walked over to the old Ford and opened the driver's side door.

"Come help me." I walked over to my truck and waited for instructions. "Open the door as I have done. You see this column?" He set his strong hands on the steel column that ran up the driver's side of the windshield. I opened the passenger side door and put my hands on the opposite column, in the same position as his. The Phantom leaned into the car, pushing down the clutch with one hand, and with the other, he shifted into neutral. "This mountain is very steep. It will destroy the truck. Are you ready?"

The Phantom and I pushed the old Ford into motion. Slow at first, the truck built momentum as it rolled out towards the edge of the mountain. Ahead of us, the slope fell away into darkness. The truck had gained enough speed to roll on its own. With preternatural instinct, we released our grip at the same time, and the truck was abandoned to the mountain. We both stood at the edge of the decline, watching the truck fall. It rolled into a tumble before it went into a free fall over a cliff. The truck disappeared into the black silence. We waited for a report, and it took a second for the gnarled explosion of crunching, screaming metal to hit our open faces. The truck and the awful noise it made eventually came to a halt.

The Phantom went inside one of the casitas and came back out with a blanket. He laid it out on the ground next to the fire.

"Otis, you should go to sleep." An immense calm fell over me as I laid down on the coarse blanket. Resting on my side, I watched the Phantom's feet walk off, and soon after, I drifted to sleep.

THIRTY-NINE

Waking up under the noon sun, my nose was crusted over from sleeping in the dust. When I opened my eyes, I felt out of place. After a few seconds, I remembered where I was, and then my reality came into focus. The night before stuck to my memory like a fleeting dream, but I had a hunch that the demise of the old Ford was very real. Tire tracks from the spot where I had parked the day before led out off the side of the mountain, erasing any doubts as to what had happened.

I walked over to where the Phantom and I had pushed the old Ford over the edge. The mountain fell away from my feet and ran down at least 2,000 feet in front of me. The path that the old Ford took must have been a long one. There wasn't any evidence of the wreckage, just the tire tracks. Any sort of recovery mission seemed like a waste of time.

Once again, I was searching through a stranger's home. I walked in and out of the tiny houses, looking for the Phantom, and I came up with nothing. The old dog reappeared and gave me a haphazard look. I patted him on the head and had a seat on the bench next to the fire ring. My only possessions were the clothes on my body and my can of tobacco. Smoking my first cigarette of the day, I sat and thought about the borderless possibilities of my future.

Up until that morning, I had been bound to the old Ford. My decisions were usually between a left turn and a right turn and the implications of each. Since I had moved away from Beatrice's apartment, my truck was always with me. I no longer possessed its safety and the freedom it provided, but I wasn't confined to it either. This wasn't a liberating freedom; rather, it was a freedom full of terror and uncertainty. I was exposed. This mountain wasn't a hostel on the beach. I was out in the jungle, the middle of nowhere. Thousands of possibilities were laid out in front of me and spread to the horizon. I could walk down the road that I came up on, or I could just walk straight down the mountain. I could wait for someone to return to the property, or I could leave that second. I wondered, 'Should I go back to sleep?' Maybe I would wake up to a different reality. Running through the different options in my head, my cigarette was getting small, and I wanted to have my mind made up by the time it was gone.

After all the thinking, I didn't settle on a plan of any sort, I just acted. There was an empty plastic jug laying out on the side of the house and a tap in the kitchen of the house closest to me. I filled the jug with cold water that came from deep inside the mountain. On the road, I walked back and forth down the switchbacks, down to the base of the mountain, and out past the shrubland where Esila had jumped out of the truck. And on I went, walking with no particular destination in mind.

It was a few hours of walking before I came upon a town. Not much of a town, more of a collection of people and buildings with no real sense of cohesion. A man selling quesadillas for five pesos each caught my eye as it seemed to be the only source of food around. I reached into my pocket and pulled out a few hundred pesos. It dawned on me that those pesos would need to last me a while. The old Ford, wherever it was, whatever state it was in, held my ATM card, and with it, my access to any money for a while.

I ate my quesadilla on the sidewalk next to the stand. While I ate, a shift occurred—a shift of the mind. I'd been in

Mexico for quite some time, but there was never a moment where I consciously decided that I wanted to be in Mexico. I was just there. It seemed like the right thing to be doing. While sitting on the curb, eating my quesadilla, I made the conscious decision that I didn't want to be in Mexico anymore.

I thought about all the people that had come and gone during my travels. I remembered my mother and father. My uncle. I thought about Ruiz and the guys at La Posada. I remembered how I had left things with Beatrice, and I wondered if Doyle was able to get out of the situation I left him in. I thought about how happy Lillian and her boyfriend were when I parted from them. I finished my quesadilla and had nothing left to do but sit on a grimy curb and have a long overdue cry.

The man who had made the quesadilla looked down at me sitting below him. He watched me cry for a second and then asked me if I was ok. I nodded to show him that I was, and the only thing I could think to say was, "Este Quesadilla es muy bueno." He shook his head and looked away, giving me a bit of privacy during my public display of emotion.

Back walking on the road, cars passed me by with great force. 'Maybe driving would be faster,' I thought. In the next town, I caught a collectivo headed back to Jalpan. The collectivo was packed full of locals sitting on homemade benches. Mostly women, who I assumed were headed to the market in town or maybe headed to work. My fellow passengers examined me with interest. A little girl pointed at me and asked her mother why I was there. Her mother shushed her and told her to look out the window. The little girl looked at the fellow passengers around her and then back to me. The ride was short and only cost me seven pesos. The next collectivo went to Rioverde and then on to San Luis Potosi. Each ride was cheap, but they were starting to add up, so I decided to try my hand at hitchhiking.

Out of San Luis Potosi and headed north, I stuck my thumb out like I had seen people do in Albuquerque. Cars passed by with a whoosh, and the heat rose up off the highway in clear rivulets. Eventually, a large truck carrying empty pallets pulled over. The man said he could take me as far as Saltillo. He couldn't take me any further. He was loading up in Saltillo and then headed back south. I hopped in, and he asked me why I didn't have any bags.

"No tengo nada, Señor." He laughed and pushed the truck into gear. As we started driving, he wound his window down and spat a stream of tar-colored tobacco from his lips.

The man, Antonio, presented a pack of ready-rolled cigarettes and offered me one. I accepted and used one of his matches to light it. He put a cigarette in his mouth and I lit it for him. Antonio didn't talk much, and I wasn't interested in explaining myself, so the pairing worked out well. I dozed off for an hour or two while he drove, and when I woke up, we were getting close to Saltillo. Antonio offered me another cigarette and we both smoked our way into town. Jumping down from the cab, I thanked him for the ride, and he told me to stay away from Monterrey. I didn't ask why because I wasn't headed to Monterrey.

It was getting to be nighttime, and I didn't know where to go, so I walked into the center of town. There weren't many people around in the square. I laid down on the steps of a church and shut my eyes. A lady came out of the church, woke me up, and got me up off the stairs. She asked me if I had eaten. I told her that I hadn't in a while, and she told me to follow her into the church, so I did.

She took me into a very simple room with a wooden table and some wooden chairs, the floor made of worn sandstone. I took a seat and the women left the room. Five minutes later, she came back to the room with a small plate of rice and beans and two homemade tortillas. I ate like a dog. The lady watched in silence as I wiped my plate clean with the last of my tortilla. She took me to a room in the back of the church where a few men and one woman were lying on cots. She gave me a tattered bed sheet and pointed me to an empty cot.

I laid down and fell asleep as if I was programmed to do so. I dreamt of horses. I was a ranch hand and I was taking a wily gelding from the barn out to a fenced in pasture when the horse started snorting and bucking. I dropped the reins, and the horse ran violent, angry, and scared. I sat on the fence watching him, waiting for him to tire out so I could pick up the reins and get him back in the corral.

When I woke up, the other guests around me were still asleep. Outside, the sun was getting ready to come up over the horizon. Standing in the front of the church, I was just in time to see an old two-tone Ford truck pull up. This vehicle was just like the one I had pushed off the mountain. Instead of a camper on the back, this truck had a beat-up empty bed. I made eye contact with the driver and he smiled. I stuck my thumb up to show him I needed a ride, and he waved me over to the driver's side window. He asked me where I was going.

"Tejas."

"Tejas? I can't take you that far. I'm headed north though, up to Chihuahua. I'll take you there, if you want." The man had a kind smile tucked up under a shiny black mustache, and he wore a cowboy hat that framed his rugged, handsome face. I hopped in and introduced myself.

Two days earlier, back when I was sitting on the curb in that old jungle town, I decided that I wanted to leave Mexico, but I didn't have a destination in mind. I just knew that I didn't want to be in Mexico anymore. It wasn't until I had heard the word "Tejas" come out of my mouth that I realized where I was headed.

FORTY

The man that I hitched a ride with was Efrain Garcia. Not too long into the trip, Efrain told me the story of his life. He owned and operated a cattle ranch outside of Chihuahua. When he was my age, he crossed the American border into Texas so that he could work at a grocery store in San Antonio. He lived in the US for ten years, where he learned English and saved up enough money to move back to Mexico. Upon his return, he bought a ranch in the area where he grew up.

Efrain's professional life started much earlier than his move across the border to Texas. When he was eleven, he left his family home behind. "Things got too rough there," he told me. He spent his childhood hopping from ranch to ranch, working odd jobs, shoveling shit, and picking weeds. His pay was usually tendered in rice and beans and a place to stay. Efrain told me that many young kids in Mexico still live like this. To emphasize his point, he said, "All I owned was a machete and my huaraches. I didn't have nothing more," he said.

"When you're a small kid and you don't have nobody to hold you, nobody is there to love you, then you don't care about nothing. When you don't care about nothing, then you can do anything. You can cross borders, you can work for no money, and you can live with five other men in the same room. I've done all these things, and none of them were as hard as that first couple weeks when I was a boy, out on my own."

By the time he was twenty, Efrain had learned how to raise cattle and run a profitable ranch. He decided that the only way he would get his own ranch was to go to America. He went on to tell me of the life he left behind in San Antonio. He had a girlfriend that he planned on marrying, but she refused to return to Mexico. "Her past was too painful to return to," he said, then added, "I wanted to live my life. She wanted to survive. We couldn't make that work, you know?"

When Efrain returned to Mexico, he bought a piece of land and found a woman to marry him, Rita. "After a lot of tries, God gave us a child," he said. He pulled a picture of his daughter from his wallet and handed it to me. She was sitting on top of a chestnut horse. He told me that she loved horses and that she was a fancy girl. He laughed as he said "fancy." "My daughter has her own horse. When I was a boy, I didn't even know a kid could own a horse; it didn't seem possible," he said. He was proud of his daughter and jealous of her. "She is a great reminder to me. She remind me that I made something of myself."

"What were you doing in Mexico?" he asked as the conversation shifted away from his story and into mine. It's not easy to tell a man who has worked so hard about all the time you've spent fucking around. Efrain listened to my stories without too much judgment until I told him about pushing my truck off a mountain. He laughed and said, "That man give you drugs. You don't seem that stupid on your own. Either that, or you fucking crazy, man." We both laughed, Efrain harder than me.

"I don't get it," he said to me out of the blue. "Your home, it sounds nice. Why you don't want to be there?"

"Things with my folks got complicated. My uncle told me that he is actually my father. All along, everybody had lied to me. I just decided I didn't want to be a part of them anymore. I figured it was best to go out on my own," I said.

"I don't blame you. I did the same thing. Do your mother and your father love you? Do they treat you well?" Efrain asked.

"They do."

"And this uncle who is your real dad, does he love you?"

"Yes, he does."

Efrain thought for a while and then said, "That's good. You're going back to a good home."

We laughed a lot during the drive. Efrain was a very funny guy and a careful listener. He asked me about raising sheep, and he seemed to be impressed by how much I knew. We smoked cigarettes and ate tamales that Efrain bought from a lady on the side of the road. We broke through the edge of the Chihuahuan desert. The smell of mesquite trees filled me with the sensation of being on the ranch. In a different country, driving to a town I had never been to before, I felt like I was home.

Efrain invited me to stay with him and his family, and I was happy that he did. When we got to his ranch, his wife, Rita, had dinner ready for us. We sat down to a full spread of Cabrito al Pastor and rice and beans. I ate so much that my skin stretched out over my belly and felt like it might split if I moved too much. I met Efrain's daughter and spoke to his wife about my travels through Mexico. She was a very friendly woman, a tiny human with silver hair and freckled cheeks. Satisfied from the best meal that I had in Mexico, I took to the front porch to watch the sunset. Efrain brought out two cigars and we smoked as the desert hills rouged up pink, then went blue, and finally fell into the black shadow of night.

The next morning, Efrain offered to drive me to the bus station in Chihuahua. From there, I could catch a collectivo to Ojinaga, and from there, he told me, I could just walk right over the border. Rita handed me a brown paper bag, translucent from the greasy delicacies inside—leftover

Cabrito al Pastor wrapped in tortillas. She hugged me goodbye, and I thanked her for her generosity.

When we got to the bus station in Chihuahua, Efrain said his goodbyes. I thanked him for all he had done for me. Before I left for the collectivo, he stopped me and offered some parting words: "I think you are a little lost right now. Don't worry, you'll find it. Just don't forget, men twice as smart as you have fallen on their face. You aren't too clever to work. Nobody is."

FORTY-ONE

I caught the collectivo to Ojinaga, and from there, I was able to walk over the border, just as Efrain said. The border agents looked at me like I was a two-headed dog and questioned me thoroughly.

"Where's your shit?" the agent said. He was a big man with dark, sunken eyes. The only explanation for why he was in such a foul mood was that he was being asked to do his job.

"I don't have anything, sir."

"How long you been in Mexico?"

"I'm not sure exactly. Maybe a year."

The agent scratched at his shaved head while he shook it side to side. He let out a big sigh. "Look, buddy. I don't know what you're trying to pull here, but we'll figure you out. Might as well save everyone the time and just tell me what's going on."

"I'm just trying to get home, sir."

"I bet you are. But that doesn't explain why you come here empty-handed after being down there for an entire year. You been wearing those same clothes this whole time?"

"No, sir. Just the last week or so," I said, bracing myself.

"Well, get ready to take them all off. Lord knows what kind of stink we're gonna find under there."

The agent walked me into a room with nothing in it. He told me to get undressed. "All the way," he said. He and another agent searched my body inside and out. "Why haven't you been showering?" the man asked after he finished his search.

After another hour of making me wait, they cut me loose. I walked out of the customs office and into the sunny blue skies of America.

Presidio, Texas, was the town that I crossed into on the other side of the border. It wasn't all that different from Ojinaga, but there were small things that I noticed. Fast food restaurants and gas stations sold gas by the gallon rather than the liter. New trucks and street lights and familiar traffic signs. I was back in the US.

I caught a ride from a man who had also just crossed the border, Andre, an artist, who when asked where he was headed, said, "I'm based in Marfa."

When I hopped in his hatchback Honda, he looked me over and said, "Traveling light, huh?" I nodded and sat back into the seat, drained of my ambitions to chat. "What were you doing down there?"

"Traveling," I said, not in the mood to talk. "You?"

"Getting materials for my next project. Took some pictures, drank some beer. A little work, a little play."

"Sounds nice."

"It was fine. I don't speak much Spanish. Been a few days since I've spoken to anyone who speaks good English."

"I'll try to keep up, I'm a little pooped."

"Don't worry about it, I'm not much of a talker."

Andre listened to jazz on the radio and smoked cigarettes that were wrapped in some kind of brown paper. After a few hours, he stopped off at a gas station to take a shit, and while he did so, he let me borrow his cell phone. I called my folks.

"Hello." It was my mother's voice.

"It's me, Otis." The silence that ensued was long enough for me to accept the fact that I was an asshole.

"Otis," my mother said after a while. She was crying into the phone. "Where are you? Where have you been?"

"I'm outside of Marfa. I've been in Mexico a while."

"Your Uncle Grant died. You missed his funeral. Did you know that?"

"No, ma'am. I did not." There wasn't anything left to say over the phone other than, "I'm coming home."

My mother hung up, and I waited for Andre to finish his pit stop. When Andre got back in the car, I handed him my phone. I turned towards the passenger side window; I didn't want him to see my face. I felt so stupid for being ashamed, which made me feel more shame, but I just couldn't let him see me like that. When we made it to Marfa, I changed my pesos to dollars and then spent it all on a bus ticket to Kermit. After arriving in Kermit, walking away from the bus stop, I ran into an old classmate of mine, Travis.

"Howdy there, Travis," I said, getting his attention. It took Travis a second to recognize me. We hadn't seen each other since high school. "I know it's a strange thing to ask, but could I borrow your phone?"

"Whatcha need a phone for?" Travis asked, looking at my tattered body and clothes.

"I just got back into town, and I need to call the house to see if I can get a ride."

"I'm parked just over there. I don't mind driving you out there," he said and motioned over to his truck. "Haven't seen you around in a while. Been years, I think," Travis said once we were driving.

"It has been years, hasn't it. This is a nice truck you got."

"Thanks, just got it last year."

"You bought it?"

"All I do is work. Figured I'd buy myself a nice truck, you know?"

"It's nice."

"So, where ya been?"

"What do you mean?"

"You said you just got back into town. Where were you?"

"Mexico mostly. California too."

"What was it like?" Travis asked.

"What's what like?"

"I don't know. All of it I guess. Never been out of the state before, other than up to New Mexico."

"It's different, but it's also the same."

Travis thought on my words, and we were silent the rest of the trip. When we pulled up to the boundary of the property, I had him drop me off on the road where the long driveway started. I thanked him for the ride and told him I'd buy him a beer next time I was in town.

FORTY-TWO

As I walked down the sand and pebble road, I smoked one of the ready-rolled Mexican cigarettes that I'd bought in Ojinaga. About halfway down the drive, I stopped to finish my cigarette out on the road. I watched the quiet buildings of the ranch from afar. Everything looked so peaceful from out there. No movement, no stirring of any kind, not a sound to be heard. Out there, nothing had changed yet.

When I walked up on it, the house was still—there were no signs that anyone was home. I knocked on the door and waited. My father answered the door. He didn't say anything, just wrapped me up in his arms and pulled me in tight. My mother wasn't there; she was in the kitchen house, working on dinner. My father and I walked out to the mess hall, side by side. We hadn't seen each other in so long, but we were both comfortable with not talking.

When she saw me, my mother dropped everything and ran up to hug me. She cried, and the rest of the folks in the kitchen said hello and commented on how much I had changed, how different I looked. When a little kid runs away from home, their parents go from anger to worry, and then when the kid comes back home, it all ends in relief. Another one of Otis Billings' lucky breaks. In the kitchen, facing the faces of the ranch, nobody pushed me to explain myself. Nobody asked me tough questions. I didn't have to confront any of the pain I had caused. Letting things pass by in silence felt like I had found safety.

After the hugs and kisses and back pats, my father and I left my mother to finish up her cooking. As we walked my father said to me, "Damn, boy, you need a bath. You smell like a Mexican street dog. Face needs a shavin' too." I thought he was just busting my balls until I caught a glimpse of myself in the mirror on my way into the shower. It had been a long time since I had seen myself, let alone studied my appearance. The man standing in the mirror was a ragged sort. Bleached-out hair falling past the eyes, a deep street tan, cheeks thinned out and hollow, a mess of stray whiskers that didn't quite make up a full beard. Somehow I had lost a good bit of weight without noticing. Instead of a stranger, I saw myself in the mirror, perhaps for the first time.

When dinner was served, all the familiar faces were there, minus the Randall family, who had moved away. Two new families had moved onto the ranch, the De Sotos and the Horns. I had changed and the ranch had changed, both in ways that I didn't fully understand at the time. It felt as though the eyes of the room were fixed on me, and whenever someone talked out of earshot, I assumed they were discussing me.

That night, I waited for my folks to go to bed before going out to survey the ranch. I smoked cigarettes as I leaned up against the pasture fence. The sheep were restless, walking in chopped steps, ducking their heads to eat, keeping their eyes up, scanning for threats. I weaved in and out of the great maze of buildings and into the barn that stored all of our hay. That familiar smell of dried-up dusty grass was so thick, it coated the back of my throat. When I left the hay barn, my uncle's office called out to me. Forbidden darkness surrounded the little cabin—a lone shadow on the halogen glowed ranch. With apprehension, I approached the cabin. This was my uncle's tomb, and I wasn't sure what the protocol was for entering a tomb. I opened the door and walked into the sleeping office.

My uncle's office hadn't changed since the last time I sat down at his desk to talk with him. Since he told me who he was. The cushion on his leather desk chair was still indented from his ass as if he had just risen from it. I sat down in the chair and felt the grooves. I rolled a cigarette on his desk and lit it, leaning back into the chair. Smoking in my uncle's sanctuary was a special type of trespass. Despite the feelings of wrongness, I enjoyed sitting in that chair. I was reminded of how I had always wanted to.

The next morning, while I was asleep, my mother came into my room and sat on my bed. I woke up to her looking at me in an adoring fashion.

"Breakfast is ready. Will you be coming down soon?" she asked with a hint of hesitation.

"Yes, ma'am, I'll get dressed and come on down."

"Your father's going to talk with you." She raised up from the bed and walked towards the door to my room.

"Before I talk to him, maybe we should have a talk of our own." My mother's face twisted a little and then softened.

"I know we need to talk, but let your father say his piece first. It's important." She waited for me to agree to these terms before she left me to get dressed.

I got my pants and shirt on, then my boots. My father looked up from his breakfast and watched me walk down the final few stairs. A plate was sitting next to him piled high with eggs, bacon, and toast.

I sat down next to my dad and dug into my plate, my stomach a black hole from being on the road. My dad set his fork down and took a sip of his coffee.

"Mom, do you think I could have a cup of coffee?"

"Sure, hun." My mother poured a cup and put it down in front of me. She looked at my father, and he took the cue.

"Your mom told you about Uncle Grant's passing, right?" he asked.

"Yes, sir. I was awful sorry to hear that. I should have been here for the funeral. I'm sorry I missed it." I remembered the kid who had run away from home. The consequences of running away were delayed because of the relief his parent's felt, but they weren't forgotten.

"We know you are, son. We sure wish you could've been here too." My father took another sip of coffee and then set his mug down. He folded his arms around his ribs and sat back a bit in his chair. "When you were a boy, you spent a lot of time with Grant. Probably more than I did."

"Yes, sir, I did."

"Did he ever tell you why he was showing you all the things he was showing you?"

"No, sir."

"My brother had a plan for everyone and everything. But he was a secretive man." My father looked up at my mom, who was watching him with a somber intent. "Your uncle died so suddenly that it threw the ranch into a tailspin. When Grant was buried and the dust cleared, we were all surprised to find your name on his will."

"He left me something?"

"Your uncle thought very highly of you."

"I guess so." I looked at my mom, and she looked sad.

"Grant left you the ranch," my father said, the words scratching his throat as they passed.

"I don't get it."

"He willed you the whole place. The ranch is yours. What's not to get?" He paused and looked down at the table, spinning his mug by the handle at a perfect ninety degrees. "I'd love to ask him why. I really would, but he ain't around to answer. I suppose he had his reasons." My dad picked up a piece of toast, intending to finish his meal, but I hadn't heard all I needed to hear.

"Who's been running the ranch?"

"We all have," he said, his toast bobbing around his mouth. He finished chewing his food. "It ain't been easy. Now that you're back, you're going to need to figure some shit out."

My dad spoke for the people on the ranch. All those eyes on me the night before, they didn't care about where I had been, they cared about where I was going, where I was going to take them.

Uncle Grant didn't bestow upon me a normal business; what he built was more like a religion, or a cult. Maybe commune is the right word. The folks on the ranch, my parents included, were Grant's disciples, and they were lost without him. In the time between Grant's death and my return, everybody was awaiting the arrival of their new messiah. It sounds dramatic now, but the pressure of that moment made this secular man think spiritually. The entire ranch had released a great big sigh of relief upon my return, and that great big sigh sat right down on my chest.

Going back to Texas, back to my childhood home, in my mind was supposed to be a temporary stay, a visit. Before breakfast that morning, I had thought about going to live in California, or maybe Albuquerque. I even thought about going somewhere new after I got everything in Texas all straightened out. Coming home and inheriting the place was like going to a wedding and realizing it was you that was getting married. The ranch was my new life, my future, whether or not I wanted it to be.

I didn't sleep that night. Instead of resting, I smoked cigarettes and thought about what the fuck I was going to do. 'Should I sell the place?' I'm ashamed to admit it, but selling the ranch sounded real good right then. Even though I wanted the easy fix, I knew the long painful route was going to have to be the way I went. I tried to remember all the things Grant had taught me. The years away had caused the memories to fade, not only of Grant's training but of Grant himself. I tried to imagine his voice and what he would have told me to do. Nothing came to me. He was gone.

FORTY-THREE

After Uncle Grant died, the folks on the ranch were like a train with no conductor—they just ran in a straight line, they couldn't read the signs or switch tracks. Money got spent on the wrong things, bills went neglected, and there wasn't a single person who thought it would be necessary to do any accounting. My dad and others were making decisions, but nobody recorded any of them. I worked every day for three months just to get the books straight, and doing taxes that first year was a nightmare.

It almost broke me, and it almost broke the ranch, but we got to the other side of all the trouble, miraculously intact. Two years after I took over, it was almost like Grant never died, at least from a business perspective. The responsibility I took on was monumental. The finances, the accounting, working with all the vendors and all the businesses—getting it all straightened out was very difficult, but in some ways, it was the easiest part. Finances and accounting are concrete, there's a formula to follow—a formula that my uncle had, at least in part, taught me, and as long as I followed the formula, the ranch stayed afloat.

Grant taught me the numbers side of the ranch, but he hadn't taught me the nuances of the people. I went from a kid with no responsibilities to a man that was depended on. The folks on the ranch now looked at me like I used to look at Grant. I always knew that my uncle was the lord of this place, but it wasn't until I replaced him that I understood the complexities of his position.

Running the operations side of the ranch and running the human resources side of the ranch were two very different challenges. Daily, I made decisions that affected mothers and fathers, the families of people that were my senior, people that had helped raise me. Telling these people what to do and how to do it was an out-of-body experience. When I first gave orders, I braced for a disastrous backlash. Lucky for me, the folks on the ranch were so desperate for a leader that by the time I got back to Texas, they were willing to accept anyone as their boss. That's not to say I didn't have my authority challenged from time to time, but I never lost favor amongst the majority.

Just as I had seen my uncle do my entire childhood, I projected a veneer of calm and control whenever I made a public appearance. On the inside, at the emotional level, I struggled. Needing all the support I could just to survive, I leaned into the people around me. My father filled in the knowledge gaps that Grant didn't have time to teach me. Grant taught me how to run the business, but my dad knew how to run the actual ranch. The tasks, the chores, the duties of the day-to-day, managing the people that managed the property—my father kept it all straight and taught me the processes that he kept in his mind. Of course, Grant had oversight, but he trusted my father with the implementations of his processes and procedures. The business was in trouble when I returned, but the sheep were still alive, the fences were still up, and the vegetable gardens were producing. This was my father's doing. He maintained the infrastructure of the place, and if it weren't for him, there wouldn't have been anything for me to save.

My mother was an expert on the social dynamics of the ranch. Without her, we would have struggled to keep people fed, washed, and educated. She could sense issues rising up in the families and had a plan in place before things had a chance to break down. It's a real testament to her abilities that the other families didn't pick up and leave as soon as Grant died. My mother, the great diplomat. She quelled fear, settled squabbles, soothed tensions from one group to the next, one family to the other. She was the family counselor, a mentor, nutritionist, chef, and a friend to all of the people on the ranch. Tough as stone and soft as virgin wool, she had a warm mind and loved to share it with others.

I talked to Efrain Garcia every single week; his guidance was crucial. He knew how to run a ranch better than anyone I knew, and he became a mentor to me. If Uncle Grant had given me a Bachelor's degree in ranching, then Efrain gave me a Master's. We spent hours on the phone together during that terrible first year. He knew how to talk me down from abandoning the seemingly insurmountable task in front of me.

He would always say, "You don't need to take care of everyone forever, you just need to get through this day. Then, maybe the next one."

Efrain was a great man, and we stayed close up until his death. His little girl grew into a woman, and she took over his ranch when Efrain passed. Just as I had leaned on Efrain, she leaned on me, and I was more than happy to pay that debt.

After a while, I was able to grasp the huge amount of responsibility that had been given to me, and from there, my life as a West Texas sheep rancher normalized. From time to time, I'd stay up all night while my mind raced through every possible disaster that could come. Looking back, I marvel at the calm my Uncle Grant was able to produce at all times. He must have been stressed as hell, but he never showed it. The behavior of my uncle was a case study on how to be a public figure. Grant was like a great politician in the way that he never allowed anyone to feel like his plan wasn't working. I realized that part of that was keeping yourself secret. The less I was seen, the less projection I had to do. Thinking back to my childhood, it became clear to me that Uncle Grant had seldom made himself available for questioning. Solitude became my friend. Dinner each night was my daily public appearance, which worked well since everyone had their mouths full.

When the madness settled, I spent some time looking inward, at myself—something I hadn't done enough of in my life. It went against every instinct that I had, but my emotional mind was able to convince my rational mind that self-reflection was the next step in becoming the person I wanted to be. Not only did I reflect on my life, but I found myself spending a lot of time reflecting on Uncle Grant's. His life, which was so mysterious to me as a child, made a lot more sense now that I was sitting at his desk. Like him, I never married, and like him, I never got too close. There have been some ladies, of course, some nice relationships, but the ranch is a different world, and it doesn't make sense for everyone. I work too much, I smoke too much, and I don't bend too often. My lifestyle isn't all that conducive to building a lasting bond. Maybe someday I'll figure it out, just like I figured out the ranch. I'll work and work, and one day, I'll show up to a wedding that happens to be mine.

The world outside has been changing ever since I came back home, but things don't change on the ranch as they do out there. When I took over the ranch, it felt like a monumental shift, and then, life went on as if nothing had changed. Things don't look much different; the day-to-day life is just about the same and we still make our living off of raising sheep. I'm right back to where I started, in more ways than location. Every day, I get little reminders of my childhood; my whole life a reeling cycle of deja vu.

FORTY-FOUR

As you may have noticed, I glossed over all of the work it took to get the ranch back in order, and to be honest, I did that because it's not that interesting. The story of the people is more compelling, especially that of my mother and my father. Confronting my past had been on my mind for years, and when I returned to the ranch, there was a real sense of urgency to do so. An urgency that I allowed myself to ignore because there was so much work to be done and so much uncertainty, avoiding the obvious tension felt easier than uprooting the painful truths. Avoiding painful truths was something I had been doing my entire life. Reflexively, I focused on the things that needed to get done, not the things on my mind. That worked for a little while, but in the end, I just couldn't shake the seed that had been planted inside of me. Not only would the seed not go away, but it was growing, taking root. I wanted to forget the whole thing and just move on. There was societal and familial conditioning that told me forgetting was the right thing to do. Just get over it. It would have been easier that way, but something in me pushed for the difficult path, advocated for the tough conversation, and I couldn't resist the urge to explore my origins.

"Is it too early to talk?" I asked my mother one Sunday morning. My father was sleeping in, and my mother was still in her nightclothes.

"I look a mess. I'm barely awake," she said.

"I think it's time."

"Oh, you do?" she asked. Her voice lost its raggedness. "Let's you and me head out onto the porch then."

She put on her winter coat over top of her nightgown and slipped her bare feet into her boots. I followed her out onto the porch, and we sat down on the pine bench in front of the kitchen window.

"I'll just tell you the whole story. You're right, it's time. It's long past time. The doctors thought Grant would get better, but he knew he was dying; he could sense it somehow. That's when he told me that he had told you. We'd all been keeping that secret so long, longer than you've been alive. I know that's obvious, but it still seems crazy to think about, a secret being older than a grown man. Of course, Grant didn't tell you the whole story. That's how he was. He had to leave a mystery for you."

"I tried to forget about what he told me."

"Not surprised by that. It's painful. That's why we all kept it quiet for so long. Never thought Grant would be the one to spill the beans. Guess I should've."

"All he told me was that he's my dad. Nothing else."

"No matter what he told you, he isn't your father. Not really. Your dad and I tried to get pregnant for a while, but we just couldn't. You know your dad, he didn't like the idea of going to the doctor, didn't want to do all the tests and have everything exposed. Small town thinking. I went in and got some tests done, and the doctor told me I was fertile as can be. Nothing wrong with me, and I wanted a baby so bad. I knew your dad wasn't going to do anything about it, and even if he did, I don't think he could have. So I came up with a plan. It seems crazy now, but I wouldn't change any of it. I wouldn't.

"After I took the tests, I went to see your uncle. I'll just tell you straight away, I asked Grant to get me pregnant. Figured he was the next closest thing to your father. I knew you'd have your father's blood in you, and for some reason that just seemed right to me. Your uncle Grant had his reservations, of course."

"Does dad know this?"

"Of course he does. I got pregnant, and Grant and I kept quiet, but then the hormones built and built inside me, and I couldn't keep it from bursting out. I had to tell your father. He didn't take it well. There was so much tension it felt like the ranch was either going to blow up or cave in on itself, and I couldn't decide which would happen first."

"How did you calm him down?"

"Grant told him that the baby and I were staying, told your father that I wasn't going anywhere, so he better get used to it. For a while, that just made your dad more mad, but he came around to the whole thing. Your father wanted a kid just as bad as I did. Neither of us wanted it the way it happened, but we got you, and once you were born, everything smoothed out, and we loved you so much that it seemed like it was worth all the pain."

"I'm gonna ask cause I gotta know. You had sex with Grant?"

"I did."

"You had sex once, and boom, you were pregnant?"

"Not exactly how it happened, no."

Looking at my mother, I saw her as an individual, a sovereign region. Her imperfections, her insecurities, her personality came out in a way I had never seen and didn't fully understand.

"How'd you fix it all? Surely my arrival didn't mend all fences."

"No, it didn't. It's nice to remember it that way, but that isn't so much how it happened. For a while, we beat around the bush, guarded ourselves, and avoided talking about it. It was a new kind of pressure. And then one day, we sat down together—your dad, your uncle, and me, and we told each other how we felt about the whole situation. It took all the strength I had to wrangle those two into the same room. Can you imagine? Nothing will ever fix what happened, but talking about it and working through our feelings made it so we could see each other's perspective."

After talking to my mom, I realized this whole situation had very little to do with me. I traveled all over this country and another country looking to hide from a reality that had, for the most part, already been reconciled. What a waste of gas.

My mother went back inside. "I'm freezing out here. I'm going to put some coffee on."

As my mother walked into the house, I was free again—a freedom I hadn't had since Grant pulled me into his office and told me his secret. Owning the ranch didn't seem like such a burden after that conversation with my mother. In comparison, repairing the relationships I had fractured felt much more daunting.

FORTY-FIVE

As soon as I accepted the reality that I was back on the ranch for good, I took over my uncle's office and his house. The house was next to barren when I moved into it, and that's because the office was where the man truly had lived his life. The little old cabin that housed Grant's office was a museum in a way, full of mystery and clues about who he was. When I was a kid, I had always wanted to explore Grant's office. It was the only place on the ranch that wasn't community property. Finally, when it became mine, I was allowed to unwrap the mysteries of the office, and in a way, Grant. Somehow I had never noticed that he had a bookshelf. Probably because it was out of view from the visitor's chair at his desk. Would have pegged Grant for a nonfiction reader, the type that read books about wars and past presidents, but the bookshelf told a different story, as he had a nice collection of fiction.

After my working day was done, my favorite thing to do was smoke cigarettes at my desk and read through Grant's collection. My private release. One day, I sat smoking and reading when a knock on the door stirred me from my book. At first, I thought the sound had come from my head. I pulled the door open, expecting to see nobody, but it was my father at the other side.

"Hey there," I said. My father didn't speak; he just stood there, sizing me up. "What's up?" I asked.

"Wanted to have a chat."

"Come on in then." My father walked in and I returned to my chair, and he sat down in the same chair that I used to sit in when I would visit Uncle Grant. A cigarette burned in the ashtray. He looked at the smoldering cigarette, whitish-gray smoke spindling off the tip, and then he looked up at me. I picked the cigarette up and put it to my lips. "What did you want to talk about?" I asked.

"I wanted to have a word with you cause there's some things I don't know about you," he said and then paused. "It's hard to say exactly why I came to talk to you, but I felt compelled to."

"Ok then. Let's talk."

"I don't know what I want to say just yet. I got a feeling more than I got a topic. Figured if I came to you, all the things that I want to say would come to me. I do know that I want to be frank with you. I want to tell you the truth, and I want you to do the same for me."

"Seems like a good plan."

"What were you doing out there on the road?"

I sat back in my chair and looked up at the ceiling. "I'm not sure how to answer that."

"You left for a couple of years, years I don't know nothing about. Then you come back this whole other person. And me, and your mom, we don't know what the hell went on out there," he said, motioning his hand to emphasize the world that existed outside of my office. "I guess that's why I'm here. Yep, I think that's it. You been home for a while, but it just dawned on me the other day. I said to myself, 'I wonder what Otis was doing that whole time.'"

I thought about his question, and then I thought about how I should answer. "Mostly fucking around, if I'm to be honest with you, which you did request that I do. I think I may have started out with good intentions, but without a proper foundation, my plans were destined to go awry, and they did."

"Did you ever write anything?"

"No, sir, I did not. Not anything of worth."

"How come?"

"Good question. Not sure I've meditated on that enough to answer it, though." I picked up my cigarette and took a deep hit from it. My jaw swung up and my lungs fired out a stream of smoke towards the rafters. "I guess it's hard to write when you don't like to be alone."

"Were you any good?"

"No, sir, I wasn't. I don't think so."

"Why not?" my father asked with the quickness of a swordsman parlaying his enemy's attack.

"For a long time, I thought it was because I didn't have the right mix of life experiences. A young man probably doesn't have enough perspective to create well-rounded characters."

"Sounds like an excuse," my father said.

"Yes, sir. I've got a lot of excuses. Maybe I didn't want to face the fact that I don't have the skill or the discipline necessary to write. I think with writing, and perhaps many other things, discipline is the skill." I broke out my pouch of tobacco from the desk drawer. "Grant knew something that we both didn't."

"And what's that?"

"That I ain't no writer. That I was destined to run this ranch."

My father rubbed his jaw; the stubble on his face made the sound of wind blowing through dry grass. "This is your destiny?"

"I suppose so. I don't know if I believe in predetermined outcomes quite like that, but I don't think Grant would leave something up to chance either."

My father's face whitened and relaxed. I took my newly rolled cigarette into my mouth and pulled a match across the strike on the side of the matchbox.

"You're quite the smoker these days, aren't you?"

I nodded my head and exhaled a puff of smoke. "Want one?" I asked.

My father gruffed out a little chuckle but didn't answer.

"You mind if I ask you a couple questions? Before you leave."

"Shoot," my father said, looking into my eyes.

"You ever talk to Grant about a succession plan?"

"Not directly. There were some hints and some comments that maybe I misinterpreted."

"You sure seemed surprised to find my name on that will. Shit, you seemed like you were still in shock five months later when I showed back up," I said with a laugh. My father's face re-reddened.

"I was surprised. Perhaps I let some wishful thinking in. When you do that, it can poison your whole mind, cloud everything up and make you see through a lens of bullshit. I can admit I'm guilty of that." My father looked down at his hands; they were folded in his lap. He spoke again, "You getting the ranch was one of the great betrayals of my life. There won't be another like it, least I hope not."

"It must have been hard for you. To keep working this place like nothing happened. To pour your soul into something that had been ripped away from you in such a way."

"It wasn't never mine. Thinking it was is where I messed up." My father stood, and then I stood. Before I could think of anything to say, he turned and walked out of my office.

That conversation dug up the feelings I had successfully buried since I returned to the ranch. There were layers to my avoidance. Mulling over my failure as a writer and the time I spent out on the road, I tried to interpret what it all meant. I treated people badly, I used women as vehicles of validation, and I engaged in a lot of one-sided friendships. I took and took and never gave anyone anything in return.

There were so many regrets about the way I had conducted myself, but the fact that I never wrote anything worth a shit was a whole other haunting. My failure to write a book somehow made all the bad shit I'd done worse. This was just more twisted selfishness on my part, but it's how I felt, and I couldn't help holding it up over all my other failures.

There was so much lying, and I needed to reckon with that. All of those times I had told people I was a writer, it was all a big lie. I had been told I was smart my whole childhood, and like a fool, I believed it. I used my intelligence to justify my actions. My obsession with my past indiscretions was all focused on the idea that there must have been people talking behind my back, laughing at my posturing and my bullshit philosophizing. The people that knew the truth, Beatrice and many others, knew that I was a fraud, and forever I remain that way—a fraud in their eyes.

Wishing to hear what they had said, I wanted to be embarrassed by them, exposed. I wanted to go back in time and indulge in the hatred of my non-believers. My self-deprecation was consuming and borderline lustful. Feeling terrible leads to the belief that terrible things *should* be happening.

Revelations about myself came often while I sat at my desk, alone with my mind. They all centered around my time on the road and my life in general. I thought about how I was able to make false promises because I was protected by the time it takes to write a novel. I justified my bullshit by convincing myself that I would write the novel later, at the next stop, the next town. I thought my lies weren't lies yet because I still had time to make them the truth. I moved around a lot, which meant I always had a new group of people to tell, "I'm working on a novel." When I left each place, I assumed the people I had lied to forgot about it. Chances were, nobody was reading the New York Times bestseller list every week, looking for my name. It was an easy lie to tell, but the only people who believed it were the people that didn't matter. Now, sitting at my desk, leading the life of a rancher, the lies were cemented, and there was no later.

I opened up these feelings and, for the first time in my life, I forced myself to feel them. I sat in them, covered by them. It was very difficult, and it wasn't always healthy or helpful, but it was better than hiding from them.

My mother was an incredible saving grace in this time, and we grew so much closer. She forced me to look at myself with clear eyes, and she let me be vulnerable in front of her. I had never talked to anyone about my emotions; I thought I wasn't supposed to. But when they started pouring out of me, I had to talk to someone because I was making myself crazy by way of my self-analysis. My mother and I talked daily, and with her help, I processed and worked through the shit I had piled up. Accepting what I had done and who I was was crucial in my pursuit to move on and be something better.

Aside from daily conversations with my mother, reading became my world. I worked all day and read all night. I closed myself off with Uncle Grant's books and read through the whole lot. About halfway through Grant's collection, I came across an unbound stack of papers tucked into a large yellow clasp envelope. It was a manuscript written by Grant. It took all of five hours, but I sat at my desk and read it straight through. Grant was a great man with many accomplishments, so I was surprised to find that this novel wasn't about him. The story was about a family of migrant workers who had moved from Mexico into West Texas. Full of hardship and sadness, the family's victories were little and their failures many. His manuscript was unpolished and needed some re-writes, but it still filled me with sadness and regret.

I had always liked to read because reading was entertaining. I enjoyed digging into the characters and plot, savoring the language and dialogue. After I read Grant's manuscript, the way I read started to change. I found enjoyment in new ways. Structure and foreshadowing and the setup of dialogue became so interesting to me that I greedily read through texts trying to uncover these devices. The author's strategy and execution of the story became just as important to me as the story itself. While reading, books became more tangible, like watching a house being framed, the mystique and polish stripped away, and I could see the bones of the craft. Noticing this shift in my reading seemed irrelevant at first, just a curious evolution.

Then one day, I was walking around the ranch, thinking about George Orwell, and it triggered a memory of something funny that had happened to me when I was broke in college. When I got back to my office, I got a yellow legal pad out of my desk and I wrote out that funny thought. For some reason, that thought pushed me to pen and paper. During my days as a "writer," I had to force myself to write through shame and a sense of duty. But then, at my desk, I wrote because I felt like it. It was the first time I had written anything since I was in Mexico. Every single day since then, I have written something down in my notebook. Sometimes it's only a little blurb or thought, and I take five minutes to scribble it down. Some days, the words pour out of me, and some days, I look at the yellow pad with its little pink lines and I can't squeeze a sentence out. Eventually, something comes to me, I jot it down, and then I put the legal pad back in my drawer. I can't help but hope that someday I'll have something written down that's worth a shit.